Dear Reader,

Sometimes a project gains momentum and simply takes wing. Such was certainly the case with this delightful collection written in honor of our authors' beloved four-footed friends!

As you will see when you read each of the authors' personal notes, their pets have inspired stories that showcase how the uncomplicated love between animals and humans sometimes provides the additional benefit of revealing the path to a lasting romantic relationship.

Our talented authors are showing us not only their creativity in the stories they have crafted for this volume, but also their generosity: each has chosen a charity devoted to animal rescue to be the beneficiary of their attention as well as their personal contribution. Advance notice of this initiative has kept Lori Foster's Web site hopping with contributions to The Animal Adoption Foundation, Kristine Rolofson has become an advocate for the Pekingese Underground Railroad, and Caroline Burnes, mother to a continual parade of pets, supports the Best Friends Animal Sanctuary.

I know you will enjoy these heartwarming stories that showcase the warmth, laughter and joy that pets can bring to their owners' lives...and loves!

Marsha Zinberg
Executive Editor, Harlequin Books

Known for her trademark sensuality and delightful storytelling, **Lori Foster** is one of Harlequin's most celebrated authors. She began writing for Temptation in 1996, and since then has sold over thirty books with six different houses, including many special projects, novellas and single titles. Her books have appeared on the *USA TODAY* and *New York Times* extended bestseller lists. Though Lori enjoys writing, her first priority will always be her family. Her husband and three sons keep her on her toes.

Kristine Rolofson read and analyzed over two hundred Harlequin romances before beginning to write and sell her own first novel. Now the author of over thirty books, she is the winner of the Holt Medallion and the National Readers' Choice award. Kristine lived in the mountains of northern Idaho for twelve years before returning to her native Rhode Island. Having married her high school history teacher at the age of eighteen, she has now been married for twenty-nine years and is the mother of six. The Rolofsons were named Rhode Island's Adoptive Family of the Year!

Caroline Burnes lives on a small horse farm in the deep, deep South (Mobile, Alabama). As a little girl, she wanted to be a cowgirl or an Indian—it didn't matter, as long as she got to ride a horse. Although she was born in Mississippi, she has a great love of the west. Caroline is also the author of the FEAR FAMILIAR series, featuring that savvy black cat detective, Familiar. She is a great animal lover and an advocate of spaying and neutering to ease the problem of animal overpopulation. She has written over thirty books for the Harlequin Intrigue line.

Lori Foster
Kristine Rolofson
Caroline Burnes

The Truth about
Cats & Dogs

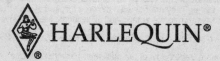

HARLEQUIN®

TORONTO • NEW YORK • LONDON
AMSTERDAM • PARIS • SYDNEY • HAMBURG
STOCKHOLM • ATHENS • TOKYO • MILAN • MADRID
PRAGUE • WARSAW • BUDAPEST • AUCKLAND

ISBN 0-373-83634-1

THE TRUTH ABOUT CATS & DOGS

Copyright © 2004 by Harlequin Books S.A.

The publisher acknowledges the copyright holders of the individual works as follows:

TAILSPIN
Copyright © 2004 by Lori Foster

SECONDHAND SAM
Copyright © 2004 by Kristine Rolofson

FAMILIAR PURSUIT
Copyright © 2004 by Carolyn Haines

CONTENTS

TAILSPIN
Lori Foster

To Whitney Price,
You're the best assistant an author could ask for!
With all the hard work you do, you've
simplified my life a lot. I can't begin to tell you
how much I appreciate it.
Thank you a hundred times over,
Lori

Dear Reader,

Thank you so much for all the wonderful mail you sent about my little dog Butch, who appeared in *Riley*. After all your enthusiasm, I had to feature him again in this anthology—but with a twist. You see, Butch now has a girlfriend, and she broke my heart.

The moment we saw her, bald, scarred and scared, we forgot about the cute puppies and chose her instead. My husband put it best when he said she had "Foster" written all over her. She's still timid, even after seven months, but she's warming to us little by little, and I love her with all my heart. Giving her a story of her own is my way of encouraging everyone to think about our little furry friends who need love so badly. The Animal Adoption Foundation is a wonderful local shelter in my area that works hard at giving abandoned and mistreated animals everything they deserve. The AAF is a "no-kill," nonprofit, non-tax-supported animal shelter, and at present they desperately need a new building. My donations alone won't be enough, but together we can make a real difference. You can find the AAF at www.aafpets.org, or e-mail them at info@aafpets.org. I hope to hear from you again, and I hope AAF will hear from you, too!

Bless you all,

Lori

P.S. You can see both of my lovable and funny Chihuahuas on my Web site—www.lorifoster.com.

CHAPTER ONE

IT WAS BARELY SIX O'CLOCK on a cloudy Saturday morning in Chester, Ohio. The sun struggled to shine without much success as Buck Boswell finished brushing his teeth, then splashed his unshaven face with cold water. Saturday mornings were meant for sleeping in, preferably with a soft, warm female. But for the next couple of weekends, that was out.

Butch, the little Chihuahua he'd been roped into baby-sitting for two weeks, was causing a ruckus. For a four-pound dog, he made a lot of noise.

Butch had already been out to do his business—the reason Buck was up so early on a vacation day—so he should have been curled up on his blankets, back to dreaming blissful doggie dreams. For the two days Buck had minded Butch so far, that'd been his routine: up at dawn, out for his morning constitutional, back to bed.

Unfortunately, Buck couldn't do the same. Once Butch woke him, getting back to sleep proved impossible. He was starting his vacation by keeping the hours of his grandpa instead of those of a thriving bachelor.

It sucked.

Riley, one of his best friends, had asked Buck to sit the dog so he and his wife, Regina, could take a cruise. But Riley hadn't mentioned that Butch rose with the roosters, only to nap again afterward.

Owning his own lumberyard and working sixty-hour weeks as a result hadn't allowed Buck much time to bond with pets. Free time was spent with his friends, his family and a selection of very nice females. Not animals.

But since he was the only bachelor left in their close circle of friends, the duty fell on him. And despite his lack of familiarity with furry creatures, he and Butch got along well enough.

So what had upset Butch enough to cause that mournful sound?

Concerned, Buck dried his face and dropped his towel. Because he slept in the nude, he'd had to pull on underwear when Butch had first awoken him. In the dark, he'd chosen monkey-print boxers given to him as a joke by Ethan's wife, Rosie. He hadn't bothered to put anything more on yet, so he cautiously poked his head around the corner to see what had Butch riled.

The dog sat at the French doors at the back of Buck's apartment, staring out at the shadowy yard.

"Hey, bud, what's the deal?"

Butch cast him a quick worried look, then went back to staring. Buck strode forward, leaned close for his own peek and narrowed his eyes to see through the hazy morning shadows. A trim figure moved across the high grass.

Sadie Harte.

Figured it had to be a woman who'd get the dog baying like a crazed wolf. Occasionally Sadie had the same effect on Buck. He didn't understand her. She was unlike other women he knew. And she made him nuts.

Sadie was the most buttoned-down, prudish, spinsterish twentysomething woman he had ever seen. To call her plain would be an understatement. But did that stop Buck from being nice to her? No. He even teased her a little, tried flirting some. He was friendly, cordial.

It got him nowhere.

In fact, despite her cold politeness, he thought she actually disliked him. In the three months that she'd been his neighbor, not once had she invited him to her apartment. And when he'd invited her to join a small get-together with his close friends, she'd refused. She'd chat with him in the yard, or give a passing greeting, but anything remotely indicative of a relationship seemed to scare her off, even one as casual as friendship.

The only time she'd been to his apartment was to ask him not to make so much noise.

It nettled him that he couldn't get her to warm up to him. Women liked him, damn it. He wasn't an ogre, he had his own business, his mother had taught him manners and he loved to laugh. Not bad qualities, right?

So, why did Sadie keep him at arm's length?

Curiosity was getting to him. Not once had he ever seen her with a boyfriend. She never had company, either. No one. Not family, not friends.

But she did take in rescue animals. Pitiful creatures with their tails between their legs, their ears down. They'd cower whenever anyone got near. Sadie was patience personified, tender and careful and caring. Too many times, Buck had stood at his door and watched her with a dog or two in the small backyard. He'd open his window so he could hear her soft voice as she cajoled an animal into trusting her.

Broke his heart, it really did. The worst part of it all was that Sadie didn't keep the pets. She helped them, and then found them good homes where they could have the love of a family, a big fenced yard, maybe kids to play with.

Today, however, wasn't the same. Normally when he saw Sadie, she had on her schoolteacher duds, as Buck liked to think of them. Even while working with the animals in the yard, she wore long shapeless skirts, flat shoes, loose blouses better suited to a maiden aunt than a young woman. Far as Buck knew, she didn't own a pair of jeans. Or shorts. Or, God forbid, a bathing suit.

She always looked prim and standoffish—and it

drove him crazy wondering what she'd look like in something more revealing.…. That was the way with men. They always wanted what they couldn't have. He wanted a peek at proper Ms. Sadie Harte.

Today was his day to have his wish come true.

Mesmerized, intrigued and a little amused, Buck leaned against the wall and took in the sight before him. For reasons he couldn't fathom, Sadie was in the yard, running from his lot to her own and back again.

In a thin nightgown.

Now he knew what she slept in. It wasn't the nudity he'd imagined many times over, but the long white gown made of thin cotton would do for future fantasies. The gown was innocent, romantic and hinted at the body beneath.

As Sadie dashed past, his gaze tracked her from the top of her head to her dew-wet feet and back up again. Sleepiness got replaced with sharpened awareness. If Sadie dressed like that more often, her social calendar would be full.

Had she just woken, too? Maybe had a nightmare? They'd talked enough for him to know that Sadie was the sensible sort, not a woman prone to theatrics. Given her wardrobe, she was really modest, too. But this morning she hadn't even donned a housecoat.

At that precise moment, early morning sunbeams burst through the clouds, making Sadie's gown slightly transparent. Breath caught, Buck took in the sight of the few subtle shadows that hinted at female curves.

The new view was damn interesting. He made note of her narrow waist, her small, high breasts and long thighs. The image of her curled in bed, half-asleep, soft and warm, crowded into his brain.

Butch howled again and scratched at the door, forcing Buck back into the moment.

"Sorry, buddy. I don't want you running after her. No reason for you both to look wacko."

Sadie's light brown, baby-fine hair danced around her head as she whipped this way and that in a crazed fashion. He'd always wanted to see her with her hair down. Because she usually had it twisted up, Buck hadn't known it was bone straight, shoulder-length, or that it had glints of red and gold when the sunlight hit it just right. Now that he did know, he wondered why she always kept it up. It looked real pretty around her shoulders.

Suddenly her small bare feet slid in the tall, dewy grass, almost landing her on her tush. Her arms did cartwheels in the air. She looked panicked before catching her balance and taking off again.

Damn it.

Buck slid the door open a little so she could hear him, but not wide enough for Butch to get out. "Sadie," he called, hoping to gain her attention without startling her. "Is something wrong?"

Her head jerked in his direction, her chocolate-brown gaze locked on his, and to Buck's surprise, she came barreling toward him. Except for her nose, which had turned pink with the morning chill, her face was pale.

"What the—?" Buck braced himself for the unexpected attack.

Screaming, Sadie jerked the door right out of his hand and nearly knocked him over in her haste to get inside. Her wet feet shot out from under her again when she stepped on his tile floor. Buck caught her under the arms before she hit the ground, aware of her slight weight and fragile bones. She was such a delicate woman—

Sadie paid him no mind. Immediately she slammed the door shut again, using enough force to rattle the panes of glass. Panting, nose glued to the glass, she watched the yard as if expecting something momentous.

Crossing his arms over his chest, Buck leaned against the wall and stared down at Sadie. At six-three, he stood taller than a lot of people. He was used to looking down. But Sadie was more petite than most, damn near a foot shorter than him.

And she was in her nightgown. With pretty, sleep-rumpled hair. And small feminine feet, now wet and dirty with grass stains.

He was still ogling her feet when Sadie jumped. "Ohmigod, there it is! There *she* is!"

Buck looked over her shoulder—and saw another Chihuahua, way fatter than Butch but not much bigger otherwise. The poor thing was soaked from running in the grass. It was also missing some fur. It had a bald forehead with other bare patches on its belly and behind. It was about the ugliest little dog Buck had ever seen, and it charged right up to his door, then put both front paws to the glass.

Sadie screamed. The shocking sound caused Buck to nearly jump out of his underwear. Bewildered, he caught Sadie's upper arm and turned her toward him.

"What in the world is wrong with you?"

"Cicada! Cicada!"

"No," Buck said reasonably, "*Chihuahua*. Probably the homeliest Chihuahua I've ever seen, but you apparently agreed to take it in…."

Sadie turned on him, stretched on her tiptoes to glare and said, "In. Her. Mouth."

Her snarling tone startled him. Buck glanced down at the female dog and…*ewww*.

Right there between the dog's teeth was a chubby, still screeching, red-eyed cicada. He shuddered in honest, horrified revulsion. No wonder the dog was losing fur if she kept things like that in her mouth.

"Good God, is she going to eat it?"

"I don't know," Sadie wailed while doing a little dance and flapping her hands. "She keeps getting…*things,* and bringing them home to me. A dead frog, a slimy night crawler, and now *this*."

The little dog whined around the pulsating bug.

"She wants in," Sadie gasped.

"Over my dead body," Buck said.

Her expression earnest, Sadie turned to Buck. She even flattened a hand on his chest, which nearly stopped his heart.

"Go out there and take it away from her," she said, her tone commanding.

Buck stiffened. Of all the things to ask, why did it have to be *that?* And she had asked it while touching his naked chest with her soft little hand, he in his underwear and she in her nightgown, leaving room for all sorts of possibilities.

He hated to disappoint her, but some things were too much. "Sorry, no can do."

Her lips trembled. "Why?"

"I hate cicadas."

Her doelike eyes widened. "But you're a man!"

"Last time I checked, yeah." At least he knew she'd noticed that much. "And stop yelling. You're upsetting the dogs."

Only Butch didn't look upset. He looked…lovestruck. From the moment the other Chihuahua appeared, Butch had gone stock-still, his head tilted, his bulgy little eyes wide. Deep in his throat, a low, husky rumble escaped. Close to a whimper, but Butch was all male dog, so no way would Buck accuse him of whimpering.

Maybe Butch had bad eyesight and didn't realize the other dog was balding. Maybe—

Sadie's hand, still on his chest, curled into a fist,

grasping a handful of hair. "She's *leaving*. You have to go get her."

When Buck just winced, she changed tactics. "Oh please. I can't lose her, but I can't go out there, either. I just can't. Not while she has that awful thing in her mouth."

Buck watched the dog trot around the corner. He shook his head, denying the inevitable. "I hate cicadas. If it were a spider, no problem at all. A snake, I'm there. But cicadas—"

Sadie jerked, nearly removing his chest hair. "She's going to get lost!"

Yeah, she probably would. Disgusted and feeling very put out, Buck gently untangled Sadie's fingers from his chest hair. He leaned down till his nose almost touched hers.

"All right. But you owe me."

Her lashes fluttered in incomprehension.

"Agreed?"

She swallowed, then gave a small nod. "All right."

Satisfied, Buck picked up Butch and handed him to her. "Hold him. I'll be right back."

"Her name is Tish," Sadie yelled in a belated effort to be helpful.

Buck crept out, his eyes darting this way and that, his ears alert to the scream of the cicada. No sign of the dog. No sign of other neighbors, either, thank God, since he wore only boxers.

In a ridiculously high voice for a man who

weighed two-twenty-five, all of it muscle, he called, "Tish? Come on, sweetie pie. Heeeere, Tish…"

He rounded the corner of the building and there she sat, her round butt almost hidden in the tall grass. She'd put down the cicada, but it wasn't moving. It just…lay there, looking gruesome and wicked with its fiery eyes exposed. Ick. Why wouldn't the damn thing fly away?

Buck drew a fortifying breath. "Come here, baby," he cajoled.

Tish tipped her head and stared. Her ears perked up, forming a wrinkle in her bald forehead. Buck could see her belly and what looked like a scar. He frowned—until Tish put one paw on the vibrating bug.

Buck's stomach lurched. How could she bare to touch it? "Come on, Tish. Be a good girl, now. No reason to be afraid, baby, I promise. I just want to hold you. That's all."

Behind him, Sadie whispered, "I bet you say that to a lot of girls."

Buck's eyes narrowed. Slowly, so he wouldn't startle the dog, he pivoted to face her. "I thought you were too chicken to come out."

The hem of Sadie's gown was soaked and clung to her ankles. She was shivering in the brisk morning air, with Butch hugged up to her chest, shielding her breasts from view. Butch didn't seem to mind. In fact, he looked real cozy.

"You're between me and the bug." Her expression was taut. "That helps."

A thought occurred to Buck and his eyes rounded. "You didn't close my door, did you?"

Sensing his alarm, Sadie hesitated before admitting, "Um… Yes. Why?"

Just what he didn't need this morning. Letting his gaze settle on hers, he growled, "Because now it's locked. And in case you didn't notice, I'm in my boxers."

She cleared her throat. "I, uh, noticed."

She had? *Of course she had,* he told himself. *They're bright yellow and have monkeys all over them.* His eyes narrowed more. "All right, brainiac, so how am I supposed to—"

Sadie started backpedaling. "Here she comes!"

Buck jerked around, prepared for the worst, but thank God, Tish had left the cicada behind. "That's a good girl, Tish. Come here, baby." He knelt down, held out his arms, and the dog…dodged around him.

Buck tried to grab her, lost his balance and landed butt-first in the wet grass. Dew instantly soaked through his boxers.

Sadie dropped Butch into his lap and took up the pursuit. After more wild scrambling and a few near spills of her own, she caught Tish. Wild-eyed with alarm, the pudgy little dog wiggled, getting the front of Sadie's gown wet before settling against her and tucking her head into Sadie's underarm.

"There you go, Tish," she crooned softly. "It's okay now. I've got you. I'd never hurt you."

Cradling the fat little dog securely, Sadie came back to Buck. She kissed the dog's ear, which thankfully had fur on it. "Thank you, Buck." She kissed the dog again, and her voice went soft and sweet. "She's more trouble than three Great Danes, but I already love her."

Watching Sadie, Buck felt a funny melting sensation in his chest. Sadie the spinster really did seem to adore the animals she took in. How hard it must be to get attached to a pet, and then let it go to someone else.

Yet that's what she did. Because even though she cared, she couldn't possibly keep them all. She rehabilitated animals, found them good homes and then said goodbye.

What an incredible woman.

Behind him, the cicada began screeching and took flight. Buck ducked, Sadie squealed. Luckily, for all concerned, it flew in the opposite direction before they had time to get too excited.

"No problem." Unwilling to wait around to see if the bug returned, Buck shoved to his feet, reached back to pluck the clinging wet material of his boxers off his ass, and nodded. "Now how am I going to get back into my place?"

A blush stained Sadie's cheeks, making her pink nose less noticeable. Her shoulders slumped and she bit her lower lip.

It was a nice, full lip, Buck realized. He watched

her teeth worry it and his heartbeat sped up. She was such an intriguing mix of contradictions. Rigid and formal in some ways, but overtly sensual in others.

He shook his head and concentrated on her eyes. They were a soft brown, almost the color of milk chocolate, framed by darker lashes, and at the moment, filled with guilt.

"I, uh, suppose you could come into my place and call the manager."

"At six in the morning?" He tucked Butch under one arm and shifted. Everyone in the complex knew better than to bother Henry before a respectable hour. "Respectable" to Henry was around noon, but Buck wasn't going to sit around in his boxers that long.

Sadie continued to chew on that soft, full bottom lip, agonizing in indecision until Buck took pity on her. "How about you pour me a coffee, maybe even throw some breakfast together, and at eight I'll call him?"

Her eyes rounded. "Coffee?"

"Yeah. It's a morning drink. Hot, loaded with caffeine. I didn't get a single cup yet, and right about now, I need it."

"I know what it *is*." She struggled again, then gave up and cradled the dog a little lower in her arms. "I have some made already."

"Great." The damp front of her gown clung to her breasts. "I'm freezing my ass off. My nipples are so hard, I could cut glass."

Her mouth fell open, and she looked at his chest.

Buck, feeling provoked by that hot, nearly tactile stare, pointed out gently, "Yours too, for that matter."

Her stunned gaze clashed with his, held for two heartbeats, then she whipped around, giving him her back.

Buck watched the gown settle around her trim hips and the plump curves of her small behind.

Ignoring his comment on her stiffened nipples—which really had tantalized him—she stammered, "Y-you want to stay at my apartment for *two* hours?"

Distracted, he murmured, "Yeah, why?" And then, realizing how unenthusiastic she sounded, he added, "Is that a problem?"

She shrugged.

"Turn around, Sadie. I don't like talking to the back of your head." And he liked seeing her expressive eyes as she spoke, the way she watched him, how easily she blushed.

She turned, but kept the dog held high. "I don't think it's a good idea, that's all."

So, Buck thought, he was good enough to save her bald, bug-eating dog, but not good enough to feed? Did she find him so distasteful that she couldn't tolerate his company for two measly hours?

He shifted again, ready to grumble at her, then saw her eyes dip past his navel. She sighed softly before remembering herself and returned her gaze to his face. This time she didn't blush, but she did look defiant, as if daring him to mention her gaffe.

Given how she kept checking him out, maybe she didn't find him distasteful at all. Buck grinned. "You think I should just sit on my back porch twiddling my thumbs till Henry wakes up? In this wet underwear?" When she still looked undecided, he added, "With a Chihuahua on my lap?"

The mention of the dog did it.

"Oh." She frowned, shrugged her thin shoulders and tucked her silky hair behind her ear. "I, uh, I guess not." And she glanced at his lap again. "That wouldn't be fair to Butch."

If she didn't quit that, the monkeys on his shorts were gonna start dancing. Having a female, even a spinster-type female, stare at a guy's crotch usually got the action started. Seeing as he had no way of hiding it, he just knew her blush would brighten up a few notches.

With perfect timing to break the awkward moment, Butch barked, then stared at Tish while making that low humming sound again. Buck scratched the dog's ear, knowing just how he felt.

"There, you see? Butch isn't as…hardy as Tish. He's freezing and he wants to visit. I think he's even a little enamoured with Tish."

Sadie's chin went up. "Obviously *he* doesn't think she's ugly."

Oops. Had that remark he'd made about Tish insulted Sadie somehow? He hadn't lied. She was bald and fat. Anyone could see that. Still, given how

Sadie doted on the dog, he should probably apologize if he ever hoped to make headway with her. "I didn't mean—"

Sadie gave him an evil look. "I think she's beautiful. She just needs some love and nourishment and then her fur will come back in and she'll be a beauty queen, you'll see."

Buck watched her loving the homely little critter, and knew that if anyone could make it happen, he'd put his money on Sadie. "You know what? I believe you."

He turned and started toward her door, but after a few steps, he realized Sadie wasn't following. He looked over his shoulder. She was staring at his butt. It was nice to be appreciated, but hey, the cold was starting to settle into his bones.

"Your fault," Buck accused, knowing his seat was wet, that the material was again clinging. "I've only had these on ten minutes, and now I'll have to change again."

Sadie stared at the boxers, an undisguised look of curiosity on her face.

"I sleep naked. I just put the boxers on to let Butch out."

"Oh." She blinked several times.

Knowing she didn't, but in the mood to tease, Buck asked in his most innocent tone, "Don't you?"

"What?"

She did have a problem concentrating. "Sleep in the nude."

She took a step back. "No!"

"Why not?" When she floundered for an explanation, Buck asked, "Get cold at night?"

She jumped on that. "Yes. I do."

He turned his back on her again, saying, "You need someone to sleep with. Sharing body heat is the best way to stay toasty." He heard her gasp, but luckily, she couldn't see his grin. Yep, things were progressing nicely this morning. "C'mon Sadie. Get a move on before I catch pneumonia."

"Right." Sounding breathless, Sadie scrambled to catch up. Her gown billowed out behind her, and at the last second, she passed him to reach the door first. With her bottom lip held in her teeth, she stood back so he could go in.

Ready and willing to take every advantage, Buck made a point of brushing against her as he entered. He heard her indrawn breath, felt the stillness that settled over her, and then she moved away.

She flapped a hand toward the tiny kitchenette. "Make yourself comfortable. I'll go dress and be right back."

Buck hated for her to do that. She looked softer and more approachable in her nightgown. If she changed, he just knew she'd pile on the layers and do up all the buttons and start behaving like a spinster again.

But if he suggested she *not* change, then what? She'd probably throw him outside in his near-naked state.

Sadie was almost out of the room, Tish secure in her arms, when Buck said, "Grab me a big towel or something, too, will ya? I want to get out of these wet drawers."

She stumbled to a halt, her shoulders rigid, her spine straight. Without turning to face him, she put the little dog down, nodded and fled the room.

Buck stood there smiling, pleased and pondering Sadie's behavior. She was so easy to read, but also confusing in her different reactions.

Considering how many times he'd caught her at it, she liked looking at him, no two ways about that. But she blushed when she did it.

She hadn't hesitated to barge into his apartment and then order him out to get her dog. Yet, she'd been reluctant to let him into her place, and she seemed stunned silly whenever he got too close to her.

He'd never seen her date. And he'd be willing to bet she'd never seen a guy in his underwear.

Was she one of those women who only had sex in the dark? Not that he minded the dark on occasion, but generally, he liked to look at a woman as much as touch her. But if she preferred the dark, he'd make do.

There was only one problem. Dumb as it seemed, he kept wondering if she'd had sex at all. In so many ways, Sadie acted just like…a virgin.

But that didn't seem likely. Women these days were experimenting before they finished high school, and definitely by college. Sadie had to be—what?—

midtwenties, probably twenty-four or twenty-five. The odds of her being *that* innocent were pretty damn slim.

But once Buck thought it, he couldn't get the idea out of his head. It teased him, sending a variety of possible scenarios flitting through his male brain, making him wonder about things he probably shouldn't wonder about.

Like just how much experience she might have. Kisses, surely. Everyone kissed. Even prim, spinsterish women.

But had she ever gotten a really *good* kiss, the killer kind that nearly pushed you over the edge and made common sense not too common?

Had a guy ever touched her breasts? Kissed her nipples? His jaw tightened just thinking about it.

Her breasts were modest, but then, she was a petite woman, so anything larger would have looked overblown on her frame. And seeing her nipples tight against that pale gown had really got to him. Before she'd hidden herself from him, he'd seen them clearly. They were small and tight…and he wanted to taste them.

Would he be the first?

That thought jolted him. Hell, she didn't even like him. He'd had to coerce her into letting him in her apartment.

And, of course, they had nothing in common. Buck wasn't even a dog person! But then, that hadn't stopped Riley from leaving Butch in his care, so did it really matter that Sadie had a lot of dogs coming and going?

He wasn't a spinster person, either, preferring women who were more like him, outgoing and full of laughter, willing to play. But from the day he'd met her, Sadie Harte had intrigued him. Because of her, there were some pretty vivid fantasies zinging around his brain. Watching her blush and listening to her stammer beat drinking coffee alone any day.

Tish trotted past him, drawing Buck's attention. He bent down to pet her, but she scampered away in obvious fear.

"It's okay, baby," he crooned, holding out his hand for her to sniff. But she cowered in the corner, her ears down, her round eyes watchful. She was truly afraid of him, as if she expected the worst. That bothered Buck. A lot. It sort of reminded him of Sadie.

Unwilling to upset her, Buck slowly straightened and took a step away. It occurred to him that the little dog deserved special attention—just as Sadie did.

Butch struggled to be free, so Buck set him down near Tish. She probably outweighed him by two pounds, not that Butch minded. His eyes were huge, his ears raised on alert, and he definitely had courtship on his mind as he began sniffing Tish from one end to the other.

Truly, love was blind.

At least Tish liked and trusted Butch; her tail wagged in greeting. Like most guys, Butch wasted no time testing the water. Only Tish wasn't having it. She was anxious to play, but amorous attempts got shot down real quick.

"Typical," Buck grunted, thinking of how Sadie had ordered him out to get her dog, then tried to refuse him coffee.

Seeing that the dogs would get along fine, Buck decided to look around Sadie's apartment. It was nice, in a female-cluttered kind of way. Lots of silly knickknacks, lush plants, a few ruffles here and there, like on the white kitchen curtains and the tablecloth on her minuscule dinette table.

On her refrigerator were a variety of photos. No men, no family, just cats and dogs of varying sizes and ages. It devastated him to think of what they had been through. It took a strong woman with a big heart to heal them. It took a special woman.

A woman without much of a social life.

Beside the refrigerator hung a calendar. Buck hesitated, he really did. But there was no sign of Sadie's return, and the temptation was too great. Because she was so standoffish, this was the best chance he'd likely ever get to know her better.

He walked over to the calendar and read the few notes she'd written in for September. Most of her days were empty, but there were four blocks with writing in them. She had marked an afternoon appointment with a vet, a trip to the dentist, a library book due back and carpet cleaners scheduled.

No dinner dates. No parties. Nothing exciting at all.

He flipped back to look at August and saw much of the same. Then back to July—and he froze.

July second, Sadie had met with a funeral director. Two days later, she'd met a lawyer. In her ladylike script were the words "Settle Mother's estate." And two days after that was "Secure death certificate."

Jesus. Buck swallowed, wondering if her mother's death had precipitated her moving into his apartment complex. The timing was right. He stared off at nothing in particular, trying to remember how she'd been three months ago, when he'd first met her. Quiet, alone. She'd spent nearly a week moving in, unloading her car each day all by herself. Back and forth she'd go, thin arms laden with cardboard boxes, lamps and small pieces of furniture.

What she couldn't carry she'd pushed or dragged in. She'd been relentless, tireless. Determined.

Buck had offered her a helping hand, but she'd refused, thanked him and gone back to work. That first day had seemed to set a precedent. No matter what he offered, she always refused.

The dogs came running past Buck's feet in a blur, ears flattened to their round heads, tiny bodies streamlined. They were a cute distraction. Tish enjoyed Butch's company, and Butch looked besotted.

Buck narrowed his eyes in thought. He had two

weeks' vacation lined up, and no real plans because it'd all be spent with Butch. If being here made Butch happy, and being with Butch made Tish happy, then surely it'd make Sadie happy, too.

Maybe he could combine things to everyone's advantage.

He rubbed his hands together as the plan formed. Ms. Sadie Harte wouldn't be able to deny him any longer.

The best way to her heart was through her dog.

CHAPTER TWO

SADIE RAN THROUGH her morning routine in record-breaking time. She hated to admit it, even to herself, but she was half-afraid that if she took too long, Buck would leave. That he was in her apartment in the first place was nothing short of a miracle.

With ruthless determination, she brushed the tangles out of her hair and pulled it back into a quick twist. It wasn't the neatest job she'd ever done, but then she'd never done her hair with a big handsome man waiting for her in his underwear.

Oh, Lord.

Hands shaking, she cleaned her teeth, even gargled for safe measure—not that she expected to be too close to Buck, but… Several times, he'd invaded her personal space.

She stared at herself in the mirror, breathing hard, unseeing. Every single time Buck had gotten near, she'd enjoyed it. It likely meant nothing; he was a big guy and just naturally took up more room than most. But it still thrilled her, even when she knew she had no business being thrilled. Buck was not the kind of man she could start dreaming about.

But he smelled so good. Hot and musky-male. The freshness of the brisk morning air had competed with his scent, creating an intoxicating mix.

She closed her eyes, took a calming breath and quickly washed her face. She never bothered with jewelry or makeup, so less than ten minutes later she was dressed in a crisp pink blouse, a brown skirt with matching cardigan, and her comfortable weekend loafers. She had a bath towel—the largest she owned—draped over one arm.

Still she hesitated. Buck Boswell was just so... *much.* So much male, so much muscle, so much appeal.

And he was sitting in *her* kitchen. In his underwear. With his impressive, hairy chest, wide hard shoulders and flat abdomen all on display.

Sadie shivered in sensual delight. She felt terribly excited and anxious and apprehensive, all at the same time.

Never in her twenty-five years had a man sat mostly naked in her kitchen. Never. She'd had men over, of course. She wasn't a complete social misfit. But they were businessmen, guys from the shelter dropping off a pet for her to nurture, or the lawyer with papers for her to sign concerning her mother's affairs.

In some ways this was very, very different.

In others, it wasn't different at all.

Determined to face reality, Sadie reminded herself that Buck wasn't here for a date any more than the other men had been. Despite his frequent attempts to be friendly, he wasn't interested in her on a personal level; she'd seen the women Buck preferred, and they were nothing like her.

If she hadn't locked him out of his apartment, he wouldn't be here now. She'd ordered him outside to rescue her dog, then repaid him by locking him out in his underwear. She wanted to groan. He had reason to be furious with her.

She'd handled plenty of large male animals that'd been angry and fearful because of past treatment. She'd soothed them, petted them until they calmed down and eventually won them over. She only had a few scars to show for her efforts. Nothing dramatic. Nothing life-altering.

Besides, Buck didn't seem all that angry, and she doubted he went around biting women. And she definitely wouldn't be petting him.

Her heart gave a tiny little trip even as she formed the thought.

But no. He wasn't interested in intimacy, even if she felt that daring. And she didn't. Really. But the thought of stroking his powerful body made her flush, and then snicker at the absurdity of it.

Done being a coward, she forced herself to leave the room. When she rounded the corner of the hall, her eyes went immediately to the small kitchen table, and found it empty. Her heart sank before common sense took over. He wouldn't have left, not in his underwear. Not when he'd be insistent that she let him in.

Curious, she moved a little more quickly into the family room—and almost tripped over him.

Sprawled on his stomach on the carpet, taking up most of her minuscule floor space, Buck was trying to coerce Tish into coming closer. Butch sat beside him, impatiently watching, whining a little, and barking every now and then.

Her heart almost melted. From the day she'd met Buck, she'd been amazed at his size. He clowned around a lot, and he loved to tease and laugh, but there was no denying his strength. His biceps were so big, even using both hands she wouldn't be able to circle them. His shoulders looked like boulders and his thighs like tree trunks. He could intimidate most anyone just by standing there, and he'd certainly intimidated her.

Yet now he was trying his best to sweet-talk her little bald dog. Such an amazing contradiction.

In silence Sadie tracked the long line of his powerful body, from his rumpled brown hair, down the deep furrow of his spine framed by bulging back muscles, across his tight buttocks, along his thick thighs, his hairy calves and finally to his enormous feet.

He was the biggest man she knew. He was the only man she'd ever seen in his underwear. And he had the gentlest, sweetest voice—

"Want me to roll over so you can check out the other side?"

Sweetness changed to amusement when he addressed her, and Sadie's eyes nearly crossed. She glanced at his face, but he wasn't looking at her. He watched Tish, his lopsided smile giving him an endearing look.

She cleared her throat, summoned up a credible lie and said, "I was just trying to decide if this towel is big enough."

"Right."

Time to change the subject, and fast. Sadie coughed. "It's nice that you're trying, but Tish's really shy. She won't come to me willingly, either, and she's especially afraid of men."

"I'll win her over, eventually." He winked, then rolled to his feet and stood in front of her, towering, imposing.

Sexy.

When Sadie just stared up at him, he held out a hand. Reflexively, she jumped back, thinking he meant to touch her. One of his eyebrows lifted, and she saw his hand was held out, palm up.

Oh. She gave him the towel. "You can hang your shorts over the back of a chair to dry if you want."

He smiled, then started for the kitchen. "Sure. Give me one minute—and no peeking."

As if she would! Well…she might. If she knew she wouldn't be caught.

The dogs followed on his heels, and Sadie found herself alone in the tiny living room. She waited, peeked down the hall, and waited some more.

Incredible. A naked man was now in her kitchen. Her belly pulled tight as she pictured it all too clearly in her mind.

"Coast is clear," Buck called.

Being the cautious sort and already flushed from her vivid imaginings, Sadie crept in until she saw that he was indeed covered. Phew. What a relief.

Sort of.

Not that his wearing a towel was that much better than his wearing boxers, but it hid more of him, from beneath his navel to just below his knees. Still, he sat in the stiff kitchen chair, thighs open, one long leg stretched out.

She'd always heard that men had no modesty. This pretty much proved it. Right now, if she bent over just a little, she'd be able to see—

"The coffee smells good."

Sadie met his mocking gaze and had the horrible suspicion he'd read her thoughts. Mortified, she turned her back on him. "You could have helped yourself." As she said it, she got two mugs down from the cabinet.

"I wouldn't be so presumptuous."

That had her smiling. He was by far the most outrageous human being she knew, and she doubted he could spell *presumptuous*. She peeked at him. He'd hung the silly monkey-covered boxers over the back of a chair. The bright yellow in her white kitchen seemed as out of place as Buck himself.

"After saving Tish, I owe you. Especially since I locked you out."

He shrugged a massive shoulder as big and hard as a boulder. "I should have warned you that the door would lock. My fault."

Generous, too. And kind. Why had she never noticed these attributes before?

But she knew the answer. She'd been hurting from the loss of her mother and the upheaval of moving from the only home she'd ever known. She hadn't had the emotional strength to let anyone else into her life, especially not a man like Buck—so powerful and strong and…threatening.

At least to her peace of mind.

Besides, she'd known Buck wasn't the type of man to pay her much attention. He was big and sexy and he almost always had a smile on his face. He'd never been lacking female company, either. Sadie often saw him grilling steaks in his backyard with a woman draped around him.

She'd hear them laughing, and be drawn to look, regardless of her own sense of decorum. Buck liked to kiss and tease. He was a toucher, always stroking the women he had around. Not in a sexual way, though she was sure he indulged in plenty of that in private. But anytime he had a woman near, he was either holding her hand, casually caressing her arm, or running the backs of his fingers across her cheek.

He liked to tickle, too, she'd discovered. More often than not, that game would end up with Buck hoisting the woman into his arms and carrying her inside. Sadie would watch with a sick sense of yearning.

Not that it did her any good to pine after men. For the most part, they ignored her.

Only Buck wasn't ignoring her now.

"I really am grateful," Sadie told him. "I know we haven't always hit it off." To cover that halfhearted apology for past transgressions, she set a steaming mug of coffee in front of him and quickly inquired, "Cream or sugar?"

"Neither, thanks." He sipped, nodded. "Good. Maybe that'll help wake me up."

Tongue in cheek, Sadie asked, "Hard night?"

"Not in the way I would prefer." He tipped his head toward Butch, who trailed behind Tish like a caboose on a train. "I'm not used to having the little guy spend the night. My friend, Riley—you've probably seen him at my place before…?"

"With the red-haired woman, yes." She'd noticed Butch with him, too, of course. Not only was he smaller than most, but a red Chihuahua with black brindling stood out because of the unusual coloring.

"That'd be Regina. Or Red, as Riley calls her."

Riley was one of Buck's quieter, calmer friends.

He oozed menace and confidence, but also gentle concern, especially with his wife. Still, even he took part in the boisterous laughing when three or more of the men got together.

"Riley's had Butch over plenty of times," Buck said, "but this is the first time I'm dog-sitting overnight. Butch keeps odd hours, which means I have to keep odd hours, too."

Sadie turned to the refrigerator to rummage for food. They had two hours together and feeding him would help pass the time.

"If he's the reason you were up so early this morning, I can only be grateful. Otherwise I'd have been dealing with that cicada on my own." She leaned around the door to see Buck. "And I hate to admit it, but I'm not sure I could have."

"Don't blame you. Cicadas have to be the nastiest bugs around."

That he'd agree with her made her feel less ridiculous. "Eggs and bacon okay?"

"Sounds great."

She heard her delicate little parlor chair creak as Buck settled back. "Now. About what you said…"

"Hmm?" Sadie dug out her frying pan. Cooking for a man would be a unique experience. Her father had walked out when she was young, leaving her mother to raise her alone. As an only child, Sadie had no brothers, and her mother had never remarried. Because her mother's health had always been frail, she'd never been a big eater. How many eggs would a man like Buck need?

She eyed his enormous form, decided on two, then changed her mind to three.

"About us not always hitting it off."

She nearly dropped an egg. She didn't want to discuss that, but apparently, she'd have to. She probably shouldn't have said anything, but after his heroic rescue this morning, she felt she owed him an apology.

To keep from looking at him, she began laying bacon in the hot skillet. "I'm sure that was more my fault than yours."

Buck leaned forward, bracing one elbow on the table. "Well, now, I don't want to rile you, but until today, you have always seemed kind of cold."

Sadie's back stiffened. "Cold?"

"Unfriendly," he said by way of explanation. "Standoffish. Maybe a little—"

"I get it." She glared at Buck.

He grinned. "Okay. Don't bite my face off."

Blast. She turned back to the stove. Her words had been sharper than she'd meant them to be. But just because she hadn't jumped all over him as most women did, he'd labeled her cold? She bit her lip, slapped two more slices of bacon into the pan, and said through her teeth, "Again, I apologize."

A loud, masculine sigh accompanied the creaking of the chair, and suddenly he was behind her. He didn't say a word, but the sensation of being cornered had her breath catching in her throat. Heat radiated off his big body, touching her all along her back. And she could smell him again, the delicious smell of warm male.

She couldn't turn to face him.

"I riled you."

"No." Sadie denied that with a quick shake of her head.

"I'd like to get to know you better, Sadie."

Oh, Lord. Her stomach dropped to her feet. She'd imagined this scenario many times, but the reality was a lot more nerve-racking.

His long hard fingers wrapped completely around her wrist, emphasizing the disparity in their sizes. He lifted her arm and his rough thumb coasted over a small scar, then another. "How'd you get these?"

With her heart ramming into her chest wall, speech was nearly impossible. "Dog." She cleared her throat. "Make that plural. Sometimes the dogs are... nervous with me."

"You let them bite you?"

"I don't exactly *invite* them to, no. But it happens." He was being so casual about touching her that she regained some—but not all—of her aplomb. "Most of the dogs I take in have been mistreated, abandoned, starved. Naturally, they don't trust humans, with good reason. Anything can startle them."

His thumb continued to caress her wrist, sending her senses rioting. "Hmm. Like what?"

He expected her to indulge in this conversation with him so close, his hands touching her, his expression intent? For most women, it'd be nothing out of the ordinary. For Sadie, it was unheard of.

She cleared her throat and tried to keep her voice steady. "Noise really bothers them. And when they're scared, they lash out. A dog might bite, a cat might scratch. They don't want to hurt me, but they're so afraid."

He frowned.

"It's not their fault. When I first bring them home, I try to give them security and quiet, lots of love and comfort. If they hear a loud noise while I'm trying to get them used to me—"

"A loud noise, like a laugh?"

He caught on all too quickly. She ducked her head. "Sometimes."

Carefully, Buck tugged on her wrist until she turned completely toward him. The top of her head reached his bristled chin. His mouth had gone flat and hard, his jaw tight.

She stared at his chest. He was just so…so *large*. And hard. And sexy.

What would it be like to run her fingers through that dark, curling chest hair? She knew it was soft because she'd already touched him there, earlier when she'd demanded his help. At the time she'd been too worried about Tish to really appreciate the feel of him. If she nestled her cheek—

He lifted her other arm and examined it, too. "I'm a jerk."

She had to quit daydreaming. "No, you're not."

"That's why you don't like it when I have friends over and we make so much noise. That's why you won't ever join us."

After all his help that morning, she had to be entirely honest with him. It was horrible to admit, but she had to be fair. "The noise can upset the animals, yes. But I don't join in because I'm not very good in social settings."

He bent his knees, lowering himself to look her in the eyes. "Yeah? How come?"

He was so close that she breathed in the heat of his skin. She felt tight from her toes to her eyebrows, and everywhere in between was jumpy. But the big goof probably had no idea what he did to her, how his nearness turned her inside out. He wasn't flirting.

No man ever flirted with her.

Sadie stared at his right nipple and whispered, "Since moving here, I've been really busy."

Skeptical, he said, "Busy, huh?"

She nodded. "Between work and caring for animals, I don't have time to socialize."

"But I'm right next door."

He lifted her free hand and pressed it to his chest—right over the nipple she'd been ogling. Oh, Lord, oh, Lord. To not contract her fingers required all her concentration. She wanted to test his strength, knead him like a cat.

"You could bring your animals with you if you want."

For a moment, Sadie wondered if she was dreaming. Buck couldn't be serious. Not only was a man in her apartment, but now he was offering to let her visit, and with animals in tow?

Why would he make such a generous offer? "I'm…I'm usually not good company. Sometimes the dogs keep me up too late. They have nightmares just like anyone else and I get cranky without enough sleep."

She sneaked a glance at him and saw she'd amused him again. Forging on, she added, "When I don't make as much progress as I like, it gets to me. That makes me crabby, too."

With Buck holding one hand, and her other braced on his rock-hard chest, she had to blow away the lock of hair that had fallen in her eyes. She should have taken more time when pinning it up.

Buck was silent for a moment, watching her so intently, her knees felt ready to buckle.

In a voice that sounded remarkably seductive, he said, "You're a real sweetheart, you know that?"

Her gaze shot up to his face. "What?" Had he just complimented her?

He tucked her hair behind her ear for her, smiled and said, "I'll help cook while you tell me about Tish."

No! He couldn't say something like that and then act like nothing important had happened.

She wanted to know what he meant, but didn't have the nerve to push him. "You can cook?" She no sooner asked it than she felt like a dolt. He certainly didn't look malnourished.

"Yeah, I can cook." He lifted her hand from his chest, kissed her palm and then nudged her out of his way so he could reach the stove. "Nothing too complicated, but breakfast is a must." He turned the bacon with a fork before dropping butter in another skillet for the eggs. "You can make the toast. I'll take four slices."

Like a zombie, Sadie got out the loaf of bread and headed to the toaster.

"So why is Tish bald?"

That brought her around. Sadie glared at his broad back. At least he hadn't said "ugly" again. She glanced at the little dog, now curled in a ray of sunshine with Butch snuggled up to her back. If Tish moved, Butch jumped up in expectation, only to lie back down when Tish failed to do anything astounding. Too cute. Both of them.

"Her previous owner let her breed with a dog that was too big. She had a really hard pregnancy and couldn't deliver the puppies on her own. The vet had to do a cesarean section."

"They do that to dogs?" He dropped eggs, two at a time, into the sizzling skillet. "Cesareans, I mean."

"When they need to. It wasn't just the size of the pups that gave her problems. She was undernourished, physically stressed in her labor, and someone had just left her on the shelter stoop."

Buck turned from the stove to stare at her with an unreadable expression. "The puppies?"

"Were fine. All five of them." Anger tightened her voice and left her stomach in knots. "Poor Tish didn't know what was going on. She was so afraid and in painful labor. The trauma of surgery, especially the anesthesia, can make the fur fall out. But it'll come back."

Buck paused, then he, too, looked at the dog. "Poor little baby."

At the sound of his voice, Tish lifted her head and stared at him.

Sadie's throat ached, and her heart hurt. "Whoever had her also hit her."

Without looking away from the dog, Buck stiffened. "How do you know?"

"The way she flinches if I lift a hand around her, as if she's expecting a blow. She's so afraid, she fights me every time I put her collar on her, and more often than not, she struggles until she can get out of it. I can't put it on her any tighter without hurting her, and that I won't do." She glanced at Buck. "That's how she got loose this morning."

Buck looked as disturbed by the truth as she felt. "So don't put a collar on her."

"If I don't, she might get away. I can't bear the thought of her getting lost and being alone again."

Buck turned away from the stove, a contemplative look on his face. Then he walked to her patio doors. Tish quickly darted out of his path, which meant Butch followed. Both dogs watched him from several feet away.

Sadie's apartment wasn't as upscale as Buck's. Where he had French doors, she had sliders. He looked out, rubbing his chin in thought. "I could build you a little fence for her. Nothing permanent, so it wouldn't get in the way when the maintenance guys cut the grass. But she's so small, it wouldn't take much to contain her. That way, you could wait to put the collar on her until she starts to like you."

Offended, Sadie said, "She already likes me. That's why she keeps bringing me gifts."

"Gifts?"

"The…bugs and stuff."

"She brings you a cicada because she likes you?" He grunted. "Good thing she doesn't hate you, then."

Ignoring that, Sadie explained, "We're getting along. Tish's just cautious."

"Like you?"

Sadie went still. She was cautious, but she had thought she hid it well. "What do you mean?"

Buck returned to the stove and expertly flipped the

eggs. "Anytime I get too close to you, you poker up like you think I'm going to bludgeon you or something."

No, she pokered up like she thought she might jump his gorgeous bones. It didn't matter that she was plain and inexperienced. She was as curious as any woman, with all the same desires. But because of her natural shyness, the overwhelming responsibility she'd held for a sick parent, and her own high standards, she'd had very little chance to indulge those desires.

Sometimes she felt ready to explode with frustration. And putting her next to a guy like Buck, a guy who oozed confidence and sex appeal, was like waving a flame around a keg of gasoline. She didn't want to do anything to embarrass herself, so she tried very hard to contain her interest.

Naturally, she couldn't tell him any of that. "I, uh, that is…"

"You don't date much, do you?"

If by "not much" he meant never, then…

"Sorry," he said, not sounding the least bit sorry. "I don't mean to be nosy. Well, I guess I do. But I don't mean for it to embarrass you."

Sadie fell back against the counter. Her thoughts went this way and that, trying to figure him out. What possible reason could he have for wanting to know about her lack of a social life?

The wall clock ticked loudly while she considered it. The dogs stared at her in expectation. Sadie straightened. She had a man in her kitchen. And not just any man, but Buck Boswell. He was showing interest. He was more naked than not. Shyness be damned, she had a right to ask.

She cleared her throat. "Why do you want to know?" Her voice emerged as a hesitant squeak.

He carried both plates to the table. "A guy needs to find out these things."

She looked at the dogs, and they looked back. No help there. They wore identical expressions of confusion. She turned back to Buck. "But…why?"

He moseyed over to the toaster and stared at it as if willing the bread to pop up. "We're neighbors. We're both single. Close to the same age." He looked up at her. "I'm thirty-one."

He seemed to expect some reply, so Sadie said, "I'm twenty-five," and he nodded.

"We both have Chihuahuas, too. That's a lot of stuff to have in common."

He had to be kidding. In truth, they had nothing in common.

"I was hoping to visit more," he said. "Hang out a little with you and Tish. But I don't want to intrude if you're going to be busy."

"Visit more? Hang out?" *Real intelligent, Sadie.* Soon he'd consider her a blithering idiot, as well as a wallflower.

Buck shrugged away her stammers. "Yeah. Nothing formal." He looked down at her, his green eyes warm and speculative. "For now."

For now? Was he saying that, later, he'd want to get more formal?

"I mean, we have two dogs to deal with, right? Butch isn't nervous like Tish, but he doesn't much like to be left alone. No matter what I do, he's on my heels."

Sadie pointed out the obvious. "He's not on your heels now."

That made him grin. "No, he's busy trying to woo Tish, but I'm still in his sights. He might not like it if I left. So maybe we could hang out together at my place or yours. Maybe watch a few movies or something."

"Oh."

He smiled down at her. "You like movies?"

"Yes." She loved movies. They were a form of entertainment she could enjoy in her own home, with her pets nearby.

"Great. Seems like Tish would get used to you quicker if you were around more, right?"

Sadie bit her lip. "I didn't intend to leave her alone, except when I go to work."

"But see, that's the good part. I'm on vacation, so I don't have to go to work. I could be here while you're gone, and maybe she'd get used to me that much quicker, too."

His sincerity held her in place as surely as if her feet were nailed to the floor. "I suppose." She couldn't believe this. Buck Boswell, a hulking bachelor with a score of women at his beck and call, was trying to sell her on the idea of him spending more time with her.

Or was it that he wanted to spend time with Tish? Sadie frowned, more than a little confused.

"If I'm here enough," Buck continued, "she'll start to trust me. And if she trusts one human, she'll trust another, right?"

Sadie nodded. "That sounds, uh, reasonable."

"And then maybe…" He smoothed his big hand over her hair, once again tucking it into place. "You'll start to trust me a little, too."

No one, except her mother, had ever felt free to touch her so casually. To keep from falling over, Sadie took two deep breaths. She had no idea what was going on.

His voice dropped when he murmured, "Your hair is really soft." His thumb grazed her jawline. "Your skin, too."

Sadie's insides started a slow burn. She was about to melt when the toast popped up, making her jump a foot.

Buck reached for the toast before she could. "So tell me, you seriously involved with anyone right now?"

She was seriously involved in a *fantasy*. "No."

He took a second to absorb her fast reply. "Casually dating anyone?"

Sadie shook her head.

He stared at her, brows slightly drawn, expression probing. "Dating at all?"

Why did she have to be so fair-skinned? Her

blushes didn't make her look pretty. They just made her look scalded. "No."

"Why not?" Buck slathered an obscene amount of butter onto the toast while awaiting her answer.

What to tell him? The truth? She actually shuddered. No, some humiliations should be kept private forever. Like being stood up on prom night. Her blush intensified with the awful memory of standing there in her fancy dress with her fancy hairdo, feeling so giddy and anxious—and two hours later, finally accepting the reality that her date wouldn't show. Being the sophomore joke had been enough to last her through the rest of high school.

She locked her knees. "There hasn't been much time." Her eyes sank shut at that awful fabrication. She had all the time in the world and he probably knew it.

"So you used to date, but don't much anymore?"

She refused to bare her soul, to totally expose herself and her lacks. She was a grown woman, not a wounded child. Her chin lifted. "Are we going to eat this morning, or keep talking?"

"Let's do both." He turned to carry the toast to the table, and almost tripped over the dogs. Butch knew better than to think he'd get table food, but Tish apparently had no manners. She jumped, barked, begged.

"So now you like me?" Buck inquired of the little dog with a smile.

"Sorry." Sadie hurried to the cabinet and got out the box of doggie treats. "When we first got her, she was so thin that everyone hand-fed her, just to make sure she'd eat. Now she thinks any food near a hand is hers for the taking."

"It fattened her up, so I'd say it worked."

Sadie couldn't take offense at that comment; Tish was as plump as a little penguin. She dug out a small bone-shaped treat, then thought to ask, "Is it okay if I give Butch one, too?"

"Sure." Buck sat the food on the table and again crouched down to pet Tish. She lurched away with a yelp, making him sigh. "That's okay, baby. I understand."

The way he knelt left his towel wide open over his spread knees. Sadie leaned forward to peek, but could only see his upper thighs. Nice, muscular thighs.

Buck turned to smile up at her. Either he didn't notice what she was doing, or he chose to ignore it.

"I *really* want to hold that little dog."

"I know. Me, too. Eventually she'll let us."

He turned back to the dog. "I'm always patient when I want something."

His tone of voice was sweet and gentle. Tish watched him, creeping closer, inching toward the table.

"Good girl," Buck crooned softly.

Slowly, he reached out to her. He was almost touching her when Tish snatched his colorful boxers off the back of the chair and ran off.

Startled, Buck shot back to his feet. "Hey!"

Sadie watched her run around the corner and into the living room. "Uh…"

Butch ran after Tish, and Buck was next in line. Sadie followed. The dogs had gone under her couch. When Buck knelt down to look underneath, both dogs barked at him, trying to warn him off.

"What the hell is she doing with my underwear?"

Sadie stared at the picture he made, on his knees peering under her furniture. "I don't know." And as Buck stood to face her, she said, "I can get them for you later, when she comes back out."

Buck hesitated, then, amazingly enough, stood, slung his thick arm around her shoulders and led her back to the kitchen.

"I suppose that'll be okay."

Awareness made Sadie so stiff she could barely walk. Buck's arm was heavy and warm, his embrace casual. He kept her tucked in close to his side. When they reached the kitchen, he pulled her chair out for her, waited until she got seated, then joined her at the table.

"So tell me what you do. I know you work at the shelter, but what's your job there?"

He began eating, not paying her much mind, and that made it easier to converse with him. "I work as a vet's assistant."

He nodded. "I sort of figured it'd be something like that."

"I've always loved animals."

"It shows."

He was so open and friendly, he made it easy to talk. "I'd always wanted to be a vet, but I never got my schooling finished for it."

"How far did you get?" In two large bites, he finished off a piece of toast.

Watching him eat amazed Sadie. Without looking like a glutton, he polished off the food in short order. She pulled her gaze away from him to taste her own eggs. Delicious.

"I got accepted to a veterinary college," she admitted, and hoped she didn't sound boastful.

"Yeah? You have to have a really high GPA for that, right?"

She remembered how thrilled and proud her mother had been. Buck sounded almost as admiring. "Yes. Admission was selective, but I'd already completed a pre-veterinary curriculum with a strong focus on the sciences. Anatomy, physiology, chemistry, microbiology and some clinical sciences."

"Wow. Heavy subjects. So what happened?"

Sadie toyed with her fork. "My mother needed me at home." So that he wouldn't misunderstand and think her mother selfish, she rushed through the rest of the explanation. "She'd raised me on her own. For as long as I can remember, it was just the two of us. She did a great job, but she was sick for years."

"Sick how?"

"Cancer." Just saying the word made Sadie relive the hurt. "She'd go into remission, feel a little better, then go downhill again. Each time it got worse and worse, and her recovery from treatment took longer. The cancer began to spread." Her voice started to shake. It hadn't been that long since she lost her mother, and talking about it still hurt. "I didn't want her to be alone."

Buck pushed his empty plate away. His brows were drawn with concern and sympathy. "You took care of her?"

"Me and a nurse who visited three times a week."

"How old were you when she first got diagnosed with cancer?"

Looking back, it seemed her mother had always been ill, but Sadie knew that wasn't true. It was just that when most young women were breaking away from home, striving for independence, she'd had to stay close to her mom. "We first found out she had breast cancer when I was almost fifteen. She had surgery, and things seemed okay for a year or so. Then they found more cancer. Lung. Bone." She swallowed and pushed her plate away. She couldn't eat another bite. "Eventually brain cancer."

Buck reached across the table and took her hand. "Must've been really rough."

Watching her mother weaken over time had been a living hell. But she'd borne it all alone. There'd been no one, other than peripheral strangers—doctors, nurses and a variety of legal people—to offer her any support or assistance.

For years, she'd been hungry for human contact, and to compensate for that lack, she'd turned to the animals she'd understood best. But now Buck held her hand as if he really cared. Sadie was amazed, and very grateful.

"Toward the end, she had very few good days."

Buck turned her hand over and rubbed her palm with his thumb while looking into her eyes. Sadie felt touched everywhere. Not just on her skin, but in her heart, too. For once, the icy memories didn't linger. They got soothed away by the intrusion of other, warmer emotions.

It was the oddest feeling, like falling into a deep, heated pool. Silence stretched out between them. She saw Buck's eyes narrow marginally, saw his shoulders tense.

He said, "Finish your breakfast, okay?"

"I am finished." Her upset was over, but now she was too excited and anxious to eat.

The dogs came back into the kitchen, distracting them both. Tish crept, keeping her eyes on the humans. Butch just pranced beside her, waiting as Tish dragged the colorful cotton boxers to a sunny spot in front of the sliding doors. She laid them down, used her nose to push them this way and that, digging, tugging with her teeth, before circling three times and dropping into the middle of the material with a grunt.

Butch, openly confused but unwilling to be left out, glanced at Sadie and Buck, back at Tish, then curled into her side.

A slow grin came over Buck's face. "I think she likes me."

Sadie actually giggled. "If she's willing to sleep in your underwear, then she must."

He turned to face her, still holding her hand captive. "And what about you?"

"I don't want to sleep in your underwear."

Buck accepted the joke with a laugh. He tugged her closer, leaning toward her at the same time. "But do you like me, Sadie? Because I like you. A lot."

And to Sadie's utter shock and excitement, he kissed her.

CHAPTER THREE

BUCK FELT AS THOUGH SOMEONE had just knocked him onto his terry-cloth-covered ass. It was a simple kiss, a featherlight brush of his mouth on hers. No tongues. No real heat.

And his whole body was buzzing.

He pulled back just a little to take in Sadie's expression. Her eyes were closed, her feathery lashes leaving shadows on the smooth texture of her flushed cheeks. She swayed a little toward him.

Damn.

When he'd started all this, he'd meant to go slow, to get to know her better, figure out why she didn't seem to like him.

Given her expression now, she liked him all right. But Sadie had more burdens than any single woman should have to bear. She was shy and sweet and so damn generous.

He leaned in again, but this time he let his nose graze her throat, inhaling the sweet female scent of her. You'd think a woman who played with animals from sunup to sundown wouldn't smell so nice. But she did. He felt…intoxicated.

And if his friends knew his thoughts, they'd laugh themselves silly.

Ethan and Riley and Harris, his best buddies for some time now, all considered him too goofy to ever settle down. Their wives probably agreed. He'd once heard Rosie call him a "goober." And then Clair, Harris's wife, had qualified that he was a "big lovable goober." Whatever the hell that meant. It didn't sound very complimentary, but the women had said it with affection, not insult, so Buck hadn't taken offense.

He knew he wasn't intense like Riley, and he sure as hell wasn't heroic like Ethan and Harris, who were both firefighters. He was just himself, easygoing, ready to laugh. He loved his lumberyard, his family and his friends. He loved women, and he especially loved sex. He was fortunate in that he'd inherited some good genes, resulting in a body that was tall and strong and well-muscled. All the men in his family were big—and plenty of women appreciated that.

He enjoyed good health and business success, so he'd never needed to take life too seriously. But bless her heart, Sadie hadn't been given that choice.

As he'd told her, she was a sweetheart. Petite and shy and loving. Determined and smart, but so withdrawn. He wanted to bring her out of her shell. He wanted to watch her laugh.

He wanted to get her naked and feel her softness

everywhere, and he wanted to hear her scream with a mind-blowing orgasm.

Yeah, he wanted that most of all.

"Buck?" Her voice was tentative, confused.

He sniffed his way up to her ear, brushed his nose across the downy hair at her temple. "Yeah?" he whispered, feeling more aroused by the second.

She cleared her throat, very stiff and still. "What are you doing?"

"Smelling you." He leaned back to see her face. "You smell good enough to eat."

A rush of scarlet filled her cheeks. "I, uh…"

"I don't mean right this second. We'll save that for later."

She looked ready to faint, prompting him to chuckle. He fingered the high neckline of her cardigan. "Aren't you too warm in this?"

"No." She clutched the neck together in a protective gesture.

"You sure?" Slowly, using the same care he'd shown with Tish, Buck pried her fingers loose. "It's comfortable in here, Sadie." Her top two buttons were undone, so he let his fingers drop to the third button, right above her breasts. It slid free. "I'm only wearing a towel and I'm not cold." Just the opposite, in fact.

Her eyes were wide and slightly dazed, her breath low and uneven.

When he finished undoing all the buttons, he

urged her to her feet and carefully pried the sweater off her shoulders. She was so fine-boned and fragile, he took extra care with her. Standing by her made him feel like a great ox.

She stared at him with wary apprehension and what he could have sworn was hopefulness.

He dropped her sweater over the back of her chair. "Okay?"

Practically panting, she licked her lips, blinked twice and nodded. Her breasts rose and fell beneath the pink blouse.

So damn sweet. He cupped her face. "Can I ask you something really personal?"

She stared at his mouth. "What?"

"When was the last time someone kissed you silly?" He waited, wondering if it'd been a week, a month, or longer. She seemed very unsure of herself and what he had planned.

On stiff legs, Sadie took a tiny step closer to him, then another. With incredible caution, she lifted her hands and let them touch his chest. Her fingers spread out, tangling in his chest hair, while her thumbs rubbed small inquisitive circles on his skin.

It drove him wild.

With her attention on her hands, all he could see was the top of her head. "Look at me, Sadie."

She did, tipping her head way back. Her lips parted.

"Answer my question."

Her expression was shy, embarrassed, resigned. She lifted one delicate shoulder and sighed out her reply, "Never."

"Never?" Disbelief made his voice sharper than he'd intended.

She shook her head and admitted with a grimace, "I've never dated. Never had a boyfriend. Never... done any of that stuff."

Conflicting emotions raged through Buck. Tenderness was at the forefront, so strong it nearly choked him. Damn, but he wanted to pull her onto his lap and cherish her.

Lust ran a close second. He was only a man, and knowing that no one had done *anything* with her before him turned him on. He'd be her first in every way, and there were so many things he could show her, teach her, let her experience.

Pity was there, too, because no woman should have been so ignored. He wished like hell that he'd forced his way over sooner, instead of letting her remain alone for so long. He'd stupidly wasted three months.

Behind everything else he felt was the need to stake a claim. Not just a friendly, neighborly-type thing, either. He wanted to somehow bind Sadie to him, and the easiest way presenting itself was through sex. Because of her inexperience, intimacy would mean more to her than it did to the women he usually spent time with.

"I'm going to kiss you, silly, okay?" It felt strange to announce his intent, but he needed to know that she understood, that he wasn't taking advantage of her naiveté.

"If…if you really want to."

Oh, yeah, he wanted to. He cupped her face, tipped her chin up and tried to quiet the wild drumming of his heart so he could do this right. "I want to."

It'd been a hell of a long time since he'd had to concentrate on a kiss. Usually it was the way he touched a woman, with the purpose of bringing her to orgasm, that made him concentrate. Not the foreplay, and for sure not the preliminary kissing.

The urge to devour her mouth was strong, but Buck managed to go slow, moving his mouth over hers until she softened and sighed. He licked her bottom lip, liked it enough to do it again, then gently nibbled. Her breath caught.

"Open up for me, Sadie."

With an excited little moan, she did, and Buck again cautioned himself to go slowly. He held her still and tentatively explored the moist heat of her mouth, letting her get used to his tongue, to the added excitement of a French kiss.

Damn, he'd forgotten how much fun kissing could be. He'd forgotten the sexiness of it. He opened one big hand over the back of Sadie's head to keep her close, and slanted his mouth over hers, deepening the kiss, feeling the heat rise between them. He realized he could kiss her all day and not get enough.

Shyly, her tongue came out to touch his. He felt a sexual jolt so powerful he couldn't hold back his groan.

He lifted his head and looked at her, amazed by his own reaction. He'd had plenty of hot, wet-tongue duels in his day, most that he knew would lead to hotter, wetter sex. But none had affected him quite like this.

Sadie's eyes were only partially open, her cheeks warm, and as he watched, she slowly licked her lips, as if savoring the flavor of their kiss.

Another groan tried to crawl up his throat. He wanted to lower her to the kitchen floor and show her just how clever his tongue could be.

Instead, he pulled her into his chest to hold her close. It took him a full minute to find his voice. In the meantime, he stroked her back and rubbed his chin against the crown of her head.

Finally, wondering at her thoughts, he asked, "Well?"

"Wow."

She sounded as breathless as he felt, which made him smile. "You liked it?"

She snuggled closer before asking, "Could we do it again?"

She'd be the death of him. "Oh, yeah. But I gotta take a break first."

Sadie reared back, blinking fast. "I'm sorry. I didn't mean to be—"

Buck put a finger to her mouth to hush her. Her lips were full and soft, slightly swollen. "If I kiss you again right now, I'm going to lose it. I don't want to rush you."

With no hesitation at all, she said, "You're not."

Her fast reply was so endearing, his grin went crooked. "I will be if we don't slow it down a little."

"But I don't mind."

Damn, she obliterated his control. "Sadie—"

"You don't understand, Buck. I didn't think anything like this would ever happen to me."

She looked so vulnerable, it bothered him. "That's just crazy." He knew damn good and well that other men had wanted her. But her eyes were now wide and sincere.

"No, it's not. Men like you don't look at me twice."

"Men like me?"

"Nice men. Attractive men." She again ducked her face, leaving him to look at the top of her head. "I've been asked out a few times, but it was by men I wasn't interested in. Maybe my standards are too high. Maybe I expect too much. But I just couldn't encourage a man I wasn't attracted to."

"Who asked you out?"

Her little nose wrinkled. "There's this one guy who cleans at the shelter. He…smells funny. And his hair always looks dirty."

In a dry tone, Buck said, "Cleanliness doesn't qualify as part of a high standard."

"There's also this man who won't get his cat

spayed. Three times now he's dropped off litters at the clinic." Her brows puckered. "I don't like him."

"Anyone who doesn't take proper care of their pet is a jerk, and of course you wouldn't date a jerk." He tipped his head to see her face. "What about in high school or college? Surely—"

She shook her head, cutting him off before he could finish the question.

"Well, why not?" *Everyone* dated as teenagers. Even if she'd just gone to a few school dances, they counted.

Her bottom lip was caught in her teeth. Sadie touched his chest, absently toying with his chest hair. Buck didn't think she even realized what she was doing.

"Sadie?"

"I didn't date then, either."

Buck could tell the topic was difficult for her. He had a feeling it was important, though, so he pushed her. "You said you trust me."

Her sigh was long and exaggerated. "Back in high school, a few guys asked me out. But I had to turn them down."

"Because?"

"They just asked me as part of a dare. Like a…a joke."

Suspicions rose. "What makes you say that?"

"Because once, only once, I said yes." She lifted her chin, catching him in her dark gaze. "It was prom night, and I got stood up. That next week in school, everyone was laughing about it."

Aw, hell. His gut cramped. Stupidly enough, he wanted to find the punk who'd bruised her feelings and pound on him. "It was his loss."

Sadie smiled, then laughed. "I doubt he saw it that way."

"So you're attracted to me?" Buck deliberately took her off guard with that question, changing the subject at the same time.

"What?"

"You said you couldn't get involved with a guy you weren't attracted to. And since we'll be getting involved…" He waited, but she didn't deny it. "I figured you must be attracted. Right?"

She stared at him in disbelief. "Of course I am. What woman wouldn't be?"

He had to laugh. The confusion on her face was priceless. "Honey, plenty of women turn me down."

"But…why would they?"

Buck tucked her face into his shoulder so she wouldn't think he was laughing at her. "You're going to make me conceited."

He felt her lips touch his skin. "No. But you are sexy and strong and handsome and funny."

"Sadie, stop."

"It's true."

Her compliments should have pleased him, except that he knew she drew unfavorable comparisons between them. "You're not too strong from what I can tell, but you're definitely sexy."

She snorted, and coming from Sadie it seemed a very odd sound.

Buck caught her face and turned it up toward his. "It's true. You're about the softest thing I've ever touched." He kissed each of her eyelids and felt the flutter of her long lashes. "Your eyes could eat a man alive."

She looked away in embarrassment.

"And your big heart just turns me to mush."

Her gaze swung back to his. "My big heart?"

"The way you love the animals." She'd shared so much, he figured he should share a little, too. "Do you know, I've stood at my window and watched you with them? A few times, I even hung out in the yard, wanting to join in." He flicked the end of her nose. "But you never asked me to."

Her brows shot up. "I didn't think you'd want to."

"So now we're both learning something."

Tish let out a squeaky bark, drawing their attention.

Sadie groaned. "Oh, no. She wants out again."

The dog stood on Buck's underwear, her ears back, waiting.

"I can help you get the leash on her."

"Easier said than done. She runs from me, and as you've already seen, she's hard to catch."

Buck decided to try his luck. But sure enough, as soon as he got close to Tish, she grabbed up his underwear and ran off with Butch in hot pursuit. They shot under the couch and out of reach before Buck could stop them.

Sadie stepped up behind him. "See? This is why I had to buy a carpet shampooer."

"Why?"

"Because she wants out, but she's afraid of me, so she sneaks off and ends up…piddling on the floor."

Buck grinned. Piddling, indeed. "Let's put our collective minds to this one. We're bigger, definitely smarter and human. I might not be the swiftest guy going, but no way am I going to be outwitted by a Chihuahua."

Sadie sat on the chair opposite him. "Any ideas?"

Buck bent and looked beneath the couch. Butch, normally so nice to him, had turned into Demon Dog. He snarled and growled, placing himself in front of Tish.

"You'd think I was a marauder of Chihuahuas the way he's carrying on," Buck complained.

"He thinks he's guarding her."

"Easy boy. She's all yours." Butch was not reassured, given the way he continued to bristle. Then, a thought coming to mind, Buck said, "Wanna go out? C'mon, Butch. Wanna go out?"

Butch's ears perked up and he barked in excitement. He started to crawl out from under the couch, but when Tish didn't follow, he whined.

Buck moved to stand behind Sadie's chair. "Let's be really quiet. Don't move, okay?"

She shrugged.

"C'mon, Butch old buddy. Let's go outside."

Again, Butch came out, then grumbled and whined until Tish poked her little bald head out. She had Buck's underwear clamped in her teeth. She eyed the humans, then crept toward the patio doors.

"Where's the leash?" Buck asked.

"On the wall by the door. But don't pounce on her. If you do, she'll never learn to trust me."

"I haven't pounced on you, have I?"

"Uh...no."

"Remember—trust." He slipped out from behind the chair. Butch saw him and started yapping in happiness. Slowly, Buck knelt down about five feet from the dogs. "Come on over here, Butch. If you do, she might."

Butch never turned down a nice pet session, so he did as instructed. Buck spent a long time just stroking the dog, playing a little, lavishing attention on him. Tish watched from a safe distance in fascination and obvious yearning.

She reminded Buck of Sadie.

He turned to her. "Sit with us. Slowly. Tish knows you better than she does me."

Sadie sidled over to them, took the leash off the peg on the wall, then knelt down beside Buck. She scratched Butch behind his big ears. Finally, after a long, long time that strained Buck's patience but didn't seem to bother Sadie at all, Tish took a few steps toward them.

She halted, eyeing them warily.

They deliberately ignored her, hoping that without their attention on her, she'd feel safe and join in. Eventually she got close enough to lean on Sadie's foot. The yellow underwear hung from the side of her mouth, looking like a flag.

Sadie cautiously reached out and scratched the dog's chin. As long as she didn't raise her hand or move too fast, Tish was tolerant. But the second Sadie went to pet the top of her head, Tish flinched away.

Buck's voice was soft, hiding his frustration. "It's okay, baby girl. No one's going to hurt you." He held out his hand, palm up. Tish sniffed, but wouldn't rejoin them.

Butch didn't like being ignored and again insisted on going outside as promised.

Very, very slowly, Buck caught Tish. She went spastic, howling and moaning and kicking.

He held on to her, and she held on to his underwear.

If it hadn't been for the dog's fear, Buck would have been amused. "You can keep my drawers, baby girl. Whatever you want."

Sadie, fretting like a worried mama, hurried to get the leash on her and open the door. Buck scanned the yard, thankful it was empty, and set Tish outside. To their surprise, she didn't fight the leash as long as Butch stayed beside her.

And Butch, bless his savage little animal instincts, didn't move more than an inch away from Tish. It was almost comical watching them. They kept bumping into each other, tripping over Buck's colorful boxers.

Sadie sat in her one and only lawn chair, and Buck stood beside her, holding the reins on the dog. "Tish makes a better leash for Butch than the one Red usually uses for him."

Sadie grinned. "He's protective."

Buck bent and kissed her temple. "Most of the male species suffers the same affliction."

Because the dogs were happy, they spent a long time outside. The sun shone directly on them, warming their skin and burning the chill out of the morning air until the day felt pleasant. The dogs were sometimes playing, sometimes just lying in the sun-warmed grass. Tish forgot all about her leash.

Sadie watched the dogs with a pleased smile, and Buck watched Sadie.

The sunlight did amazing things to her hair, and showed the perfection of her skin. In the bright light, Buck could see that her lashes were tipped with gold, and there were a few faint freckles over the bridge of her nose. He thought she looked beautiful, especially when she smiled so sweetly.

After a while, he lifted her from the seat, sat down, then situated her on his lap.

"Want to make out?"

"Here?" Her scandalized gaze darted around the empty yard. "Someone might see us."

"Who? Most everyone is still in bed, and even if they're not, they still couldn't see us. My apartment is empty, and your apartment is on the corner."

He enjoyed seeing her face heat with guilt.

"Come on, Sadie," he teased. "You know you want to."

She hesitated only a moment. "I do."

The dogs were currently dozing, so Buck was able to engage all her attention.

It was wonderful.

True, he wore no more than a towel. But it was his vacation and doing nothing more important than smooching with Sadie just felt right. It was frustrating, to be sure. He hadn't indulged in this much innocent kissing since junior high school. Sadie's enthusiastic involvement made it even harder. She followed wherever he led. If he kissed her throat, she murmured in delight, then reciprocated, putting her soft lips against his heated skin. If he stroked her narrow waist, she followed suit by smoothing her hands over his chest to his abdomen.

Her innocent exploration was more exciting to him than the lovemaking of other women.

When enough time had passed, Buck reluctantly went inside to call Henry. The manager grumbled and groused, but finally agreed to meet Buck at the back of his apartment when Buck explained he was damn near naked.

Sadie giggled at his predicament. But she quickly

sobered when Buck picked up a disgruntled Butch and started to leave. She walked him to the door, her feet lagging, her eyes downcast.

They stopped at the door. "Have lunch with me?" Buck asked.

Immediately her expression brightened. "Yes."

He shook his head. She wore her heart on her sleeve, leaving herself so open to hurt. It worried him. "I have a few errands to take care of, but I can be done by noon. You like pizza?"

"Yes."

"I'll pick it up. Wanna come to my place?"

She shook her head. "I can't leave Tish..."

"So bring her with you." He leaned forward and took her mouth in a warm kiss, already anxious to see her again. "You're a package deal, right? No problem. Butch would chew my ankle if I didn't invite her along."

Laughing, Sadie said, "All right, then. We'd be happy to accept."

CHAPTER FOUR

BUCK HAD JUST RETURNED from buying groceries when a knock sounded on his front door. Thinking it might be Sadie, he opened the door with a fat smile—which twisted to a scowl when he saw the faces of his friends Ethan and Harris.

"What are you two doing here?"

Harris shoved his way in. "What kind of welcome is that?"

Butch rounded the corner in a near-hysterical tangent, slid to a halt when he saw it was only Harris and Ethan, and immediately quieted. His tail stopped wagging, and his little face showed his disappointment.

Buck decided that he and Butch were in a bad way. They were two bachelors who'd accepted their fates, but hadn't yet informed the ladies of the new plans.

Ethan stepped past Buck. "Hey, Butch." Then to Buck, he said, "You been torturing the little guy? He doesn't look too happy."

"He probably thought you were Tish."

"Tish?" Harris straightened in interest. "What the hell kind of name is that for a woman?"

"I think it's cute," Ethan argued. "She sounds like a woman with big boobs."

Harris laughed. "And an IQ of two."

"Looks who talking," Buck accused. "Has anyone accused you of being bright lately?"

Smug, Harris said, "Yeah. Clair."

"She doesn't count," Ethan argued. "She married you, so she has to keep your ego healthy."

"Actually," Buck interjected, before they could start a debate on Harris's intelligence or lack thereof, "Tish is fat and bald and this morning, she stole my underwear."

Both men wore comical faces of horror, until Buck began to chuckle. "She's my neighbor's dog. A Chihuahua. Butch took one look at her and fell madly in love."

"Poor guy," Ethan said sympathetically. "I know just how rotten that feels."

"Right," Harris sneered. "You knew Rosie *forever* before you realized you loved her."

"Wrong. I always knew I loved her. I just didn't realize I was in love with her. Besides, you're no better. It wasn't until you saw naked photos of Clair that you got the love bug."

Harris, ever sensitive about the photos Clair's past boyfriend had taken without her knowledge, grew taut with anger.

"No fighting. It'll upset Butch." Buck turned his back on them and headed for the kitchen. "So do either of you yahoos believe in love at first sight?"

"No," Harris said.

"No way," Ethan agreed, then he added, "But Riley must."

Buck paused in the middle of putting cans of cola into the fridge. "That's right. He took one look at Red and was a goner, wasn't he?"

"In a big way," Ethan agreed. He snagged a cola before Buck could put it away. "It was almost embarrassing, the way he branded her right off."

"I wish he was here."

Harris and Ethan looked at each other. Slowly they grinned with conspiratorial humor. Harris, being the bigger goof of the two, said, "Tell Uncle Harris what ails you."

"Go to hell."

"A woman ails him," Ethan said. "I know the signs."

"It was only a matter of time, you know." Harris grabbed a can of cola, and together, he and Ethan made a toast. "Here's to happily married men."

Buck said, "Marriage hasn't matured either of you at all."

Ignoring that gibe, Ethan said, "So tell us who the lucky lady is." His brows pulled together in consideration. "Is it Beth? I remember you were partial to her, but I gotta tell you, Rosie doesn't like her much."

"Rosie doesn't like any woman who smiles at you, Ethan, but no, it's not Beth."

"Then it must be Rachel." Harris held his hands out in front of his chest as if juggling melons. "There's a lot of her to love."

Buck narrowed his eyes. "Clair's gonna kill you when she hears what you said."

"Well, for God's sake, I was just kidding around. Don't tell her!"

Just then, a knock sounded on Buck's French doors—and there stood Sadie with a squirming Tish in her arms. Buck's underwear was half wrapped around the dog. Belatedly, Sadie noticed Ethan and Harris and appeared ready to bolt.

Buck wondered if he could somehow magically make the guys disappear. He ran through his options—but one look at them told Buck a team of wild horses couldn't drag them away. He gave up and opened the door.

Taking her by surprise he whispered, "Hey," and bent to press his mouth to hers in a warm kiss.

When he lifted his head, she looked speechless, breathless and too warm. She glanced at Harris and Ethan, who smiled at her in turn, and her blush intensified.

"I can come back later," she blurted. "I didn't mean to interrupt—"

Harris literally leaped forward. "You're not. Come on in."

Ethan pul' ?d a chair out for her. "Have a seat. Can I get you a cola?"

She looked overwhelmed by her welcome. "Well…"

Buck had to grin. Damn, but he had great friends. They were total idiots at times, which was part of their charm, but he could never doubt their loyalty.

Butch came barreling around the corner, saw Sadie and Tish, and there was no curbing his exhilaration. He turned circles, barked maniacally, and all but demanded that Sadie put Tish down.

"Young love," Harris crooned with a hand over his heart.

He tried to pet Tish, but she almost threw herself out of Sadie's arms trying to get away. Sadie juggled her to the ground, Tish snatched the underwear away from her, and together with Butch, she made her hasty escape.

Harris stared. "My God, she hates me."

"Probably heard about your reputation." Ethan grinned.

"Ha, ha." But Harris was both appalled and wounded by the dog's rejection. Buck knew just how he felt.

Sadie tried to reassure Harris. "She's very shy. She hasn't even gotten used to me yet. It wasn't personal."

"She was mistreated," Buck explained.

"Mistreated?" Ethan demanded. "Who would mistreat that little thing?" Buck told them all about what Tish had been through, then he went on to describe Sadie's role in caring for the animals. He left nothing out, extolling her dedication and caring.

She blushed as Harris and Ethan heaped praise on her for her generosity. Within minutes, the two men were settled at the table, drinking his cola and eating his pizza and hanging on Sadie's every word. Whenever she paused, they asked another question. Their interest was genuine, but Buck also knew they were deliberately welcoming her, trying to make her feel at ease.

There was something about Sadie that brought out a man's protective instincts. Her big heart, yes, but also her naked vulnerability, the way she left herself so emotionally exposed.

Buck thought about throwing them out, then decided it'd be nice for Sadie to get to know them better. He'd have her alone soon enough.

Or so he thought.

Two hours later, Harris and Ethan were still going strong. The dogs had reappeared for a drink and a doggie treat, then gone off again for the alone-time Buck craved.

He'd done little more than think about making love to Sadie. At first, he'd resisted the idea, thinking it might be better to ease her into it. Maybe spend a week just necking, then a week petting…but he knew his control wasn't strong enough for that. Not with Sadie.

And there was the very real concern that if he waited, she'd misconstrue his impatience for lack of interest. He couldn't have that.

He brought his attention back to his guests in time to hear Sadie say, "Yes, it's incredibly hard to give the dogs up, but I always make sure they go to a wonderful and appropriate home."

"So," Harris asked with visible hesitation, "would I be eligible to take one? Clair's been talking about getting a pet since we'll be moving into our own house soon." Then to explain, he added, "Ethan's wife, Rosie, is a realtor and she's always finding great deals on houses. The one we offered for is a handyman special, and since Buck is a real handyman, I couldn't pass it up."

Ethan nodded. "Rosie made kids and a dog and a damn picket fence all a stipulation before saying yes to my proposal." He winked. "I've been working most diligently on the kid part. Since that's not happening real fast, maybe I could surprise her with a dog. What about us? Do we qualify as suitable?"

Because Sadie barely knew Harris and Ethan, she glanced at Buck.

He nodded. "You're visiting with bona fide heroes, honey. Firefighters. Ethan's even been written up for daring deeds, and Harris once went back into a fire to save a kid's guinea pig. Neither one of them would ever neglect or abuse an animal. And their wives are terrific, too. You couldn't find a better home for a dog."

Harris pretended to sniff. "Damn, Buck, now you've made me all weepy."

Ethan laughed. "True friends always make each other sound good."

"Thank you," Sadie said with a smile. "I'll definitely keep you in mind."

Buck took Ethan's elbow. "Speaking of friends and what they do for each other—it's time for you two to hit the road."

Ethan allowed himself to be hauled out of his seat. Harris rose on his own steam with a lot of feigned offense. "What? No dessert? No coffee? See, this is why you need to get hitched. You're a lousy host."

Buck surprised them both by saying, "I'll see what I can do." He didn't turn to see Sadie's reaction. He'd find out how she felt about a real relationship soon enough.

As he practically dragged Harris and Ethan to the front door, they yelled back their farewells to Sadie, then started sniggering and elbowing Buck as he tried to shove them out onto the stoop.

Buck gave up. "So what do you think?"

Bobbing his eyebrows, Harris whispered, "Still waters run deep."

"Very sweet," Ethan added. "And gentle."

Buck was so relieved, he grinned. He'd been half afraid his buds wouldn't recognize Sadie's appeal. It wasn't in your face, like a lush figure or a stop-traffic face. She didn't have a load of sexual confidence or snappy charisma. She wasn't a fashion plate.

Sadie was subtly attractive.

So much so, he'd been afraid they might not see her appeal at all. God knew he'd missed it at first. But through Sadie, he was learning the truth about cats, dogs…and women. He was learning the truth about himself, and what he really wanted out of life.

He wanted Sadie.

Anyone so quietly kind and caring deserved a lot of love.

Buck had a hell of a lot of love to give.

"Thanks," he told his friends. "And goodbye."

Harris had his mouth open to say more when Buck shut the door. For good measure, he locked it. He could hear the male laughter of his friends as they strode away.

Bending down, he peered under his couch. Butch and Tish were curled tightly together in the yellow underwear. He could hardly tell where one Chihuahua started and the other ended. Cute.

Tish opened one eye, saw him and inched farther back.

"It's all right, baby girl. I won't bother you. Go back to sleep now." She kept watching him as if waiting to be pounced on.

Sighing, Buck decided that sooner or later, he'd win her over. He really, really wanted to hold her.

Sadie stood in the kitchen doorway. "The dogs are hiding?" she asked.

Buck straightened; their gazes met. Sadie's lips were parted to accommodate her fast breathing. His muscles tensed, his abdomen clenched.

It was time—and they both knew it.

"Yeah." He walked to her and held out a hand. "How long will they nap, do you think?"

Sadie put her hand in his. Her attention was on his mouth. "Long enough. At least, I hope so."

His smile felt silly and right and full of anticipation. His heart turned over. Damn, but she was perfect.

And starting now, she was his.

SADIE WENT DOWN THE HALL to Buck's bedroom with her heart tripping, her stomach fluttering and her thighs shaking. Anticipation stole her breath.

Her hand felt tiny in his. She watched the play of muscles in his broad back beneath the soft cotton shirt. He was so sinfully, deliciously, unbelievably gorgeous.

And he wanted her.

Sadie didn't care if it would be for an hour, a day, a week. It didn't matter; she wasn't about to turn him down. Whenever she fantasized, it was of a man like Buck, a man who was physically big and strong, but emotionally gentle and loving, who filled her dreams.

No other man she knew had ever been so concerned for an animal. When he spoke to Tish, it was as if he related to her. That took confidence, in himself and in his masculinity. Though she'd deliberately kept her distance, she'd always admired him. And after seeing him with her dog, her heart was lost.

He tugged her into his bedroom and shut the door. Facing her, his gaze molten and very direct, he murmured, "I don't want the dogs to wander in."

"No?"

"I'm not into exhibitionism."

He liked to joke. "I doubt they'd understand."

She didn't understand. Not yet anyway. But soon.

He leaned against the door. "You put your cardigan back on."

Excuses tripped on her tongue, but nothing coherent came out.

Lazily, Buck reached out with his long arms and began undoing the buttons for the second time that day. "It's okay. I like undressing you." His eyes lifted briefly to her face, then returned to her sweater. "Do you mind?"

Did she mind what? Nervousness took hold, making it hard for her to think beyond the obvious desire to know him physically.

"Would you be more comfortable in the dark? I can shut the blinds, but the truth is…I'm dying to see every soft, pink inch of you."

Oh, God. If he said things like that, she'd never

get through this. Sadie licked her lips. "No one's ever looked at me before."

His expression heated even more. "I know."

He pushed away from the door, and with his fingers busy on the last button of her sweater, took her mouth. The kiss was unlike the ones earlier in the day. He ate at her mouth, consumed her, made her burn.

"Damn." His laugh was shaky as he stripped off her sweater. "I should be honest and tell you that your virginity is an enormous turn-on. I can't wait to take you, to see your face when I push inside you, when you come…"

Sadie sucked in a startled breath. She couldn't wait, either. "You first."

Buck paused. "Me first what?" He half laughed. "If I come first, I'm afraid the gig is up. I'd need at least an hour to—"

"No." Her face burned. "I meant…would you undress first? Then I won't feel so…naked."

He shrugged one hard shoulder. "Sure. Modesty isn't one of my virtues." Reaching back, he grabbed a fistful of his shirt and yanked it off. He dropped it onto the floor beside them. Smiling at her, he lifted one foot and tugged off his shoe and sock, then removed the other.

Sadie's heartbeat accelerated. Buck wasn't an overly hairy man, but there was a nice patch of brown curls between his well-developed pecs, and farther down, trailing from his navel into his jeans. She al-

ready knew that hair was silky soft and that his skin
was warm and taut.

He opened the snap of his jeans.

"Okay?" he asked, watching her closely.

"Yes." More than okay. She'd already seen him in
his underwear and a towel. Now she wanted to see
everything.

He shoved the jeans down, taking his underwear
off at the same time. He kicked them aside, straightened—and let her look her fill.

Holy moly. Everything in her felt tight and liquid
and hot. Embarrassment ebbed, replaced with fascination. Sadie had never seen a naked man up close.
It was so nice that her first was the epitome of masculine perfection.

Raising her gaze to his face, she said, "You're
amazing."

A startled laugh escaped him. "Look all you want,
honey, but you know, you can touch, too."

That was all the encouragement she needed.
"Thank you." She leaned up against him. "Kiss me
again, okay?" It'd be easier for her to explore his
body if he wasn't looking at her with such probing
expectation.

His tone was more serious than she had expected
when he said, "Anything you want, Sadie."

And then his mouth was over hers, treating her to
a long, slow, tongue-teasing kiss that made her toes
curl in her shoes.

Sadie started with her hands on his shoulders. His skin was hot and sleek, but she preferred the feel of his hairy chest. When her palms grazed his nipples, he gave a small growl of pleasure, and then his hands were on her breasts, too.

Even through her blouse, she could feel the heat of his palms, the strength. He cuddled her breasts, shaped them, and finally his thumbs moved over her nipples, circling, barely stroking, but eliciting a gasp of surprise at the sharp intensity of the sensation.

"Nice, huh?" he murmured against her mouth.

"Yes." She knew her reply sounded a lot like a moan.

"You'll like it even more once we get your clothes out of the way."

As far as hints went, that was pretty clear. "All right."

He showed his appreciation of her reply with another voracious kiss, while his hands left her breasts to tackle the buttons on her blouse. These were smaller than the ones on her sweater, and not as easy to undo. But Sadie had little thought for her own clothes with Buck's powerful body bared for her pleasure.

She let her fingers trace the tense muscles of his abdomen, tease the silkier hair beneath his navel, then she dipped lower. His penis jutted out, hard and warm. Fascinated, she cupped him in both hands.

With a low growl, Buck seemed to forget about undressing her. He dropped his forehead to hers. In a rasping whisper, he said, "I love having you hold me, Sadie."

A little awed, she spoke without measuring her words. "You're so hot and so soft."

"Not soft at all."

"No, I didn't mean that. Your skin is velvety. I didn't expect that." She continued to explore him while Buck made sounds of mingled pain and pleasure. "And you feel alive. You're even throbbing."

His hand curled over hers, forcing her to squeeze him a little tighter, then stroke. Once. Twice. "Okay. That's enough of that." With a raw, broken laugh, he pulled her hands away, kissed each palm, then put them on his shoulders. "Safer ground, at least for now, okay?"

Confused, Sadie asked, "I did it wrong?"

"You did it too *right*. And no way in hell do I want to come early on your first time."

"Oh." He was so frank in his speech, she should have been embarrassed again, but somehow, his lack of embarrassment reassured her.

She'd forgotten about him unbuttoning her blouse until he dragged it off her shoulders. Her bra was plain white cotton with no decoration at all.

But Buck didn't even seem to notice. Once the blouse was gone, he reached around her and un-hooked her bra with practised ease. He stepped back, leaving the bra to hang loosely on her slender frame. His gaze burning, he used just his fingertips trailing over her shoulders to drag the straps down her arms.

The bra slipped, then fell free past her elbows. Sadie let it drop to the floor.

Refusing to be too timid, she put her shoulders back and kept her spine straight.

Buck's gaze was so hot, so admiring as he stared at her breasts, that she didn't feel too small despite her modest bust. Throwing his own words back at him, she whispered, "I don't mind you looking, but you're welcome to touch, too."

"Yeah?" he asked with a slow grin. "Thank God. I'm not sure I could mind my manners right now."

But he didn't just touch her. No, he shocked her senseless by catching her waist, lifting her to her tiptoes while he bent down, and then his mouth was over her left nipple, his rough tongue licking, curling around her, and then he sucked.

"Buck." Sadie tunneled her fingers through his hair, holding on for dear life.

He gave a rough groan and moved to her other breast.

She felt the draw of his mouth everywhere, in each of her breasts, in her trembling thighs, and most especially low in her stomach, where a tingling ache expanded on waves.

"We gotta lose the skirt now, too, baby." He set her back on her feet and hurriedly opened the zipper down her side. "I'm sorry, I know I'm not being very patient." He went down on one knee and pulled her skirt to her ankles. "But it's crazy how bad I want you."

Sadie stared down at him, touched, flattered, turned on. "Whatever you want, Buck."

He helped her step out of her shoes and skirt. "I want this. Don't faint on me, okay?"

That was all the warning Sadie got before he cupped her fanny in his hands, pulled her forward and kissed her through her white cotton panties.

"Ohmigod."

"Yeah," he murmured, and even his breath felt erotic and tantalizing. "You smell delicious."

Never in her life had Sadie imagined a man saying such a thing while doing such a thing.

His tongue pressed against her, seeking, and her knees wanted to buckle. "I...I need to sit down."

"Not yet," he growled. "Once you're on the bed, things are going to get out of control pretty quick." He squeezed her bottom, kneading her, then hooked his thumbs into her waistband and eased her panties down. "Step out, Sadie."

She had to brace herself on his shoulders to do that. When she stood before him naked, she expected him to stand. He didn't. He put his thick arms around her and hugged her close, with his cheek on her belly, his hands opened wide on her back.

"You're beautiful."

Sex talk, Sadie thought, and smiled. While her muscles turned to mush, she stroked his hair and wondered how long this euphoria could last.

It wouldn't be long enough for her.

Buck leaned back and looked up at her. "You don't believe me?"

Her smile twitched. "It doesn't matter." She cupped his jaw in her hands. "You can't know how happy I am to be here with you. Not just with any man, but with you, Buck."

His gaze holding hers, he dragged his palms down her back to her bottom, then the back of her thighs. "Why?"

"Besides the obvious?"

His fingers rose higher again, this time between her thighs. His gaze never wavered. "What's the obvious?"

"That you're sexy and handsome and have an incredible body."

That gave him pause, but only for a moment. Sadie felt his fingertips touching her intimately from behind. Another thing she'd never imagined!

"What's not so obvious?"

"I…I can't talk while you do that."

"Yeah, you can."

One finger teased at her tender lips, gently probing without quite entering her. Sadie felt her own wetness and had to close her eyes to think.

"Tell me," he insisted. "Why me and not some other guy?"

"You're good to Tish. You're gentle with Butch." She opened her eyes so she could make sure he understood. "And you make me laugh."

He pushed his finger deeper, his expression strained, his breathing harsh. "You're so damn tight."

Sadie tipped her head back and moaned, as much from what he said as what he did.

"Am I hurting you?"

She shook her head. "No." She knew in her heart that Buck would never hurt her. Not physically. But he was bound to break her heart when their time together ended.

He kissed her belly. His tongue dipped into her navel, trailed a damp path down to her pubic curls, then he used his thumbs to open her. "You're wet, Sadie, but I want you wetter. I want to know for sure that I won't hurt you. You're just so damn small, and I'm not—"

"No," she agreed with a smile. "You're not." That she could smile at the moment, that even now Buck amused her and made her feel lighthearted, was nothing short of a miracle. He was a miracle. And for now, he was all hers.

She felt his tongue searching, and had to lock her knees. "Buck, I really need to lie down."

"In a minute." He worked a second finger into her, pressed deep, slowly withdrew, and pushed in again.

"Oh, God." Giving up, Sadie automatically widened her stance and let him do as he pleased, because what he did pleased her, too.

He nuzzled closer, his breath burning, his tongue damp and soft, seeking until he curled it around her clitoris. Her heart and lungs threatened to explode. Her body shivered all over.

And then he was suckling again, this time with such devastating effect that she almost couldn't bear it. Sensations grew, twisting inside her, shaking her, all the while expanding, receding, then coming back stronger—and she knew what was about to happen.

She clenched her fingers in his hair to stay upright and let the awesome shock waves roll over her.

Somehow she ended up on her back on Buck's bed. His mouth was now at her breast, sucking strongly, while his fingers remained inside her, keeping her orgasm alive. Sadie twisted and groaned. She couldn't silence her cries or hold herself still.

Finally, after long agonizingly amazing moments, Buck kissed his way gently up to her temple. He pulled her close and just held her.

Sadie stared at the ceiling in blank surprise. She'd never dreamed…never quite imagined… "Buck?"

"Hmm?" He kissed her ear and hugged her.

"That was *wonderful*."

He shoved up on one elbow and, though he wasn't smiling, she saw the glint of humor in his green eyes. "You're something else, you know that?"

She shook her head. She'd always thought she was pretty darn ordinary, in a plain, easy-to-ignore way.

Buck looked down at her breasts and began tracing one nipple with a fingertip. "I expected you to be really shy."

"I am."

"I expected you to be uptight. I thought I'd have to work at getting you to relax." He bent and gave her a quick kiss, which made her blush considering where his mouth had just been. He grinned. "But you're a hedonist at heart, aren't you?"

Sadie considered that. "I enjoyed what you did." She turned a little toward him so she could stroke his chest and abdomen. "And you make me feel comfortable. You're so matter-of-fact about everything. I didn't quite know how this would work, but it just seemed natural with you."

He nodded, looking far too grave. "Right. With *me*." He sat up and opened the bedside drawer. "Remember that, okay?"

Sadie watched as he located a condom and rolled it on.

"You're going to finish making love to me now?"

"No. I won't finish now. I'll take my time. But I am dying to get inside you. And after we both come, maybe we'll nap or get a snack or watch a movie." He stretched out over her, held her face and kissed the bridge of her nose. And in a voice husky with arousal he said, "Then we can start all over again."

"Really?" Sounded like a great plan to Sadie.

"Oh, yeah. You're spending the night, okay?"

Before she could answer, he kissed her deeply. He went on kissing her until she punched his shoulder and demanded he get a move on.

Laughing, Buck said, "Yes, ma'am." He reached down between their bodies, opened her and slowly pressed in.

Her breath caught.

His jaw clenched.

He was big, and she felt incredible pressure.

"Stay with me, Sadie." He braced himself on stiffened arms, which increased the pressure between her legs. He squeezed his eyes shut, clenched his jaw, then had the nerve to say, "Relax."

"I don't think I can."

He groaned. "Bend your knees, honey. Lift into me." To help her, he lowered himself onto one elbow and wedged a hand under her hips. "That's it."

His fingers clenched on her bottom, he let out a long, exaggerated groan, and then he sank deep.

Sadie cried out, not in pain but with mind-numbing pleasure. Buck didn't slow or give her time to get acclimated to his size. He pulled out and drove in again. Both hands went to her bottom, tilting her up to take more of him. His body was warm and heavy. The friction was incredible.

She wrapped her arms around his neck, her legs around his waist, and tried to follow his rhythm.

But far too soon, he stiffened. Sadie knew he was about to climax and curiosity distracted her. Until he opened his mouth on her throat and gave her a love bite. It was so wicked, such a sexual act of possession, she felt her own orgasm swelling again and she embraced it. It was different this time, with Buck a part of her. It was more powerful, and more satisfying, to be able to squeeze him tight inside her body.

Her limbs trembled and throbbed. Vaguely she was aware of Buck trembling, too, his muscles all straining, his growls raw and broken. Moments later he lowered himself onto her, but immediately rolled onto his back so that she was on top.

For several minutes they lay there like that. Then Sadie felt him pull out of her, and even that was an enjoyable experience.

"My backside is cold."

He grunted and blindly reached for a sheet, dragging it up and over her. "Sleep woman. I need to recoup my strength."

His heartbeat was a steady thumping beneath her cheek. His arms were around her, his hands now cuddling her bottom, presumably to warm it. And she felt so lax, so utterly replete, that she dozed off without a single care on her mind.

CHAPTER FIVE

TWO NIGHTS LATER, Buck accidentally woke Sadie in the middle of the night when he climbed back into bed. They'd spent the entire weekend together, alternately playing with the dogs, eating, watching movies, and making love.

Just that evening, after she'd gone limp in his arms from a long, screaming climax, Sadie had told him that she hadn't realized life could be so relaxed and enjoyable. She broke his heart when she said things like that, and made him more determined than ever to make up for her selfless and lonely childhood.

On the outside, Sadie continued to look shy and timid. But deep inside, she was wild and without reserve. She made no bones about loving sex. She wanted to try everything, claming she had a lot of catching up to do.

Buck was more than happy to oblige her.

He wanted to cherish her, and toward that aim, he kissed her all the time, for no reason and for every reason. If she fixed coffee, it deserved a kiss. If she yawned, he thought it was cute and had to nibble on her lips.

When she struggled with Tish or had to clean up a mess from the dog, he offered to help. And when Tish dragged a hideous half-dead bug into the house, Buck got rid of it for her, then hugged her and kissed her again and again until she stopped making awful faces.

He'd even tackled another cicada for her. He hoped she realized that, with his aversion to the red-eyed monsters, he wouldn't have done that for just anyone.

Sadie obviously hadn't heard him leave the bed earlier, given her suspicious look now. "Where've you been?"

For a woman who'd spent her life sleeping alone, she'd quickly accustomed herself to having him take more than half the bed. She compensated by sprawl-ing over him. Buck liked that.

He deliberately snuggled close, making sure his cold feet brushed hers. She yelped and pulled her feet up to his calves.

"I was outside."

"Doing what?"

"Herding Chihuahuas." He smiled and kissed her shoulder. She had the silkiest, most baby-fine skin he'd ever felt. She was soft everywhere, and it made him nuts. "Butch wanted out, and of course, Tish had to follow. But she got past me without her leash, and then Butch shot out, too. I chased Tish, and Butch chased me."

Sadie snickered at the picture he painted.

In mock annoyance, he said, "Hey, catching her again wasn't easy. But at least I had enough sense to pull my jeans on this time."

Still grinning, looking tousled and sexy and sweet, she sat up. "You should have woken me up."

Buck pulled her back down into his arms. "You were dead out, so I didn't want to bother you." He cupped her naked breast, loving the feel of her.

Loving her. *Damn.*

"Buck?"

"But you're awake now," he drawled.

Sadie's voice went deep and she sank down against him. "I am. Very awake."

Buck pulled her beneath him. Words of love tried to break free, but he knew it was too soon. Sadie needed a little time to get used to the physical side of having a man in her bed before he dumped the emotional stuff on her, too. Even while kissing her shoulder, he murmured, "It's four-thirty in the morning. I should let you sleep."

"I have to be up for work in an hour anyway."

He trailed kisses along her throat. "That's an extra hour you could sleep." He'd already learned Sadie's secrets and knew that she was especially sensitive on her throat, behind her ear, and beneath her breasts. Of course, she went wild when he licked at the inside of her thighs, too, and higher—

Her hand closed over his cock and Buck stilled.

"Know what I'd rather do in that hour?"

Oh, he could just imagine. She was a generous lover, but also wicked enough to enjoy tormenting him. "I don't know if I can bear for you to tell me."

With her free hand, she pushed against him until he obligingly went onto his back—giving her free rein over his body.

"I want to kiss you all over."

Excitement trembled along his nerve endings. He'd never live through this. "Okay."

Smiling with newfound female power, Sadie climbed atop him. She did seem to enjoy his body; she made plenty of comments on his strength and size.

"You relax, okay?"

He laughed. "Not a chance, honey."

Her lips grazed his. "Then at least hold still."

Lord help him. He locked his hands behind his head and promised to try his best. It sure as hell wasn't easy. Twenty minutes later, Sadie was on her knees between his thighs. She'd been slowly—and he did mean slowly—working her soft mouth down his body.

Now she held his cock in one hand, his balls in the other, and it was heavenly torture. "Hussy," he teased with a low groan. "Put me out of my misery before I break."

Laughing, she whispered, "All right." And then she bent, kissed the head of his erection, opened her mouth and swallowed him.

Buck stiffened with a wrenching growl.

Her tongue swirled, gave one final lick and she lifted her head. "Hold still."

"Can't."

Her small fist stroked. "Keep trying." And she took him in her mouth again, all the while cuddling his balls, working him. She was a fast learner, and teaching her was its own form of pleasurable agony.

To make matters worse, the moonlight shone through the window, putting her small round breasts on display. It was enough. Too much. He caught her shoulders and pulled her up onto his chest.

"Buck," she complained.

"Sorry, babe." He groped on the bedside table for a condom, while holding Sadie still with his other hand. He ripped it open with his teeth, then handed it to her. "Here, put this on me."

"Oh." She straightened, eyed the protection and smiled. "Okay." She wore that concentrated, fascinated expression that made him hot as a chili pepper. "Like this?"

With awful precision, she rolled the condom halfway down his length.

His teeth clenched. "You little tease." He hurriedly finished the job while Sadie chuckled, but she stopped laughing when he lifted her, positioned himself and drove up into her.

Her fingers curled against his chest, stinging in force while proving her own measure of excitement.

"Do whatever you want, Sadie," he managed to say. "Fast, slow, I don't care, as long as you keep moving."

Luckily for his peace of mind, she was in a fast mood. Buck held her breasts, lightly tugging at her nipples while she labored over him, rising and falling, again and again. He was so deep this way, and he loved being able to watch her face as her climax overtook her. She didn't hide from him, but at the crucial moment, she did fall onto his chest and let him take charge.

All she could do was moan.

Buck loved it. He loved her. He even loved her difficult little dog.

Soon she'd fall in love with him, too. He was counting on it.

SADIE ENJOYED HER JOB at the shelter, but because she always had a pet waiting, she never lingered after work. The need to rush home was even more urgent with Tish, because she knew that, more than most, the little dog needed reassurance and human contact.

That hadn't changed. But now she also had Buck to come home to. So she smiled as she drove, thinking of how he'd hug her when she walked in, how the dogs would run to greet her. Everything was so perfect, it scared her.

If she told Buck she loved him, would he misunderstand? Would he assume her feelings were no more than an infatuation, because she'd never been intimate with another man? Or would he realize just how special he was to her?

She didn't know, and for that reason, she hesitated to put her feelings into words.

Until Buck, she hadn't known how much was missing in her life. But knowing was a two-edged sword, because now she knew what she could lose, too, and that was one reality she didn't want to face. She'd faced enough already.

Sadie was so lost in thought that as she turned down her street she almost missed Buck on the sidewalk in front of the complex's parking lot. She slowed the car to take the turn, and stared in awe.

He wore a big smile filled with pride. And no wonder. He had both dogs on a leash—and Tish wasn't fighting him.

Exhilaration exploded within Sadie. She pulled into her parking space and turned off the ignition. Buck was striding toward her, both dogs politely trotting along, to greet her.

Sadie got out of the car and stared. "She doesn't look afraid."

"Nope." Buck couldn't stop grinning. "It was a chore getting her to try the walk, but having Butch next to her helped. At first she kept watching me, but soon she was too busy trying to keep up with Butch."

Sadie laughed. "She has your sock in her mouth."

"I know." He shrugged. "She stole it out of my

laundry, which is gross. I tried to give her a clean one, but you know how she is. I figured as long as her mouth was full, she couldn't chomp on any bugs. It's a fair trade-off."

The sight of Buck, all six-feet-plus inches of him, bulging muscles and obvious strength, walking two very tiny dogs, made her throat tight with emotion. He was so secure in his masculinity that he could love two Chihuahuas without hesitation.

How could she not love *him?*

Sounding a little hoarse, she said, "You're a miracle worker."

"Nah." He tipped his head and his eyes were warm with affection. "I learned patience from you."

He said that with so much sincerity and affection, she felt tears sting her eyes. "Thank you."

"No big deal." He grinned down at the dogs. "These two are like chick magnets. Women of all ages were beeping their horns, stopping to chat, oohing and aahing at me. One older woman called me 'sweetie' and patted my cheek. Another, um, younger woman slipped me her phone number." Buck retrieved the crumpled piece of paper from his pocket.

Before Sadie could get too worked up about that, his grin widened. "'Course, some guys passing by laughed their asses off at me, too."

Sadie watched him toss the phone number into a nearby trash can. Relief washed over her. "That wasn't nice of them."

"They're just jealous." He knelt down and held out his hand. Butch came right to him. Tish lowered herself until her belly touched the ground, flattened her ears and wiggled nearer until Buck could tickle her chin. In a voice as soft as butter, Buck said, "They wish they had dogs as fine as these two."

Well, Sadie thought. If she hadn't been in love before, that would have done it.

Buck pushed back onto his feet. "Come on, gang. Let's get inside and see about dinner."

He strode to Sadie, put his arm around her, kissed her warmly, and together they went into his apartment.

BUCK SPENT EVERY FREE MOMENT of his two weeks' vacation with Sadie. While she worked, he kept the dogs. When she got home, he greeted her at the door. She'd see him, smile and throw herself into his arms.

Tish continued to steal Buck's things. Whenever she could manage it, she'd grab something and pull it under the couch to make a bed. Good thing Buck had a big couch to accommodate the yellow underwear, the sock, a T-shirt, dishtowel, ragged work glove and leather shoelaces from his favorite boots.

The last hurt, and he half blamed Butch for that, because both he and Tish liked to chew the laces. Buck learned real quick to put his boots in the closet, well out of reach of small jaws.

They fell into a routine of sorts that seemed to work for everyone. Buck made sure the dogs had been out before Sadie got home so they could fix dinner together without doggie interruptions.

She was a good cook, but then so was he, so they took turns, and every so often they had dinner delivered.

After dinner, they took the time to play in the yard with the dogs. Before bed, they'd sit on the floor. Buck would hold Butch while doing his best to entice Tish into his lap. So far, it hadn't worked. She'd stopped being so jumpy, but she remained a long way from trusting.

Still, to Buck, they felt like a family—and he wanted to protect that. He wanted Sadie and Tish to be happy. But tomorrow, Riley and Regina would return home. They'd take Butch, and that would be one more thing for Tish to adjust to.

The September nights were unseasonably cool, making it necessary to wear a jacket or flannel when sitting outside. But neither Buck nor Sadie wanted to give up the time outdoors with the dogs. Buck had created a removable, adjustable fence that covered about ten square feet. Each day they set it up differently so the dogs could explore new areas.

The fence worked out great, except that with more freedom, Tish found more bugs. At least half the time she went outside, she caught a spider or a grasshopper or a night crawler, which she always presented to Sadie.

Thankfully, she hadn't located any more cicadas.

Butch was a more discriminating Chihuahua and didn't care for bugs. He even seemed a little creeped out when Tish caught them, but he always ended up helping her, as if it were a game.

The little dogs had become inseparable friends, and Tish seemed happiest when she was with Butch.

Now Sadie sat curled next to Buck on her small back porch. Without looking at him, she wondered aloud, "Maybe I should bring in another dog, just so Tish won't be lonely when Butch has to leave tomorrow."

Buck swallowed. He hated that idea. "Oh sure, that's fine for Tish. Maybe she'll even forget about him. But what about Butch? Think how lonely he'll be." He glanced at the dogs, and had the perfect opportunity to prove his point. "Look at the little guy. He's snuggled up against Tish as if she's his better half."

Sadie sighed. "I know. Maybe…that is, if you wanted to…"

Buck waited, almost holding his breath. "What?"

"You could bring him over every so often to visit."

He scowled at her. Her suggestion was far from what he'd hoped to hear. "I could do that." He stared at her, trying to read her thoughts. "Or I could take Tish to see him. The wives have everyone over at least once a week."

"The wives? That's what you call them?"

"That's what they are." Sadie had already been to one of those gatherings last weekend to meet Clair and Rosie. The dogs had played while the people had conversed. Sadie had seemed to like them, and Buck knew they liked her. Things were moving along in that regard. "We, meaning the guys, had kinda figured the wives would put an end to us hanging out together. But we were wrong. We still hang out, we just usually do it with the wives there. Not that they mind if we take off to fish or play cards late one night or something."

Sadie stared at him, arrested by this outpouring of confidences. "I'm sure they're very understanding. Why wouldn't they be?"

Buck felt like an idiot. "All I'm saying is that Regina wouldn't mind if we brought Tish with us, and even when Rosie's the one doing the cooking, or Clair, they like Butch, so I know they'd love Tish, too."

They'd better, because Tish was going to damn well be part of his family. As he'd told Sadie early on, he understood they were a package deal. The little dog had been through enough without being left behind.

Buck was waiting for Sadie's reaction when Harris and Clair rounded the corner of the building. "There you are," Harris said, as if he hadn't just interrupted Buck's attempts to settle the future.

"We knocked at Buck's," Clair explained, "but when we didn't get an answer, we decided to check out here."

Butch raced to greet them, and Harris knelt down close to the low fence. Tish cowered back into the farthest corner of her contained play area.

"She's still so shy," Harris said with a worried

frown. "It just breaks my heart. I swear, Sadie, I don't know how you do this."

Butch allowed Harris to pat him a few times, then he ran back to Tish.

Sadie sent a fond smile to Tish. "Some cases are harder than others." She stood. "Can I get you something to drink?"

Harris shook his head. "No, that's okay. We just stopped by because I have a suggestion." He gave Buck a surreptitious glance and then cleared his throat. "There's a house for sale next door to Riley's."

Buck stilled. His brain went blank. "There is?"

"It's small," Harris hurried to explain, "and like the one we picked, it needs some work. But if you bought it, the dogs would be close together." He winked—and Buck caught on.

Bless Harris, even he had a good idea every now and then.

Clair knelt down and offered her hand for the dogs to sniff. "Assuming you'd want to keep Tish," she told Sadie. "I mean, I know you're supposed to be getting her ready for a family, but she's…special." She glanced at Sadie. "Isn't she?"

With her bottom lip caught in her teeth, a sure sign she felt unsure of the situation, Sadie nodded. Her voice was faint, and touched with emotion.

"Very special. I'd already thought of keeping her." She glanced at Buck, then away. "She's going to need a lot more care before she's comfortable with being held. She's shy by nature, I think, and whatever she went through set her back more than I'd realized."

Harris cleared his throat. "If she was able to see Butch every day, that'd help, don't you think?"

"Yes, being with Butch comforts her."

Buck watched Sadie, foolishly wondering if she loved Tish enough to marry him, buy a house and make a home.

"How much is the house?" Sadie asked. Then she added, "I'm not sure I could afford it."

Harris again glanced at Buck. "With your combined incomes…"

Buck stood, cutting off Harris's suggestion. He wanted Sadie, more than he'd ever wanted anything else in his life, but damn it, he didn't need his friend to propose for him, and he didn't want a house to be the reason she married him.

She had to love him.

"You said you were just stopping by. You on your way somewhere?"

Taking the hint, Clair said, "We're having dinner with my boss and his wife. We just wanted to tell you about the house." And because Sadie had asked, Clair turned to her. "It's cheap enough that Rosie doesn't think it'll stay on the market long."

"Thanks. We'll check into it." Buck stepped past Sadie. "Come on, I'll walk you to your car."

Sadie also stood. "Thank you," she called to them before Buck could haul them away.

After they'd rounded the corner and were out of earshot, he thumped Harris on the back. "Thanks."

Clair smiled. "We figured it couldn't hurt to put the thought in your heads."

"The thought's been in mine almost from the first. Sadie's the one who needs to be convinced. And I'm working on that."

"Work fast," Harris suggested. "Riley and Red will be back tomorrow, and the house won't last."

"Gotcha." But Sadie didn't deserve to be rushed. She deserved a slow, romantic courtship. Still, when he thought of Tish alone, without Butch as a companion...

When he returned, Sadie was sitting in a sunny spot inside the fence, stroking Butch and crooning to Tish. With his arms crossed over his chest, Buck stopped to stare down at her. "So, what do you think?"

She continued to pet the dog. "About what?"

His temper edged up a notch. He pointed a finger at her. "You know damn good and well about what. The house."

She ducked her head and shrugged. "I don't know. What do you think?"

Frustrated, Buck stepped over the fence and sat beside her. "You are planning to keep Tish, aren't you? Because I gotta tell you, if you don't, I will."

Sadie's head jerked up. "Really?"

"Damn right. She needs someone to love her a lot.

Forever. She needs calm and quiet. In just the two weeks I've known her, she's gotten back more fur."

Sadie looked caught between laughing and crying. "She looks like a sleek little seal now, doesn't she?"

"She's beautiful." Buck touched Sadie's cheek, and he was appalled to see his hand shake. "Just as you said she'd be."

Sadie's eyes were sad, and her smile wobbled. "She's fatter, too."

"She reminds me of a little sumo wrestler, especially when she's sneaking up to steal something from me." He peered down at her. "She's not exactly graceful."

Sadie leaned against Buck and laughed.

Buck melted.

And suddenly, Tish crept over.

They both froze. The little dog had her ears flat on her head, her big brown eyes watchful—and hopeful. She slowly, so very slowly, did an army crawl…right into Sadie's lap.

"Ohmigod," Sadie whispered.

Butch blinked his big eyes in stunned surprise at this change. Since he'd been in Sadie's lap first, Tish was now half sitting on him. She outweighed Butch by at least a pound, and for four-pound Butch, that pound was a lot.

But he didn't complain.

"Slow," Buck whispered, "Go real slow." He reached out with one finger and tickled the dog's chin. Her worried gaze transferred to him, and her tail lifted in a one-wag thump. She looked very undecided about things, but she didn't run off.

Holding his breath, Buck carefully tickled his way over her muzzle, to her ear, and then to the top of her little round head, which was no longer bald, but soft with chocolate-brown fur.

Tish let out a long, doggie sigh, dropped her head onto Sadie's thigh and closed her eyes.

"You did it, Sadie." Buck's heart swelled so big, it felt ready to pop out of his chest.

Enormous tears swam in Sadie's eyes. "This is stupid," she whispered on a shaky laugh, "but I feel like bawling."

"Yeah," Buck admitted, "me, too."

Sadie leaned on his shoulder. "Butch has to have most of the credit."

Reminded of his goal, Buck was quick to agree. "It'd be a damn shame to separate them now, don't you think? I bet Regina would love the idea of letting them play together. She's taken only freelance jobs lately so she could be home more with Butch. And when she has to be away for regular business hours, she or Riley come home at lunchtime. If we were right next door—"

With her head still on his shoulder, Sadie squeaked, *"We?"* She twisted to see him. "You think we should buy the house—"

"Together." He smoothed his hand over the dogs, taking turns petting them. "It's a good plan."

She stared at him in mute surprise.

That irritated Buck. "You know the dogs would like it."

Sadie nodded. "Yes. But…would you like it?"

He touched her cheek. "I'd love it."

She bit her bottom lip, drew a deep breath, then nodded. "I'd love it, too."

The tension left Buck in a rush. Then Sadie said, "Because I love you."

His back snapped straight. "What did you say?"

His strangled voice startled the dogs, and he rushed to calm them with soft pats.

Sadie held his gaze. "I love you, Buck Boswell. You're the most wonderful, loving, giving man. Even in my imagination, I didn't think anyone like you could exist. But here you are, sitting in the yard, petting little dogs and offering to buy houses and being so wonderful…how could I not love you?"

He almost hyperventilated. "I love you, too." He wanted to grab her up and swing her around and laugh out loud. But he didn't want to upset Tish. "I've loved you since the day you ran into my place in your nightie, demanding I go head to head with a killer cicada."

She blushed. "I am sorry about that."

"I'm not. If Tish hadn't caught the nasty bug, we might not have gotten together. And I never would have realized that you and one tiny bald dog were the very things missing in my life."

She didn't laugh the way he expected. Instead, she bit her lip.

Buck kissed her, licked her bottom lip to soothe it, then asked, "What is it?"

"Will you marry me?"

He stared at her, then burst out laughing. The dogs barely paid him any mind, but Sadie blushed hotly. "I would have been on one knee within the next five minutes. Thank you for saving me the trouble."

Her cheeks turned pink. "I'm sorry. I didn't mean to…"

"I love you. Everything about you," he reminded her. "Thank you for proposing to me, and yes, I accept."

"There'll probably be more dogs. I can't give up what I do."

The cautious warning only made him grin again. "Okay by me. After all, the dogs are nothing compared to my loony friends."

Her smile warmed his heart. "Your friends are wonderful."

"Yeah, they are."

"Do you think we should get ahold of Rosie and make an offer on the house right away?" She bubbled with new enthusiasm.

"Yeah." He stood, pulled Sadie to her feet, and then his voice lowered to a husky rumble. "We'll get right to that."

"After?" Sadie asked, and her voice, too, grew rough.

"After," he agreed.

A FEW MONTHS LATER, they closed on the house. Once they moved in, Sadie did indeed bring in more dogs. But with the means to keep them, she couldn't bear to give them away.

They ended up with three—which Buck claimed was fair, since he had the same number of buddies.

Ethan ended up with two dogs, and Harris had a dog and a cat. Every get-together did resemble a zoo—not that anyone minded.

In fact, the men began speculating that the dogs needed kids to play with. And judging by the love and attention they gave their pets, the women had no doubts that they'd make doting fathers.

Butch and Tish remained the best of friends. Whenever there was a crowd, they crawled under a couch together—curled up in Buck's yellow boxers.

Sadie claimed that Tish saw the boxers as a security blanket.

Buck saw Sadie the same way. His life had always been good.

Now, with Sadie as his wife, it was perfect.

SECONDHAND SAM

Kristine Rolofson

For Mary Harrigan,
one of the most dedicated and caring
rescue people I've ever met.
Thanks for letting me help the dogs.

Dear Reader,

Thank you for buying this book and helping to raise money for animal rescue organizations.

Three years ago my dog died. Now Charlie, a gold ten-pound Lhasa mix I'd adopted eleven years earlier from the local pound, was no ordinary dog. He was one of those intelligent and devoted animals of which legends are made. But his heart gave out at age fourteen and I was devastated.

So what do you do when your heart is broken? Well, I foolishly thought that if I could find another little dog like Charlie my troubles would be over. I visited shelters, spent hours on the www.petfinder.org Web site and volunteered to be a foster mom for Atlantic Maltese Rescue. I volunteered with my local Animal Rescue League and wrote "Pet of the Week" articles for the newspaper. And, like my heroine in this story, I used my passion for vintage fabrics, trims and buttons to raise thousands of dollars sewing Christmas stockings for rescue groups.

And then a chance came to foster an elderly Pekingese, one who had been found nearly dead in a West Virginia snowbank. Not many people believe me when I tell them about the Pekingese Underground Railroad (aka PUR), a group of volunteers who, in hundred-mile increments, drive homeless Pekes to new adoptive homes, but last year a wonderful PUR volunteer drove two days on icy January roads to give me a skinny redheaded Pekingese who was blind, one-eyed and deathly ill from huge mammary tumors. She smelled like a Dumpster, snored like a trucker, had few teeth and looked nothing like Charlie, but it was love at first sight. "Miss Lillie" survived surgery and many other ailments to become the prancing, dancing queen of my house and the inspiration for this novella.

To say thanks to the many wonderful people I've had the privilege to work with, I'm donating my advance and royalties to Atlantic Maltese Rescue (www.adoptamalt.com), Northeast Pekingese Rescue (nepekerescue.org), Hearts United for Animals (www.hua.org) and the Animal Rescue League of Southern Rhode Island (www.southkingstown.com/arl). And if you want information on how to help stop puppy mills or if you want to donate old curtains or drapes (no, you don't have to clean them first), trims or buttons for stockings, please contact me at P.O. Box 323, Peace Dale, RI 02883, or via e-mail, knr8361@cs.com.

Always,

Kristine Rolofson

CHAPTER ONE

SAM WONDERED if his heart was broken or if the pain he felt in the region of his chest was due to breathing the musty air of the church basement. He'd been hauled down there by his best man to meet with his bride's father, a husky former Olympic wrestler, who'd choked back tears as he'd informed him that the wedding had been cancelled.

The one-hundred-seventy-four guests, due to arrive within the hour, would be told there would be no wedding. Apparently, the bride had sent her apologies; the bridesmaids had returned crimson dresses to their hangers; and the mother-of-the-bride had thrown a crystal vase filled with red and white roses against the locked door of her daughter's hotel room.

"I suppose it must be for the best," his former future father-in-law had sniffed before blowing his nose on the red silk handkerchief he'd pulled from the jacket pocket of his size fifty-two tuxedo. "Though for the life of me I can't see how. I don't know why she made this decision now, of all times."

Sam could have told him. He could have said,

"Your daughter never *could* make up her mind, sir. Have you ever seen her try to order from a restaurant menu? Decide which black dress in her closet to wear? Select new sheets and towels for her apartment?"

But he kept silent, afraid that any words out of his mouth could be construed as bitter. Or worse, angry.

"Uh, Sam," the older man said, flushing red before he reached inside his jacket once again. "She wanted to make sure you got—well, here it is." He handed Sam the six-carat diamond engagement ring.

"Thanks." He swallowed his disappointment, shook hands with the man who'd fathered the woman Sam had had the bad luck to propose to, accepted the sympathetic slap on the back from his best man, and untied Darcy from the metal post by the stairs. The ring, selected by his fiancée after too many trips to every jeweler in town, was slipped into a satin-lined pocket of his tuxedo jacket, to be immediately forgotten.

"Let's go get drunk," his best friend said.

"At ten o'clock?" It was to have been a morning wedding, followed by a champagne brunch in the Emerald Room of the city's most exclusive hotel. Sam had hoped for dancing, had even picked out the band, but the bride had opposed participating in anything but the most sedate and elegant reception. Susan was nothing if not sedate and elegant. He had liked that about her, not being a sedate or elegant kind of guy.

"Sure," Jim said. "What else do you have to do?"

"Call my parents, I suppose." His mother had come down with a bad case of the flu last week and had been too sick to travel to the wedding. His father wouldn't leave her, of course. Not even if he had been thrilled by Sam's choice of a bride, which he hadn't.

"At least Darcy won't have to go to the kennel again." Jim led the way up the stairs to the back of the church. A side door took them to the parking lot, now with only three cars.

"I tried to bring him there this morning, but he started howling—well, you know what he sounds like when he gets going." The English mastiff, a brute of a dog with the heart of a poodle, wagged his tail and licked his master's hand.

"Like all the hounds of hell have gotten loose?" Jim chuckled. "Yeah, I remember."

"Susan would have a fit if she knew I brought him to the church."

Darcy pranced over to a snow-dusted bush and lifted his leg. The two men, dressed in identical black tuxedos and red cummerbunds, stood with their backs to the wind and ignored the bitter cold December air.

"What Susan likes or dislikes doesn't matter anymore," Jim reminded him.

"Yeah." That was a strangely freeing observation, Sam noted, though he would have liked to have married. They'd been together for more years than he could remember and he didn't know what to expect next. He was alone, he was thirty-three and he couldn't imagine starting the dating process all over again.

Darcy walked to Sam's SUV and sniffed the back tire before peeing on that, too.

"Come on back to the house," Jim said. "I've got a bottle of scotch that'll cure anything, even a disaster like this."

"I appreciate it." He unlocked the doors of the three-year-old Escalade and opened the back door for Darcy. "But I think I'm going to head back to D.C."

"You shouldn't be alone this weekend. Stay with me and Caroline. Darcy can play with the kids and you and I can watch football and yell at the Redskins."

"Thanks for the offer, but I don't think I'd be good company. Right now all I want to do is get out of town. Tell the rest of the guys that I'm fine, will you?" The six ushers were to have met in the lobby of the hotel in half an hour, where they would have been chauffeured to the church in time to seat the guests.

"Sure. I'll go over to the hotel now," Jim promised. "I'm sure they've heard what's going on. Susan's father probably spread the word before he came here."

"Thanks." Sam opened the driver's door and slid inside. He'd inherited the Escalade from his father, who'd wanted a luxury SUV to drive after a particularly harsh New England winter. He'd had it for a year, until Sam's mother's arthritis had prevented her from climbing into it without pain. Susan had wanted to trade it in for something smaller and more politically correct, but Sam liked the Escalade. He was a large man with a large dog and he liked having room.

"No problem," said his best friend. "Take it easy."

"Yeah," Sam said, before closing the door. He would take it easy, all right. After he did whatever it was a groom did when he'd been dumped an hour before the wedding.

He wasn't going to cry in his beer, drown his broken heart in whiskey or confront Susan in room seven-twelve of the Hilton Emerald Hotel. No, he had his pride, his dog and a week's vacation.

Sam Grogan was free.

Whether he wanted to be or not.

"QUIET," JESSICA HALL TOLD the barking dogs. "I have to think."

Two of the Pekes paid no attention to her command, not that she expected them to. But a few moments of quiet would be appreciated, especially now that she sat in her wounded van, its hood propped open for inspection, parked next to a gas station six hundred miles from home.

"I'm really sorry, ma'am," the young mechanic had said, looking sincerely upset about having to give bad news. "You've got a leak in your transmission. I can fix it, but it will sure take some time to get a new transmission, or even a rebuilt one. And the money, well, ma'am, you'd be better off putting the money towards a new vehicle, if you know what I mean."

"Thank you." She'd thought of her pathetic bank account and a Visa card that wouldn't bear the cost of an expensive car repair. And she did need a new car. Or a new used one.

"Shh," she told the one of the barking dogs, a red Pekingese the shelter called Harriet. The dog looked at Jess and panted, her little red tongue sticking out of her mouth in typically comical Pekingese style. Harriet was the noisy one, Jess had learned in the two hours she'd had the dogs. Ozzie, too thin and somewhat nervous, was also red, but he made no noise unless Harriet started barking. Samantha, the quiet one, simply hid in her crate and peered out with one frightened brown eye, and Jess didn't think she could see much out of that one.

"Ma'am?" The mechanic returned and knocked on the glass.

Jess rolled down the window and let the cold air sweep inside while the mechanic nervously wiped his hands on a dirty rag.

"I put some transmission fluid in," he said. "If you go slow you might make it to Richmond before it all leaks out. Least there you can get a place to stay. And maybe somebody there'll be able to fix it for you faster 'n me."

"Can I buy some of that, just in case?"

"You want to put it in yourself?"

"If I have to, sure. Maybe you can show me where it goes." She hopped out of the van and had a quick lesson in transmission fluid.

"You let it go dry and you'll blow the engine," he warned, looking uncertain as he handed her a plastic jug filled with liquid. "Be real careful heading home."

"I will, thanks."

He followed her to the driver's side of the car and peered into the back seat while she retrieved a credit card from her wallet. "You sure have a lot of dogs back there. You headed north?"

"I hope so." She smiled, which made the kid turn red to the tips of his ears. "Thanks for your help."

"Yes, ma'am."

Ma'am. That was a new one. She was twenty-eight, not exactly matron material, but to a teenager she supposed she looked like a much older woman. A woman with an old van, old dogs and a thermos half-full of lukewarm coffee. Jess dug her cell phone out of her purse and proceeded to call for help. She left voice mails with Janice, the Pekingese Underground Railroad coordinator who normally would have handled this transport, and with Mary, her partner at Big Hearts for Little Dogs. "Help," she said. "This is Jessica Hall. I'm stuck in Virginia. Can someone foster two dogs for a week or so?"

As much as she hated to leave her van, she would fly back to Rhode Island and, if PUR couldn't transport next weekend, she'd borrow someone's car and drive back to get the dogs herself. Samantha, the oldest dog, was in bad health. She would take her on the plane with her. Surely there would be an airport in— she checked her map again—Richmond, if she could make it that far. She didn't want to count the miles between this small town and Interstate 95. She'd keep driving, at least until someone called her back with a better plan.

Sitting in a gas station worrying about her car wasn't an option. The attendant returned with her charge receipt and she was ready to go. She and three homeless Pekes didn't have any choice but to keep moving forward.

Jess drove slowly, heading east along the road. It was a cold, gray Saturday morning. She hoped it wouldn't snow, though the weather report on the local radio station this morning had predicted the strong possibility of a storm. She hadn't worried, though, planning to be well on her way north before the storm descended upon the mid-Atlantic states.

Thirty-four miles later she stopped for a hot cup of coffee and a chance to take the dogs out to relieve themselves on the frozen grass beside the Krispy Kreme parking lot. She left more voice-mail messages, checked the road map and, as she began to pull out of the parking area, swerved to avoid hitting the largest dog she had ever seen.

Then came the crash.

CHAPTER TWO

UH-OH. DARCY JUMPED back on the grass and started to shake. Sam would know what to do. He'd been inside their favorite place in the world getting a treat. A super-sugared hot Krispy Kreme treat. And Darcy, relieved to have escaped a week at the kennel and a lifetime of Sam's girlfriend, Smelly Susan, had jumped out of the car and danced for joy as soon as Sam had opened the door to put his coffee in the cup holder. No more Susan. They were both free to be together without Smelly Susan and her voice, a voice that pretended to be nice but underneath said, *I don't like dogs.*

Darcy knew he should have seen the van coming. He'd forgotten he was in a parking lot, but he'd smelled other dogs—he'd *heard* other dogs—and he'd wanted to say hello. He'd wanted to bark and share his happiness with new friends. He'd wanted to play. Sam should have reminded him to watch out for traffic, but Sam had his hands full with his cup of coffee and box of doughnuts. Sam was sad. He'd been playing Johnny Cash songs again, something he did whenever he felt bad about something.

It had been, as Sam would say, "a close call." Football talk for "luck," the dog knew. Darcy tried to stop shaking, especially after Sam called his name. He barked as loud as he could at the van when he heard dogs barking their complaints from inside of it, but he didn't move off the grass. Not until Sam grabbed his collar and assured himself that his hairy best friend was okay. Then Sam swore under his breath and Darcy found himself shoved into the car and told to "stay."

It wasn't one of his favorite words, but he knew by the look on Sam's face that he'd better do as he was told.

Besides, he had a box of Krispy Kremes to keep him company.

"STAY!" SAM SHUT the most disobedient mastiff in Virginia in the car and hurried across the parking area to the maroon van, whose front end had collided with a Dumpster. Bad enough to have escaped a ruined wedding, but now he seemed to be dragging mayhem with him wherever he went. Sam couldn't resist glancing over his shoulder to make sure that the doughnut shop hadn't burst into flames or collapsed within itself.

But the barking coming from the van drew his attention back to the problem at hand: Darcy had just caused someone to drive into a Dumpster rather than hit a dog. Sam had just turned to call him back to the car when Darcy had loped toward the van. Fortunately the driver had missed the dog; *unfortunately* the van hadn't missed the Dumpster piled high with construction materials from something that was being built next door.

"Hey!" he called, hoping like hell that no one was hurt. He saw a woman's delicate profile in the window and when she turned to face him he saw that she was young, maybe midtwenties. Clouds of light blond hair framed a pretty, heart-shaped face.

Not that he was interested in women—pretty or not—right now. In fact, he intended to join an all-male gym, hang out in sports bars and take up smoking cigars to guarantee he would no longer be exposed to those strange creatures who could turn a man inside out with one look.

He was done with women. It would be a long time before he'd let another one tie him in knots and talk about honeymoons, wedding rings and whether to redecorate his apartment or hers.

The driver of the van rolled down the window, which intensified the barking sounds coming from inside the car and revealed pale skin, large blue eyes and lips that were turned down as if she was in pain. She said something he couldn't hear, so Sam stepped closer.

"Are you okay?" he asked again, louder this time.

"I spilled my coffee," she said. "There was a dog—"

"Mine," he admitted.

"I tried not to hit him."

"You didn't. He's fine. But you hit a Dumpster."

"I know. This isn't exactly my lucky day," she said over the loud yapping of dogs he still hadn't seen. She turned to the back seat. "Quiet! It's okay!" The barking stopped for about ten seconds before resuming.

Several people came over to the van to look at the damage and to assure themselves that the driver wasn't hurt.

"Are you sure you're okay?" Sam asked again after telling two elderly ladies and a cable television installer that everything was fine, the driver wasn't drunk and the dogs were not barking from pain but from excitement.

"It's just some spilled coffee," the woman said, wiping her denim jacket with a wad of paper towel.

"Can I give you a lift home?"

"I'm not from around here. I was trying to get the van to Richmond to either get it fixed or fly home this weekend."

"It was broken before this?" He stepped back and helped her open the door to climb out of a van he guessed to be about fifteen years old.

"We were limping along. I guess I shouldn't have pushed my luck and stopped for something to eat."

"Lady," someone said, "looks like the radiator's leaking fluid."

Sam walked with her to the front of the van to look

for himself. If she'd been driving a sedan, things might not be so bad, but the blunt-nosed van had taken the brunt of its collision on a corner of the Dumpster. Whatever problems the Ford Windstar had before, they were now a hell of a lot worse.

"Oh, dear," she said. "I guess this is as far as the van is going to go for a while."

"We can get it towed," he offered. "We're right outside of town, so you shouldn't have any trouble getting someone to look at it for you."

"Maybe it's not as bad as it looks."

"Maybe." He had to admire her optimism, but anyone with eyes could see that the old clunker deserved a final resting place in a junkyard.

"You must be on your way to something important," the woman said. She wore jeans and thick-soled boots. Her blue jacket was open to reveal a stained brown sweater and a figure that would make most men drool.

Not him, though. She wasn't his type. He was through with women, whether they were sleek and elegant like his former fiancée, or voluptuous and covered with dog hair.

"Important?" He looked down to realize he still wore his tuxedo. The bride hadn't thought so, but in all likelihood she'd change her mind next week and call to reschedule. Like a wedding was a dentist appointment. "No," he said. "It's over."

The little blonde gave him a curious look, but was

interrupted by a state trooper who pulled into the driveway and turned his flashing lights on before he stepped out of the patrol car.

"Sam Grogan?" The trooper shook his hand. "Steve Betts. I was in the stadium the day you caught that seventy-four-yard pass and sent the game into overtime."

"That was a good day," Sam said, wondering how many years ago that was. "Back in ninety-six?"

"Yeah." Steve looked as if he wanted to ask for an autograph, but then he caught sight of the jeans-clad blonde and turned toward her instead. "Ma'am? What happened?"

She explained, and Sam agreed that the woman had swerved to avoid hitting his dog. He even showed the mastiff to the trooper, not that the man wanted to get too close. Darcy wagged his tail and tried to thrust his head out of the car door as soon as Sam opened it, but Steve Betts, Washington Redskins fan, backed off and talked to the woman again.

"You should get that hand looked at," Sam heard him say as he used his cell phone to call a tow truck. "I'll be glad to give you a ride over to the hospital."

"Thanks," she said, "but I can't leave my dogs right now. I promise I'll see a doctor as soon as I can."

"Ma'am." He tipped his hat and headed toward the building for a mid-morning snack.

"A doctor?" Sam followed her back to the van. "Why didn't you say you were hurt?"

"It's just a burn." She didn't seem interested in explaining. She dug through her purse with her left hand "Darn. It must have been on the seat when—"

"What?"

"My cell phone—"

She opened the door and leaned across the seat. The front of the van was a mess. He saw maps, cups, water bowls, leashes, papers, paper towels and a pile of old bath towels. She looked like she'd been on the road for a month.

The dogs started yapping again, but gave up shortly after they started. Sam figured they'd worn themselves out. He didn't like little yappy, hairy dogs. He hadn't exactly wanted to own one of the largest dogs in the universe, either, but his sister's husband had declared he couldn't sleep with his bride and a mastiff-mix mutt every night. The bed wasn't big enough and they were newlyweds. Sam's sister had cried, and Sam had relented, taking Darcy— named after someone in a Jane Austen novel—to his house to live happily ever after.

"I called a tow truck," he began, watching her retrieve the phone from the floor, "but maybe you should try starting the engine, see if it turns over."

"Good idea." She hopped onto the seat and turned the key in the ignition. The engine sputtered and died. "The transmission fluid started leaking this morning and a mechanic told me I needed a new one."

"New car or new transmission?" This was starting to sound worse and worse, and all because Darcy had taken an uncharacteristic vault across a parking lot. The damn dog was lucky to be alive.

"Either one." She smiled, and Sam fought the urge to take her to a car lot and buy her any four-wheeled vehicle she wanted. "Look, you don't have to stick around here. The tow truck will come and we'll be fine."

"I'll wait," he said. "The accident was Darcy's fault."

"Darcy?"

"The dog you didn't hit." He watched her fumble with the phone. "Do you have friends in Virginia who can help you?"

"Not exactly." She left a brief message with some-one named Janice before turning back to him. "I'm transporting three dogs from West Virginia to Rhode Island."

"You're a dog breeder?"

"No." Once again that smile, though she winced when she started to put her hands in her pockets, then quickly withdrew her right hand. "It's the Pe-kingese Underground Railroad. PUR for short."

"Pur." He repeated it the way she'd said it, "Pure," wondering if he'd heard her correctly. An under-ground railroad for dogs sounded bizarre, but then again, it was that kind of day.

"For homeless Pekes," she added, as if that ex-plained everything. He decided there wasn't time to figure it out.

"Your hand," Sam said, reaching toward her with his own. "Let me see."

"It's not that bad. I'll get some aloe and—"

"You're burned," he said, touching her fingertips carefully. Red marks covered three of her fingers and the back of her hand. "The coffee?"

"I was drinking and driving," she admitted, giving him a small smile. "It will feel better if I put some cold water on it."

"Go," he said. "I'll stay here with the van in case the tow truck comes."

She grabbed a small leather purse and hopped out of the van. "Thank you."

"No problem," he muttered, watching her hurry toward the glass entrance of the doughnut shop. "It's not like I have anything better to do."

JESS SKIPPED THE REST ROOM and begged a cup of ice from one of the young men at the front counter. Her hand stung much more than she wanted to admit. If she could pretend it wasn't that bad, then maybe she could also pretend the van wasn't that broken and this particular transport wasn't turning into the journey from hell.

This was the day she'd looked forward to the most. She'd been up early, anxious to drive the remaining miles to the shelter and meet the dogs. There was the scheduled visit with Hazel, stockings to deliver, fabric waiting to be picked up. All that and she'd anticipated beating the storm back to New England. A "slow-moving front," the weatherman had assured Rhode Island three days ago. At least it wasn't snowing.

And at least Sam Grogan, football star, had been pleasant enough to offer to watch out for the tow truck. And she'd had no choice but to trust him. The man was drop-dead handsome, with that dark hair and those wide, wide shoulders. The expression in his green eyes had held genuine concern, though he should be more careful about his dog getting loose and jumping across fast-food parking lots. The state trooper's face had lit up when he'd recognized him. Of course, how many people in tuxedos were buying doughnuts this morning? Only the ones who'd partied late last night, Jess figured, sticking her three burned fingers into the ice. The pain eased a little, especially when she scooped ice onto the back of her hand and held it in place with a paper napkin.

She hesitated before leaving the building, wondering if she should replace the coffee that had spilled across her hand and splattered on the floor of the van, but the thought of holding a hot cup of coffee again made her feel a little queasy. She wished she'd had at least one bite of glazed doughnut before crashing. Maybe her stomach wouldn't be so unsettled if there was food in it.

Jess stepped outside and took a deep breath of cold air before she headed to the van. The football player was inside, behind the steering wheel, sipping coffee and talking on a cell phone.

"Checking messages," he said, when she opened the passenger door. "Or trying to. I'm still getting used to this thing. I've figured out how to call out, but I'm never sure if I've shut it off or not." He snapped it shut and slipped it into the inside pocket of the tuxedo jacket.

"Don't let me interrupt," she said, taking her fingers out of the ice so she could close the door. One of the dogs barked again, setting off the other two. Jess told them to be quiet and miraculously they obeyed. "Thanks for watching them."

He turned to face her and rested one arm on the steering wheel while he held his coffee in the other. "They're a lot less trouble than a mastiff, believe me. Do they always stay in those little crates?"

"In the car, yes. I take them out for bathroom breaks, of course." She put her fingers back in the ice and tried not to wince.

"Let me take you to the hospital," he offered. "They can give you something to put on it, to take the pain away."

"It's not that bad," she said. "Really, it's not." And even if it was, she couldn't sit in an emergency room for hours while the dogs froze in the car.

"Are you always this stubborn?"

"Yes."

"Ah," he said, looking out the front windshield. "He's here."

"That was fast." The tow truck, its flashing lights announcing its arrival, drove past them and then backed up alongside the Dumpster. The driver got out and waved to Sam.

"Hey, Mr. Grogan," the young man called. "What can I do for you?"

"You *know* him?"

"I put in a call to an old friend." He took his coffee and hopped out of the van. "Wait here for a sec."

"But—"

"Please," he said, a frown creasing his perfect, handsome face. "It's the least I can do after the trouble Darcy and I have caused."

The man was right, but that didn't make it any easier to accept his help. These kinds of things didn't happen to her. Oh, there had been transport volunteers who didn't show up, sick dogs, a Peke that wasn't a Peke at all—luckily she'd been able to turn him over to someone with Maltese Rescue and he'd quickly found a home with a retired schoolteacher— and more than a couple of wrong turns, late nights and hours spent waiting in traffic on Interstate 95.

But two days ago, when she'd decided to drive the entire transport herself—three volunteers dropped out at the last minute—she'd foolishly assumed her beloved van would live forever, or at least until she could afford to replace it. She'd told herself she didn't have any choice. This was the last chance to get these dogs. They'd been in a high-kill shelter and wouldn't last much longer. And poor little Samantha needed surgery, not euthanasia.

She would figure this out, Jess decided, watching Sam Grogan talk to the grinning driver of the tow truck. There was still a little room on the credit card and plenty of time to fix a van. She'd be on the road in no time at all.

CHAPTER THREE

"IT'S NO TROUBLE," Sam assured the woman for the fourth time. "Well, actually it's a *hell* of a lot of trouble," he admitted, hoping she'd smile again. "But I'm not going to drive away and leave you and the yapping trio stuck at the Krispy Kreme."

"They're not yapping."

No. Now they were panting. When he looked over the front seat toward the three crates lined up along the bench seat, he saw black faces and pink tongues through the cage doors. "Do they always stick their tongues out like that?"

"Yes. It's a Peke thing." She hesitated before unhooking the seat belts that held the crates in place. "Are you sure you don't mind?"

"I told you," he repeated. "It's not that big a deal. We'll follow the tow truck to the repair shop. It's not far away."

"Well, I really do appreciate this." She handed him a crate and started unhooking the next one. "So you're a football player."

"Was." He watched her fumble with the seat belt on the middle crate. "Let me do that."

"I've got it." To prove it, she handed him another crate with a panting hairball inside. "The state trooper was impressed. I thought he was going to ask for your autograph."

"There are a lot of Washington Redskin fans here."

"What do you do now?"

"Now I talk about sports."

"On television?"

"Yeah." He turned away to take the dogs to his car. He didn't want to talk about his job, not now. He was supposed to be on vacation this weekend—the Redskins had a "bye" and didn't play again until a week from Monday night, in Miami. He was supposed to be in Hawaii tomorrow, on his honeymoon with the new Mrs. Grogan— not that Susan had wanted to change her name to his. Old-fashioned, she'd called it. He figured she'd change her mind. He'd also thought she'd grow to love Darcy. Neither had happened.

Darcy greeted him with a wagging tail and a slobbering kiss to his shoulder when Sam lifted the tailgate. His ears perked up when he smelled the red-haired visitors.

"Be nice," Sam told him, setting the crates carefully on the rubber mat. "Don't scare them."

Darcy wagged his tail a bit uncertainly and whined as if he couldn't understand what the dogs were doing inside the crates instead of playing with a big, lonely mastiff. The barking started up again, but stopped when Darcy stuck his nose close to one of the cages.

That was only the beginning, Sam realized, carrying another crated Pekingese to his car while the woman—he really had to find out her name—followed him with shopping bags filled with gifts and a large backpack. Sam also carried a bag filled with various important dog items, such as food, bowls and bottled water.

"You don't exactly travel light," he said, earning a shy smile from the dogs' guardian.

"The stockings are for a shelter in Fredericksburg."

"Stockings?"

She placed the shopping bags along the side of the car, where Darcy wouldn't be able to step on them. "I make them to raise money for animal shelters. See?" She lifted a tissue-filled Christmas stocking out of the bag to show him. Made of fabric with flowers, it had a lace cuff decorated with old buttons and a faded pink velvet rose.

"Uh, that's real nice." It looked like something that would be sold in one of those upscale boutiques Susan loved to frequent, which was a little strange considering it was in a cardboard box in the back of the Escalade.

"It's not exactly a guy thing." She smiled at him again. "Your wife might like one and I'd be glad to give you one to—"

"No wife," he said, cutting off her words. He should have been standing in the church right at this moment. He'd looked forward to the ceremony, to the solemn promise to take Susan as his wife, "'til death do us part." The only disappointment he'd antici-pated when he'd dressed for his wedding was that his parents weren't going to be there to celebrate the day with him. Just as well now. Funny how things worked out for the best, just the way his mother liked to say.

"I'm sorry," Dog Woman said, her voice soft. When he glanced up into those blue eyes, he saw that she looked absolutely heartbroken.

"Sorry?"

"Well, about your wife. You looked so sad when you said you weren't married that, w-well..." she stammered, "I thought—"

"You thought I had a wife and she left me?"

"I thought you had a wife and she died."

"Stand back," he said, before slamming the tail door shut. "I've never been married. I have no wife, dead or alive. You don't have to look at me like that."

"Like what?" She followed him around to the pas-senger door, which he opened for her.

"Like you feel sorry for me." Which was exactly what he'd dreaded, come to think of it. That's why he wasn't with his friends right now.

Her eyebrows rose, and those lovely eyes wid-ened. "Well, of course I did. You *did* sound pathetic and you *are* wandering around in a tuxedo on a Saturday morning as if you can't find your way home after a wild Friday night."

"It was not wild," he said, wondering why he bothered to explain. "And I'm not 'wandering around.' I was supposed to attend a wedding this morning." He shut the door and went around to the driver's side to get in. Dog Woman didn't look happy.

"Have I made you late?" She looked at her watch, then back at him. "What time do you have to be there?"

"It's over," he assured her. "It was over and I came here to get a cup of coffee and something to—damn it, Darcy, where are they?"

The mastiff hung his head over the front seat, but didn't attempt to lick either one of the people sitting there.

"Please," Dog Woman said, "tell me he doesn't bite or growl or attack women and small dogs."

"He's never attacked anything larger than a bakery box."

"Uh, nice boy," she murmured, patting Darcy's brindled head. "You said he's a mastiff?"

"Mostly. We think he has some boxer and maybe even some Great Dane in him, too. Do you want coffee?"

"No, thanks."

"I'm going to take the drive-through," Sam explained, starting the car. "I think Darcy ate all the doughnuts when I left him alone in here."

"He does look a little guilty."

"Yeah," Sam said, backing the car out of the parking space. "He should. He's caused a lot of trouble this morning."

"It's not his fault," the woman insisted. "In fact, I think it's me. I've been jinxed all day. My van was leaking transmission fluid and I was on my way to a repair shop and trying to figure out how to get the Pekes back to Rhode Island."

"That's where you're from? Rhode Island?" He managed to get into the line of cars waiting their turn at the microphone. The place was mobbed this morning. It was a miracle Darcy hadn't been hit when he'd made his escape from the SUV.

"Yes. My name is Jess Hall, by the way."

"Sam Grogan." He turned to look at her, telling himself he was only being polite. She was prettier than he'd thought when he'd first seen her, but Sam didn't let that affect him, no way. He didn't really want to know her name or where she was from or if she had a boyfriend—he'd happened to see that she wore no wedding ring or engagement diamonds. He didn't want to know anything more about her other than she was a do-gooder dog lover who couldn't afford a decent car.

He'd offered to take her to the hospital to treat those burns on her hands—she'd refused. He'd offered coffee and doughnuts—she'd refused. All that was left was to give her and her possessions a lift to the repair shop and his responsibilities were over. He could go home and get drunk. He could get out of this damn monkey suit and cancel his reservations at that fancy resort in Hawaii.

He was through with women. And the sooner he got this one back on the road the better.

While Jess Hall went into the auto body repair shop to talk to a mechanic, Sam sipped his coffee, ate a couple of doughnuts and ignored the pleading eyes of a dog that had already eaten a week's worth of fat and sugar.

And he reluctantly turned his phone back on.

There were twenty-seven voice messages. He wondered for a split second if Susan had changed her mind and wanted him to return to the church—not that he would, but it would have been an interesting conversation to have with his former fiancée—but most of the messages turned out to be from friends who said they were sorry to hear about the wedding being cancelled. Twelve of those were from five guys, reiterating the need to meet at Sam's apartment and entertain him for the weekend. Sam supposed they thought he wouldn't want to be alone.

There were three messages from his father, who'd had a phone call from Susan's father. The first was calm, asking Sam to call as soon as he felt able to talk. The second sounded more worried, with his mother's tearful admonitions in the background. *Call your mother* were the only words on the last voice mail. Which meant Sam Grogan Senior meant business, especially since he'd used his severest tone and didn't care how grown-up his son thought he was.

Sam toyed with the phone for a second. *Sorry, Dad. I was stuck at Krispy Kreme this morning with a crazy dog woman who drove into a Dumpster.* He smiled, despite everything, and hit the button that would connect him with his folks.

By the time Jess Hall returned to the car, Sam had explained everything to his parents. Well, almost everything, he thought as the little blonde opened the car door and hopped inside.

"So, where are you now?" his father asked, clearly worried. "You're not alone, are you? Is Jim with you?"

"No, I'm heading home. I stopped to get coffee—"

"Which is not good for you," his mother, a confirmed tea drinker, pointed out.

"I'm cutting down," Sam assured her, which he did at least once a week.

"I wish we were there, the way we would have been if I hadn't gotten sick. We could have been there for you, when you needed us." He thought she had started to cry again. "I'd like to tell Susan a thing or two."

"Mom, everything is going to be fine." He glanced toward Jess, who looked as if she was trying not to burst into tears herself.

"Where are you?" his father asked again. "You're not driving while you're on the phone, are you? I hate it when people do that. Just drives me nuts when—"

"I'm in a parking lot outside of Frank's Auto Body Shop. Darcy had a little accident—" His mother gasped, so Sam hurried to explain. "He's fine, but the woman who avoided hitting him ended up with some car trouble." He saw Jess fumble around in her purse until she found a wad of tissue.

"A woman?" His mother perked up. "Please tell me she's young, beautiful and single."

"Oh, for heaven's sake," Sam Senior sputtered. "What are the odds of that?"

"Well," Sam drawled, glad his mother had stopped sniffling into the phone, "it's true. She's some kind of dog rescue person who drives them from West Virginia to Rhode Island. I have three dogs in the car right now. Four," he corrected, adding Darcy to the list.

"What kind of dogs?" his father asked.

Martha had become positively chatty. "I'll bet we're right on the way. Tell her to stop in Westport and we'll fix her a nice meal. She could even spend the night if she wants. Give her directions, Sam."

Sam laughed and turned to Jess. "My mother says you're to stop at their house and have something to eat. They're in Westport, Connecticut, and you're welcome any time."

"Thank you," Jess said. "Maybe next time."

"Speaking of being welcome," his father said. "Why don't you come home for a few days? Your mother's feeling lots better and having you around to spoil would cheer her up."

"Next time?" His mother sounded disappointed. "What's wrong with her car, Sam?"

He turned to Jess. "She wants to know what's wrong with your car."

"Too many things to fix," she answered. "And, according to the mechanic, not worth the money to fix it, though he'll do it if I want, but it's going to take a couple of weeks to get parts. Big, expensive parts."

"I think it's totaled," he told his mother. Jess groaned.

"Then you should drive her and her dogs to Rhode Island," Martha declared. "What is it, about three hours from here to Rhode Island, Sam? How long did it take us to go to Newport last summer?"

His father was quick to answer. "Three hours is about right. You know, your mother has a good idea. You were coming here anyway."

"No, I wasn't," Sam corrected, but he knew he was talking to two people who wanted to see him and reassure themselves that he was going to be okay, cancelled wedding and broken heart notwithstanding.

"I'll make my famous meatballs," Sam Senior informed him. "What's her name? Does she likes meatballs? Will you be here tonight?"

"I don't know," he said, answering the last two questions. "It's started to snow here."

"Well, take your time," his mother advised him. "We'll be here."

"What kind of dogs?" his father asked again. "Not more like Darcy, I hope?"

"No. These are small hairy dogs. Pekingese."

"Oh, my goodness," his mother said. "This is turning out to be quite a day."

And that, Sam decided, pretty much summed it up.

CHAPTER FOUR

"IT'S NOT TOTALED," Jess told him after he put his cell phone down. "Not exactly."

"How much is it going to cost to fix?"

She told him the estimate. Even saying the figure aloud was painful and she watched Sam wince, which was exactly what she had done when she'd heard the price.

"It's not worth it," he replied. "It's how old? Twelve years? Ten?"

"Twelve."

"With how many miles on it?"

"Almost one-eighty."

He looked at her as if she was mentally incompetent, but Jess knew she couldn't afford to fix the van, not even if it was the best financial decision possible. The van was old, her checking account small, and her Visa spending limit wouldn't cover the cost of parts, never mind the labor involved. The mechanic had offered to buy it for his teenaged son to fix up, and she'd accepted.

"I'll take you to a car dealer—there are plenty to

choose from along this stretch of road. You can buy something else and be on your way in an hour."

"I can't," she said. "My best friend's husband sells cars and if I bought a car from anyone but him— They're expecting a baby," she added, as if that made any difference to a stranger. "He'll give me a good deal," she added. "Better than I'd get here."

"I'll buy you a plane ticket," Sam Grogan said as if he actually thought she would accept such an offer.

"Thank you," she said. "But that's not the problem. It's what to do with the Pekes. I can take one on the plane with me, but I can't ship the others as cargo. It's too cold and besides, it's too risky."

She watched as he finished his coffee and looked at the snowflakes hitting the windshield. He didn't say anything.

"I'll get a motel room and wait for someone from Peke rescue to rescue *me*," she said. "Someone will call back soon and we'll figure it out. If you'll give us a ride to an Econo Lodge, that would be great." She dug her cell phone from her purse. "I'll call them and find out the closest location."

"My father wanted to know if you like meatballs."

"Why?"

"I'm heading to Connecticut this weekend," he said. "And my parents—nice people but full of advice—suggested I give you a ride." He peered at the snow and frowned. "It could take quite a while to get there. I usually can do it in six, six and a half hours, if the weather and the traffic aren't bad."

"You're offering to take us with you?" She wondered if he'd been tackled too many times during his football career.

"I've had a change of plans for the weekend. My mother is recovering from the flu. My parents were supposed to be visiting me, but they had to cancel when she got sick."

"They were coming to the wedding?"

"Yes." He crushed the empty cup. "But it turns out they didn't miss anything."

"Oh." It must have been an important wedding. Someone in the family, she assumed. It had been cancelled at the last minute or Sam Grogan wouldn't be wearing a tuxedo. It was more than a little surreal, going from her leaking van to a shiny Escalade, being driven by a handsome sportscaster in a black tux. The tie was missing, the shirt collar undone, but it only added to the disheveled charm of a handsome man. And, oh, was he handsome. Not her type at all, of course. Tuxedoed men didn't show up on her doorstep and whisk her off to formal balls. Sportscasters and football players were as close—and as far away—as her television screen. They didn't drive her around town. Until today. Today was the most bizarre day she'd had in a long, long time.

The mastiff rested his enormous head on her shoulder.

"He won't stop until you pet him," Sam said. "But he won't go away if you do pet him."

"Kind of a catch-22 situation." She rubbed the dog's ears and he leaned closer, touching her cheek with his nose.

"So, Jess Hall, what do you want to do? I have to stop at my place for some clothes, but we can be on our way right after that."

"Well…" She hesitated. Every horrible story she'd ever heard about serial killers, rapists, murderers and psychopaths flashed through her head. "I don't know."

"I've been approved by the state police," he reminded her. "You're welcome to call my parents and keep them talking on my phone until we get there." He handed her his phone.

"Give me their names and address." She took a piece of paper from her purse and wrote down what he told her, then she called home and left the message on Mary's machine. She copied his car registration from the glove compartment, checked his driver's license and left another detailed message with the transport coordinator.

"Do you want to call the newsroom, too?"

He didn't look at all upset by her precautions. In fact, he seemed curious as to what she would do next.

"No. I'm used to following my instincts about people. And you do seem perfectly safe."

"I'm the height of respectability," Sam Grogan

declared. "But you probably shouldn't go around accepting rides from strange men."

"You're not strange," she pointed out. "The policeman knew you and so did the tow truck driver. By the way, the mechanic told me to tell you that you were all wrong with your game predictions for Sunday." He'd also asked her if this was the weekend that Grogan was getting married. "You had no intention of going to Connecticut this weekend, though, did you?"

"No." His smile faded and he looked away from her and turned on the engine. Darcy whined. "Up until a couple of hours ago, I had other plans."

She knew not to ask what they were. It made sense now. He was supposed to be at a wedding. His wedding. And he'd gotten cold feet and run away to Krispy Kreme for coffee and a place to hide. She'd seen a show on *Oprah* last spring about jilted brides and wedding disasters.

"Okay," Jess said. "I'm really grateful for the help. Thank you."

"You're welcome. Can we get going now, before the snow gets worse?"

"Sure." She fastened her seat belt and shoved her possessions back into her purse. "I'll walk the dogs when we stop at your place."

There was still the stop to make outside of D.C., where Hazel waited with the boxes of old fabric to exchange for the stockings. Somehow Jess didn't think this was the right time to mention it.

DARCY DIDN'T MEAN to cause problems for Sam. And he wasn't sure he liked the idea of sharing his car with three noisy little dogs with their flat noses, black faces and snuffling sounds. They snorted like pigs, in his opinion. And they looked stupid with their tongues sticking out. At first he thought they were doing it on purpose, to make him laugh, but now he figured they just did it because they didn't know any better. Maybe it felt good.

He opened his mouth and let his tongue fall out, but aside from panting and drooling, normal stuff, not much happened. The darn flat faces looked at him but didn't say anything. The male didn't even blink and the two females looked sleepy. Darcy put his tongue back in his mouth and considered his company. They smelled nice and doggy, like they'd come from a place with lots of other animals. He could sniff them for days and not run out of new scents.

But he wished they had a little more conversation. Heck, it wasn't easy being the only dog in the house. And as much as he liked riding around in the car, it would be more fun if there was another dog to share it with.

Poor Sam. He was a little stressed at the moment, driving through the snowflakes. Darcy wished he'd roll down the windows so he could have a taste of that snow. Sure would be good after those doughnuts.

The Flat Faces didn't look like they would know what to do with snow. Probably stick their heads into it and suffocate. Darcy whined, but none of the dogs responded except to snort again.

At least Sam wasn't playing Johnny Cash anymore.

AT LEAST THE WOMAN didn't chatter. Despite the traffic around Richmond and the snow alternating with periods of rain, Sam felt himself begin to relax for the first time in weeks.

Maybe he should have stayed in town and talked to Susan, but he really didn't have anything to say to her. Oh, if he was the kind of guy who liked scenes, he would have gone to the hotel, pounded on her door and demanded an explanation.

But he was tired of arguing with Susan. And he didn't want to have to talk a woman into marrying him. One's bride was supposed to be radiant and enthusiastic.

So instead of attending his wedding reception, he was spending a miserable afternoon heading toward Washington, D.C., and north, to comfort his parents. And he was with a pretty woman sprinkled liberally with dog hair and suffering from hot coffee burns. This whole thing was insane. At least he'd changed out of his tuxedo and into something less bizarre.

Sam peered through the windshield. At this rate they'd be lucky to get to Westport by nine tonight— "Would you mind if we stopped in Fredericksburg for a few minutes?" Her low voice broke into his thoughts.

"I thought we'd try to get past D.C. before we had lunch." He glanced over to see that she was holding a map on her lap again.

"I can wait for lunch," the woman said, "but I have to deliver the stockings. Hazel—that's the woman who runs a shelter there—is expecting them for their annual fund-raiser next weekend. And we're only a few miles outside of Fredericksburg now."

Which meant he couldn't say no, not without sounding as if he didn't care about fund-raisers for homeless animals. He had the overwhelming urge to buy all of the stockings himself and keep driving, but he doubted that she'd believe he was serious if he actually offered. "Do you know how to get there?"

"I have the directions," she said, lifting a yellow piece of paper from the road atlas.

"Read them to me." With any luck they could be in and out in ten minutes.

He should have known that nothing today would go as he expected it to. They got lost, of course. Hazel, a widow with a pillared colonial home the size of a small hotel, traded Jess boxes of musty old fabric for boxes of fancy Christmas stockings, all of which Sam carted back and forth while the snow pelted down. Hazel insisted on them staying for lunch, presented Darcy with a steak bone and immediately fell in love with one of Jess Hall's snorting passengers, the dog that Jess placed in the woman's arms to hold "for just a minute."

Yeah, he could see Jess had another reason to stop at this house.

"The little sweetheart. The darling. Oh, look at that little face and those big eyes." Hazel, a sturdy woman with graying hair and sensible shoes, held the homeless Pekes and hugged it to her ample bosom.

"She needs a bath," Jess said, "but she is awfully cute."

The dog wagged her tail and gazed up at the older woman as if she was hanging on to every adoring word. A few snorts, which Hazel pronounced as highly entertaining, made the Peke appear as if she was trying to communicate with her new friend.

"Do you have someone to adopt her?" Hazel blinked back tears.

"No, not yet. I pulled these three out of a kill shelter this morning—they were going to be put to sleep if I didn't get them this weekend. I'm going to keep her myself until I can find a foster home and put her picture on Petfinder."

"Petfinder?" Sam finished his last forkful of pecan pie. He could see the writing on the wall. Hazel was going to have a companion.

"It's a Web site that shelters use to list animals up for adoption," Jess explained, but she wasn't looking at Sam when she spoke. "Her name is Harriet," she told the older woman.

"I could be her foster mommy," Hazel said. "Or I could adopt her, don't you think?" Darcy lumbered over and rested his head on the mahogany table. Hazel absently patted his large head, but her attention was on the Pekingese relaxing in her arms. "My Wookie died last year and I never thought I'd want another dog. Until now."

Sam helped himself to another sugar cookie, this one in the shape of a reindeer, and waited for his traveling companion to see the wisdom of placing a homeless dog with their tenderhearted hostess. Not that she hadn't planned it this way. He suspected Dog Woman was sneakier than she looked.

"She hasn't had a complete vet check yet," Jess said. "She seems healthy enough, but—"

"I'll take her to my nice Dr. Otis first thing Monday morning. Do say yes, Jessica dear. There's no need for her to travel all the way to Rhode Island when she can have a perfectly good home here."

"You'll have to fill out an adoption application." Jess leaned over and lifted the male Pekingese from underneath her chair just as he was sniffing it. Sam looked around for the other one, but she was hiding in her crate with the door open, her dark face peering out at the strange new world she'd been moved to. "And there's an adoption fee and a contract to sign."

"I'll get my checkbook," Hazel said, giving the black-faced Pekingese another kiss before handing her to Jess. "She'll be my own little Christmas present to myself."

"Well, that's a happy ending," Jess said, after their hostess had left the dining room.

"Yeah," Sam agreed. "First one today."

CHAPTER FIVE

"YOU PLANNED THAT, didn't you?"

"I didn't exactly *plan* it. I *hoped* that Hazel would take to one of the Pekes." She studied the map again, wanting to discover that they'd covered more miles than they actually had. They were only twenty miles past Fredericksburg, but it felt like they'd been on the road for an hour since stopping for lunch.

"Had you ever met her before?"

"No. We e-mailed about fund-raising and one thing led to another. She said she had old fabric for me, but I can't believe how much she gave me." Christmas had come early, for her and for Hazel. She couldn't wait to get home and wash all the drapes that Hazel had collected from various people in Fredericksburg. She suspected most of the fabric came from the woman's own attic. "I won't have to buy fabric on eBay for next year's stockings."

"Is that your business, making those things?"

"No, it's just part of the fund-raising for my shelter that a friend and I run. The dogs—*small* dogs," she added, giving Darcy an ear scratch, "are in foster care."

"That dog of Hazel's has got it made now."

"Yes." She smiled and hugged her coat closer to her. "Harriet needs some pampering and Hazel's the perfect person to do it."

"I'm glad you're happy. That little stop cost us the day."

"What do you mean?" she asked, though she knew perfectly well that the weather had worsened, adding the complication of slippery roads to the bad visibility of the late afternoon.

"We'll be lucky if we make it to Baltimore before the roads ice up. Move, you mutt." Darcy, who should have been wearing a canine seat belt, rested his head on his owner's shoulder and sighed. "I sure can't drive many more miles in this."

"Where do you want to stop?"

"We'll see if we can get past D.C. first," he said, peering through the windshield being pounded by icy snowflakes.

She had enough money for a motel room. Econo Lodge hotels accepted pets. They could get dinner at a fast-food restaurant and take it back to the rooms. She would pay for Sam's room, of course. It was the least she could do after begging a ride. She'd give the Pekes much-needed baths tonight, make all her phone calls, go to bed early.

And try not to worry about how she was going to afford a new car.

She wondered what Sam's bride was doing right

now. The poor woman must be drowning in tears. He was a handsome man, and a kind one. But running out on his wedding? What kind of man would do that? Jess studied his profile and wondered what had made him run away. Fear of commitment? Possibly. In love with someone else? Not likely, or he'd be with the other woman right now instead of driving to visit his parents.

"What?" He glanced at her before turning back to the road.

"Hmm?"

"You were staring at me."

"I was just thinking," she said. Of course *he* could be the one who was deserted at the church. She almost smiled at how ridiculous that idea was.

"No."

"No?"

"No, I am not going to adopt one of those hairy little dogs."

"Maybe Darcy is lonely," she couldn't help teasing.

"Not likely." The mastiff licked his master's ear. "He goes everywhere with me."

"Did he go to the wedding, too?"

Sam's smile faded. "There was no wedding," he said, "but, yes, he was there. He put up such a fuss about going to the kennel—which is usually one of his favorite places because they specialize in caring for very large dogs—that I took him with me to the church. Lucky for Darcy the minister let him stay downstairs."

"So you *went* to the church?" Why would he do that if he didn't want to get married? Why not call it off before everyone got dressed in wedding clothes and arrived at the church?

"Yeah." He leaned forward and wiped the fogged windshield with his hand. "I went to the church."

"It was your wedding," she said. "The mechanic told me he heard it on television."

He shrugged. "Susan never could make up her mind about anything. I shouldn't have been surprised."

Susan was ten times an idiot, Jess decided. Or insane. Sam Grogan was a perfectly nice man with a set of shoulders that made a woman want to tackle him.

"But you were surprised."

He didn't respond. One very large hand punched the defroster button, causing the fan to accelerate. Darcy moved away and stretched out on the back seat. The car slipped slightly, so Sam slowed down to little more than a crawl now that they were in worse traffic than before.

"Yes," he finally said. "I never saw it coming. She's a designer, an artist, and she can be temperamental. It's part of her charm, I guess."

Jess bit back a sigh. Temperamental women were charming? That's what was wrong with the world, all right. The nicest men usually panted after the bitchy girls, one of those mysteries of the universe that no one could ever figure out.

"But why—"

"Why did she call it off? I don't know."

"What did she say?"

"Nothing, not to me. Her father told me."

"I'm sorry" was all she could come up with. This Susan woman hadn't had the decency to tell her own fiancé that the wedding was off?

"Thanks."

"Maybe it's for the best," she dared to say, hoping the man would show a little righteous anger toward the no-show bride.

"For the best?" He shook his head. "I wish people would stop saying that. I should be at my wedding reception. Tonight I would have been on a plane to San Francisco. And tomorrow? A private beach in Hawaii."

With a bitchy artist with no manners, no class and no courage, Jess would have liked to add. *Gee, what a loss.*

"WELL, YOU KNOW MY SAD STORY. What about you? Married, engaged, divorced, living with a significant other?" Sam felt almost lighthearted, an odd sensation he barely recognized. He figured it had something to do with getting off the icy highway and into a four-star hotel.

The Pekes were snoring in their crates, Darcy lay stretched out on the floor guarding them, the heat was blasting throughout the large beige and blue room, and Sam settled himself into a wing chair, with no steering wheel in sight. The last hours on the road had crawled by at a thirty-mile-an-hour pace. Lunch at Hazel's seemed like yesterday.

"None of the above," Jess Hall declared. She checked on the Pekes, gave Darcy a pat and crossed the room toward him.

"Children?" He could picture her with kids. She treated those dogs with a gentle, patient hand and she hadn't complained about standing behind the hotel while freezing snow pellets had rained down on three dogs determined to take their time doing their business. She looked better now, having towel-dried her hair and taken off her wet jacket and boots. This was her room, but he'd decided to make himself comfortable until she was ready to order dinner.

Asking for connecting rooms had been an act of genius. Paying for them without Jess's interference had been a downright miracle. The woman argued like an outraged coach.

"No children—" Her knockout smile reminded him that he was not so heartbroken that he couldn't appreciate a pretty woman.

"I don't have a very interesting past," she added.

"Well, *your* disastrous wedding isn't going to make the Sunday paper tomorrow, but I'm sure you can come up with something." He picked up the phone. "I'm calling room service. Have you decided what you want?"

"Yes. Chowder, a hamburger and fries, a pot of tea."

"This is Maryland," he reminded her. "You don't want crab cakes?"

"Forgive me." She sat on the edge of the double bed closest to the table where he'd set the room service menu. "I've never been to Maryland."

"Never? I thought you drove dogs all over the place."

"In my old van? No. I don't usually venture this far."

"So do you want the crab cakes?"

"Sure. But remember our agreement."

The agreement had been that she would pay for dinner. And he would send her a copy of the hotel bill so she could pay him back. He had no intention of doing that, of course. He'd put down a large deposit so the dogs would be allowed in the room, he'd assured the receptionist that Darcy would not sleep on the bed and he'd promised that the dogs would never be left alone in the rooms.

"Chowder and the crab cakes dinner-for-two, hot tea, decaf coffee and two pieces of chocolate cake," Sam announced, dialing room service. "Sound okay?"

She looked up from the menu. "Chocolate cake?"

"Don't look so innocent. You were at Krispy Kreme this morning."

"I'll bet you would have eaten most of the wedding cake," she said, then flushed. "I'm sorry. I shouldn't—"

Sam laughed. "You're right. I run five miles every morning so I can have dessert every night."

"I'm glad to know you're not perfect."

"My mother thinks I am," he said, then gave the dinner order to the woman who answered on the other end of the line. He added a bottle of white wine at the last minute, figuring Jess may as well help him drown his jilted-at-the-altar sorrows.

She piled the pillows against the headboard and stretched out on the bed. "You should call her. She's expecting you tonight."

"I will." *Dog Woman and I are partying in an Econo Lodge outside of Baltimore, Mom. We're going to kill a bottle of wine, talk about my honeymoon and brush dog hair off each other's naked bodies.* "We have a minibar. Do you want anything?"

Jess closed her eyes. "I'll wait for dinner, thanks."

"It could take an hour. They're backed up in the kitchen."

"Mmm," she said sleepily, and within minutes she had dozed off.

Well, she certainly wasn't nervous about being in a hotel room with him. The woman was practically unconscious. He helped himself to a mini-beer from the minibar, assured his parents over the phone that he would stay put as long as the roads were bad, and listened to the Pekes snore. He thought about turning on the TV and checking out the weather channel, but he didn't want to get up again. It felt pretty damn good to sit in the quiet and have a few minutes to relax. Between work and the prewedding festivities, he hadn't had much time just to sit and think.

And he hadn't had much time to be alone with Susan, either. She'd been so tense last night, he'd worried that something more than wedding nerves was at fault, but she'd only frowned when he'd asked her what was wrong. As if he was supposed to know without her telling him. He was beginning to wonder why he'd ever thought that he and Susan would be happy together.

Jess rolled onto her side, giving Sam an enticing view of her nicely shaped bottom. Her worn blue jeans fit her well, her sweater hugged a tiny waist, and all those blond curls looked surprisingly appealing on the white pillow.

Jeez, what was the matter with him? Ogling a woman pale with exhaustion, admiring her tidy body curled up on a motel bed… Well, he was a man, wasn't he? Sleeping Beauty here didn't look too concerned. Neither did her two remaining companions, who were snoring like truckers while the wind whipped against the large window at Sam's back.

Darcy, sensing that he might be able to get away with something, lifted his head and stood to look at the woman in the bed. One small wag of his tail was the only warning he gave before climbing on the bed to join her.

"Darcy," Sam hissed. "No!"

The dog hesitated, gave his owner an I-don't-hear-you look and lay down beside Jess. He scooted his large hind end against her knees and attempted to put his head on her pillow before Sam could clamber across the mattress to grab his collar.

"Come." Sam did his best to whisper, but he had the kind of voice that carried across football fields and into the bleachers. "Get off that bed."

Darcy played dead, but Jess opened her eyes and yelped.

"Sorry." Sam grabbed Darcy by the collar and tugged. "I was trying to get to him before he woke you."

The dog suddenly rolled backward, tossing Sam off balance—and on top of Jess Hall's tempting curves.

This time it was Darcy's turn to protest, which he did with a loud whine that set the Pekes to barking their concern.

"Sorry," Sam repeated as he attempted to move away from Jess and extricate his legs from Darcy's. Her breasts rose and fell beneath his chest and she began to laugh. Darcy nuzzled her ear and whined, which made her try to swat him away.

Which meant that her hand hit Sam's cheek—not that it hurt. No, the problem was suddenly finding his mouth so close to hers as he looked down into a pair of very wide, very beautiful blue eyes. She laughed up at him, and that was his undoing. Because of course he had to kiss her, despite the whining and yapping going on in the background.

Her lips were soft. And welcoming. And surprisingly arousing to a man who was supposed to have a broken heart. He would have moved his hand along her waist and higher, to touch those gorgeous breasts, if he wasn't pinned down by a mastiff. He might have deepened the kiss, tasting her and teasing, if Darcy had stopped wriggling. He could have swept his lips across her jaw to taste her neck…and lower, if only the knocking on the door would stop.

"I think," Jess gasped, when he released her mouth, "I think our dinner is here."

Dinner. Knocking. Room service. He forced himself to remember where he was and what he was doing—before kissing Jess, of course—and, with a superhuman show of strength, heaved himself off that delectable body, shoved Darcy to the other side of the bed and told the Pekes to be quiet.

"Room service," a man's voice called.

"Coming." Sam ran his fingers through his hair and hurried to the door, Darcy following. One of the Pekes let out a small yip as Sam walked past the crates, but at least the room was quieter than it had been a few seconds earlier. He opened the door to face a wide-eyed young man behind a large trolley laden with domed dishes.

"Mr. Grogan?"

"Yeah. Come on in. It sounds like a zoo, but it's safe."

"What about him?" He pointed to Darcy, who was

now panting at Sam's side. Sam took him by the collar and backed him up to the bathroom, shoved the dog inside and shut the door. A little redheaded Pekingese charged the moving cart, barking at the wheels and the kid's legs, before Jess scooped him into her arms and shushed him.

"Wow," the man said, pushing the cart deeper into the room. "You guys must really like dogs."

"We do," Sam and Jess said at the same time. Sam didn't look at her, though. He suspected she would be smiling, which would make him want to kiss her again.

Which, in a day of unexpected happenings, would be the craziest thing of all.

CHAPTER SIX

"IT LOOKS WONDERFUL," Jess said, eyeing the table of food being rolled toward the chairs by the window. She scooped Ozzie into her arms and away from the legs of the hotel worker. Thank goodness for the dogs. Between Ozzie and the mastiff, Jess could pretend she was too busy to be embarrassed about that kiss.

That kiss—and her reaction to it—still shocked her. In fact, waking up to find Sam wrestling with his huge dog had been quite a surprise. She couldn't believe she'd fallen asleep so quickly, but the past few days of little sleep and too many hours on the road had caught up with her. There was something about stretching out on a soft bed in a warm room that overrode any discomfort she felt about relaxing in front of a stranger.

And then he'd fallen across her and she'd laughed at the mortified expression in his dark eyes. She couldn't remember how many months—if not years—it had been since a handsome male body had tangled with hers on a bed, so she'd laughed. And he'd kissed her. She had seen it coming and she'd welcomed it.

She had held still at first, testing the feel of his mouth against hers. And then she'd warmed to what would have been a perfectly lovely moment—if room service hadn't interrupted.

A lovely moment? With a stranger on a bed? Jess frowned. The storm must be affecting her usually sensible brain.

"What?" She was aware that Sam was staring at her and the young man was walking out the door.

"I asked if you want a glass of wine."

"Yes, thank you."

"Does he bark *all* the time?"

She looked down at the yapping Ozzie and told him to be quiet, which he did. "I think he just wanted to let the stranger know that he was guarding the room. Some Pekes are like that."

"Aren't *we* strangers to him, too?" He studied Ozzie as if he was afraid the little dog would leap out of her arms and go for his jugular.

"Yes, but I think he senses we're taking care of him. The three of them would have been put down today if I hadn't gotten them out of there," she reminded him. Jess set the dog on the carpet and watched him walk past the beds and into his own crate. Darcy whined from behind the bathroom door.

"So he knows you saved his life."

"Maybe. Can I let Darcy out?"

"Not yet. He's being punished for not obeying."

Which brought them both back to what had happened a few minutes ago on the bed. She hated feeling awkward with him. Despite everything, they'd managed to muddle through the day together.

Jess pushed her hair away from her face and concentrated on Sam opening the wine bottle. He performed that task with effortless skill, of course. He and his Susan had no doubt been Richmond's Most Elegant Couple. She imagined a tall, sleek brunette who smiled for the cameras and kept her arm firmly linked with Sam's whenever they appeared in public, the kind of woman who had a closet filled with "evening wear" and matching shoes for every outfit.

"Miss Hall?" Sam handed her a crystal glass filled with white wine. He looked distracted and didn't meet her eyes.

"Mr. Grogan," she replied, lifting her glass as if toasting him. "Thank you again for rescuing me."

"You're welcome" was his only response as he lifted his own glass to hers.

She didn't miss his tuxedo. The charcoal cashmere sweater and khaki pants appeared expensive and stylish, but at least he didn't look like someone else's groom. She thought she should say something comforting about his wedding, like how sorry she was and how she hoped things would work out, but there was no way she could get such words out of her mouth. If the temperamental Susan had said "I do" this morning, Jess would most likely be stranded in Richmond still, waiting for help from PUR and for the storm to pass. There would have been no flights leaving Richmond and nothing to do but fiddle with her checkbook and watch the dogs pee against icy parking lot curbs.

"I'm sorry—" she began, but he interrupted her.

"I am, too. What happened on the bed was an accident, a mistake," he assured her as seriously as if he were announcing the Redskins were in last place and had decided to quit for the rest of the season.

"It wasn't *that* bad, was it?" She couldn't help teasing him and watching the surprise flicker across his face.

"No. I wouldn't say that."

She took a sip of her wine, and then slid between the table and the bed to one of the upholstered chairs.

"I mean, I certainly didn't expect to see you and Darcy on the bed, but you have to admit it was funny."

"Yes," he said, his mouth lifting at the corners. "An odd version of a honeymoon."

"How can you laugh about it? Didn't you want to— Never mind, that's none of my business." She took a deep breath and started over. "Sit down, Sam. I meant that I was sorry about your wedding." She crossed her fingers under the table. She wasn't the least bit sorry, not if what she'd guessed about Susan was true.

"I don't think I am." He took a seat across from her and lifted the domed lid on the plate in front of him. "Not anymore. I've been thinking about it—you have a lot of time to think when you're driving thirty miles an hour in the snow—and maybe everyone was right."

"Right?"

"That it was for the best." Sam unwrapped his silverware and tossed the linen napkin in his lap. "These crab cakes smell great."

Jess guessed that meant the serious conversation—and the subject of his wedding—was over.

"Tell me," she said, lifting the lid from her own plate, "do you know anyone who would like to foster a Peke?"

"Foster? What does that mean exactly?" He cut a section of crab cake with his fork and looked at it with undisguised relish.

"Take care of for a while," she explained. "Until we find the right home, take care of any medical needs, figure out the dog's personality and what kind of a home he'll do best in."

"These are damn good crab cakes— Is that what you do for a living, find homes for dogs?"

"No. We're all volunteers." She took a bite of the crab cake. "Wow."

"Told you."

"The big decision is whether to eat the crab cakes first or start with the chowder." She looked at him for help, pretending to herself that this was a real date. Certainly no one could blame a woman for wanting to fantasize about Sam Grogan, sportscaster, athlete and all-around nice guy.

"Whatever you want," he said, spearing another chunk of crab cake. "You can make up your own rules when you're eating in your hotel room, you know."

"And here I thought I'd be back in Rhode Island tonight." She took another sip of wine.

"What would you be doing?"

Jess thought for a moment. "Washing the dogs. Soaking in the tub. Checking e-mail." She grimaced. "Not very exciting, is it?"

"'Exciting' is overrated." He smiled at her, which had the affect of making her remember the way those lips had touched hers and what the feel of them had done to her insides. "If it wasn't for the wedding—and that's the last time I'm going to mention it—or our trip to Connecticut, I'd be home studying my notes for tomorrow's games and eating leftovers."

"Do you travel a lot?"

"Yeah." He refilled her wineglass. "And now I'm in Baltimore, having dinner with a mysterious woman from New England."

"Mysterious?"

"I don't know where you live or what you do for a living. You're not married, you don't have children, you love dogs and you volunteer to drive them around to new homes. You don't have a lot of money and you're too softhearted for your own good." When she started to protest, he pointed out, "You drove into a Dumpster rather than hit a dog."

"You're making me sound like an idiot."

Sam grinned. "Yeah, but an entertaining one. Tell me what you do when you're not hauling dogs from state to state."

"I dust." She took the lid from her chowder bowl and picked up a spoon. "I vacuum. I scrub." He waited, clearly interested. "I have my own housekeeping business."

Sam looked impressed. "That's hard work."

"One of these days I'll go back to school—when I decide what I want to be when I grow up—but for now I like the independence." What she wanted was a home, a husband, children and a huge fenced yard for any and all dogs that needed homes, but it wasn't something that Jess confided to anyone aside from her best friend. She'd sound old-fashioned and be accused of that biological-clock nonsense. Just because she liked babies and dogs and all things domestic didn't mean she wanted to run down the aisle with the first sperm donor who put a ring on her finger. Her parents had had a wonderful marriage; she'd grown up in a happy home, unlike a lot of her friends. And she wasn't willing to settle for anything less than that same kind of love.

Sam finished the crab cakes and started in on the mashed potatoes. "How did you start rescuing dogs?"

She told him about one of her clients, a busy single mother with no time for the little dog she owned, and how Charlie came to live with her for seven years until he died of heart failure. That was two years ago, she told Sam, who actually seemed to be listening. She'd been so heartbroken she'd volunteered to help with several small-dog rescue groups. What she didn't tell Sam was that she hoped that one of these days another little gold and white mongrel would prance into her life and fill the void left by eleven-pound Charlie, sleeping companion and fellow Milano cookie lover.

"What happened to the last boyfriend?" Sam poured himself another glass of wine. "And don't tell me there haven't been boyfriends."

"He met someone else."

"And broke your heart?"

She laughed. "Absolutely not!"

Poor Darcy let out another pitiful bark from the bathroom, which gave Jess the perfect excuse to change the subject. She needed to remember that Sam wasn't her dinner date, wasn't a man who would be in her life after tomorrow. However he might look and act and kiss like the man of her dreams, Sam Grogan was real. And famous. And not at all the type of guy who dated women who pushed around vacuum cleaners for a living.

She would let the little Pekes up on the bed with her tonight and tell herself she wasn't the least bit lonely. She would not think of Sam Grogan and the feel of him against her breasts or the taste of his mouth or the way he smiled when he thought she'd said something amusing.

She would sleep with the dogs and be happy about it.

LIFE WASN'T FAIR. He didn't want to be stuck in the bathroom when he could smell food. Good food. People food. Those two Flat Faces better not be under the table, begging for food and accepting treats with their stupid little tongues. The one they called Ozzie barked, too, but now he grumbled, teasing Darcy by telling him that the food smelled good and didn't Darcy wish he could come out of that room and play. Samantha, the one-eyed girl, never said anything, but Darcy thought she might be nice. He wouldn't mind giving her another sniff.

Sam had forgotten him. Sam never forgot him at dinnertime, except when Smelly Susan came over to the apartment, which wasn't often. Old Smelly didn't like dogs and didn't much like his and Sam's home. When she slept over, Darcy had to sleep in a different room, on a bed all by himself.

"Woof!"

The nice lady said, "Can't you let Darcy out of there? I saved him a piece of my roll."

Oh, boy. Things were really looking up now. Sam had finally found a girlfriend Darcy could like, even if she came with a couple of Flat Faces. He wagged his tail when Sam opened the door, but he trotted over to the lady and squeezed himself into the small space between her chair and the bed. The buttered bread was a heck of a lot better than anything that came out of that bag of dog food Sam had brought along for the trip, so Darcy made sure that he ate it fast before the Flat Faces got any ideas about coming over and sharing. He gave the lady's jeans a kiss and looked across the table at Sam, who sure seemed sad all of a sudden.

Humans were weird. Even the best of 'em didn't know a good thing when it was sitting right in front of them. Darcy licked the lady's hand and waited for another fat chunk of bread. Good thing dogs were around to show the humans what to do.

"I'M SORRY TO WAKE YOU," Sam said, trying to keep his gaze from dropping to Jess's nightgown. He concentrated on her eyes, on the wild curls that cascaded past her cheeks and down—no, he wasn't going to look past the lace collar of her flannel nightgown. Flannel wasn't sexy. Unless it was covering the body of—

"What's wrong?" She blinked, as if trying to figure out if this was real or a nightmare.

Sam, hovering in the doorway that connected the two rooms with Darcy whining at brain-aching decibels, didn't know how to explain. He'd thought the connecting rooms were a good idea, but now this kind of access seemed too darn tempting.

"Darcy won't stop whining. I'm afraid someone's going to complain if he keeps it up."

She stared up at him. "You want to leave? In the middle of the night?"

Darcy brushed past her and trotted over to the crates where one of the Pekes lay snoring. The other one, Sam noticed, was on its back in the middle of Jess's rumpled bed.

"No! I hoped you'd let Darcy sleep in here. I guess he wants to be with the other dogs."

"Okay." She still seemed a little dazed. Those blue eyes of hers hadn't quite focused.

"Hey," he said, putting his hands on her shoulders. "Are you awake?"

"I hope not." She gazed up at him. "Good night."

"Good night." He didn't move, not to release her shoulders or to take a step backward. It was as if he was physically incapable of leaving her. She smelled like vanilla and soap, a combination he never thought would be erotic, but was.

Unexplainably.

So when he dipped his head and put his lips against hers, Sam didn't stop to think about what he was doing. She was there and she was warm under his hands and she looked up at him with that "Are you going to kiss me?" look in her eyes that would make any man think, *damn right*.

He wished he'd been prepared for his own reaction. Kissing her while laughing on a bed had been one thing. Kissing her in the semidarkness at two in the morning was another. Her hair smelled like honey, and her skin felt soft when he moved his hands to frame her face. She made a little sound of surprise, but she didn't pull away. He stepped closer, so that his T-shirt-clad chest touched her breasts, covered by flannel and yet so damn close. And then he touched his tongue to hers—and the world stopped.

He felt as if he'd been hit in the gut, knocked to the turf, dumped upside down and tossed on his head. Nothing made any sense, except that kissing Jess was exactly right. Like coming home to a place he hadn't even known existed until now.

Sam never knew how long they stood there kissing each other in the open doorway that connected their two rooms. He didn't move forward; she didn't step back. As long as they didn't move, as long as they stayed with their bodies pressed together, as long as they kissed upright, as long as their few clothes remained on their bodies, then maybe this could be chalked up to some kind of midnight madness.

He'd been rejected; she was lonely. They were two adults with nothing else to do in the middle of the night. His hands slid to her waist, then higher, to touch those soft breasts. Jess groaned and pressed closer.

Something licked Sam's ankle, which made him jump sideways and bump his head against the doorframe. He swore, Jess chuckled and a dog barked from the bed.

He looked down. One of the Pekes—the one with only one eye—wagged her tail.

"Damn," he muttered. "I think we have a chaperone."

CHAPTER SEVEN

THEY'D PRETEND it hadn't happened. That was Jess's plan, and Sam seemed happy to go along with that idea when they met outside walking the dogs in the parking lot behind the hotel. Sometime this morning Darcy had returned to his owner, and Jess assumed Sam had closed the connecting door, leaving her to sleep as late as she wanted.

"Good morning," she said.

"Good morning," Sam answered, and Darcy wagged his tail and attempted to pull his owner toward the two little dogs that were mesmerized by a small pile of dirty snow. Samantha bumped into it, Ozzie peed on it and Darcy bounded on top of it. The Pekes scampered to get out of the way, Ozzie barking with great excitement.

"It's a beautiful day," Jess pointed out, needing to say something, anything. Sam hadn't shaved yet. He had that adorable rumpled look that handsome men wore so easily and he looked pleased to be outside, despite the cold wind blowing around the corner of the building. "I never thought to ask if you wanted to get an early start."

"I'm not in any hurry. Have you eaten?"

"Not yet." She picked up Samantha, who looked nervous at the noise of the strong wind. The little dog no longer reeked. Unlike Ozzie, she'd enjoyed last night's bath and her session with the hair dryer and brush; she'd snuggled against Jess as if she'd never felt anything so wonderful, before returning to the safety of her crate and pillow. "I haven't been awake very long."

"Me, either." He smiled, which of course added to his charm. Jess found it disconcerting, especially without having had a cup of coffee yet. "I guess we both needed the rest."

There didn't seem to be anything else to say. Avoiding any conversation about last night's toe-curling, heart-stopping, mind-numbing kissing session might not be as easy as she'd thought. Jess shifted Samantha in her arms and attempted to tug Ozzie away from the pile of snow.

"When do you want to leave?"

"Come here, Darce," he called, then turned back to face her. "Let's order something from room service and eat before we get on the road. It's about a three, three-and-a-half-hour drive to Westport."

"I'll have someone meet me there," she assured him.

"There's no hurry. My father is making meatballs and expects you to stay for a meal, you know. And my mother will talk your ear off."

"I'll call when I get to the house then," she agreed. "Are you sure they won't mind the dogs?"

"No." He tugged Darcy closer. "They'll be pleased to have the company. They've been lonely ever since my sister went to London on sabbatical. She and her husband are on a dig somewhere on the northeast coast of England right now." He grinned. "I was the jock of the family, Karen was the brain."

"I guessed that," she said, and he laughed as they headed toward the side door of the hotel. The wind whipped around them, but the sun was shining as if yesterday's storm had been completely forgotten.

"What do you want for breakfast?" He held the door open for her and the Pekes.

"Waffles, if they have them. Or French toast."

"I'll have it sent to my room this time. How about in an hour?"

"That's fine." She would have time to shower, fix her hair, put on makeup, brush the dog hair off her sweater and hope that her jeans didn't look too worn. She would make coffee in the little pot provided by the hotel and remind herself that this would soon be over. She and the dogs would be home tonight, which would end this strange journey. And she would be busy finding foster homes, going through adoption applications, returning phone calls, shopping for a car… Surely she would be too busy to think about Sam Grogan and his broken heart.

Because, she reminded herself, he must have a broken heart. A man didn't come that close to getting married without really wanting to, no matter what he said about how he was relieved.

"OH, SWEETHEART, I'm so sorry."

"It's okay, Mom." Sam hugged his mother, who looked unnaturally pale but still as pretty as ever. She wore a velour pantsuit and pink fluffy slippers, and her gray-streaked hair was stylishly cut, as usual. "Really, it is."

"Well," his father said, clearing his throat and clapping Sam between the shoulder blades. "Well, we're glad you're home. Your mother wasn't going to be happy until she saw for yourself that you were okay."

"I'm okay. I'm glad yesterday is over, but I'm okay."

"Now I can say it," his mother declared, releasing her hold on him. "Susan wasn't the right woman for you, not that she wasn't a nice girl, but I couldn't quite figure out why you two stayed together. She seemed a little—" His mother paused, frowned, searched for the right word.

"Indecisive?" Sam suggested.

"High maintenance," Martha Grogan said. "You have your whole life ahead of you now, honey. There must be hundreds of women who would love to go out with a big, handsome television star."

"Mom—" He started to explain that he wasn't a star but a sportscaster, but he knew she wouldn't hear a word of it. She knew he was on television—he sent her tapes of the shows—and that was that. "Let me introduce Jess, okay? She wouldn't come inside, said she wanted us to have some privacy."

"How sweet," his mother said. "Is she nice, Sam? Is she pretty?"

"Mom—" Sam kept his expression neutral. If he so much as thought about kissing Jess, his mother would see something in his face that would start her asking more questions.

"For heaven's sake, Martha, leave the boy alone." His father guided him toward the door. "Let's go get your stuff and this friend of yours. Martha, you get back on the couch and put that afghan over your legs. Just because you're feeling better doesn't mean you have to run around the kitchen asking questions and making Sam here nervous."

"I'm not nervous."

"He's not nervous," his mother added, refusing to leave the kitchen. "Go get that young lady and her dogs. I have a steak bone for Darcy and a hundred questions for you."

"A million's more like it," his father grumbled, but he was smiling when he held the door open for Sam. "Your mother's been on pins and needles ever since you called yesterday. She was sure you were just about going to die of a broken heart and—holy moly, who the hell is that?"

Sam Senior had just had his first glimpse of Jess Hall, all blond curls and blue eyes and a hot body poured into denim jeans and a snug red sweater.

"That," his son breathed, "is the woman I found at Krispy Kreme."

"I would imagine," his father whispered, "she's cheered you up quite a bit."

"Yes, sir." Jess looked up from walking the Pekes. She smiled at both Grogan men, and Sam remembered kissing that mouth and touching those breasts less than twelve hours ago. Every time he looked at her he somehow found it difficult to breathe. "She's a very cheerful person."

IT KEPT GETTING WORSE.

She liked his kisses, his dog and his parents. She loved his smile, his kindness and the way he'd coped with a disappointing wedding day. He hadn't wallowed in self-pity or passed out in a bar. No, he'd taken his dog out for doughnuts and he'd rescued a woman who came with luggage, dogs and boxes of Christmas stockings.

And yet Sam looked at her as if *he* was grateful for something as he sat across the dinner table eating his father's *promised* meatballs, complete with spaghetti, salad and thick slices of Italian bread.

"You must stay for dinner," Mrs. Grogan had said when Jess talked about calling home for a ride. "I'm feeling much better today and I'm not the least contagious. A couple of days ago I thought I was at death's door, but today? Well, today I'm much more optimistic." This was said with a friendly smile and after letting Ozzie climb up on the couch to lie at her feet.

Mr. Grogan, whose sturdy good looks echoed his son's, had gone out of his way to make her feel welcome. "We're so glad you were with Sam yesterday," he had confided when she'd gathered dishes to set the table. He'd said it as if she'd volunteered to ease Sam's pain, as if she was an old friend. "Martha and I felt better knowing that he wasn't alone."

"I think he's going to be fine," she'd whispered. "Really. He was a little sad at first, but then he seemed better."

"Yes," Mr. Grogan said, and winked at her. "I can see that."

It was all too tempting, after traveling with Sam and kissing Sam and now spending time with Sam's parents. Tempting to fall the tiniest bit in love with him, to believe—just a little—that fate had intervened and brought Sam knocking on the window of her dented van because they were meant to be together, like an opening scene in a movie.

But a sensible woman such as herself did not go falling in love after a mere thirty-six hours with a man, no matter how special that man was turning out to be. Nope. Oh, she'd seen enough people fall in love with *dogs* at first sight. Take Hazel and Harriet. Jess pictured the elderly woman and her little Pekingese living happily ever after. Why couldn't it be that easy for people?

"You really should spend the night." Mrs. Grogan now held Ozzie in her lap and the dog was upside down and fast asleep, his little pink tongue sticking out. Poor blind Samantha refused to come out of her crate, despite Darcy whining at her. The mastiff lay in front of the crate, his head on his paws, staring inside as if he could will the little female to come out and play.

"I can't," Jess said. "But thank you. I'm going to call a friend of mine and—"

"I'll take you home in the morning." Sam passed her the basket of Italian bread. "Whatever time you say."

"Mary said last night that she'd come get me," Jess explained, looking past Sam to the darkening sky out the dining room windows of the comfortable ranch house. Sam's parents had raised their children here—Mrs. Grogan had made sure Jess had seen the photos displayed on the bookshelves beside the fireplace—and Mr. Grogan said they were content to stay exactly where they were, a few miles from the ocean and close enough for "Sammy" to visit whenever he could.

"There's no need," Sam said. "Unless you have to work tomorrow?"

"No, but—"

"Good," Mrs. Grogan said, snuggling Ozzie closer to her. She kissed the top of the dog's head and his tail wagged in appreciation. "It's so much fun to have some company now, and I'm not sure I can let little Ozzie leave me yet."

The two Grogan men looked at each other and

then toward Mrs. Grogan, who was happily unaware of the horrified expression on her husband's face.

"Now, Martha," he said, "the last thing we need around here is a dog."

Mrs. Grogan ignored him. "Jess can sleep in your sister's room, Sam. Show her around while your father cleans up the kitchen."

Jess knew she could have protested and Sam would have given in. She should have called Mary as soon as she arrived in Westport, but she hadn't. She'd been having too much fun pretending that she was Sam's official girlfriend making a visit home to meet his parents, instead of a hard-luck passenger he'd pitied in a parking lot.

So she stayed. And later that evening, after the Grogans had said good-night and gone to bed, Sam took her in his arms in front of his sister's bedroom door.

"I've never kissed a cleaning lady before." His mouth dipped closer, brushed her lips, teased with light, feathery kisses.

"I guess there's a first time for everything," Jess managed to say. And then it was a long time before she could say anything at all.

CHAPTER EIGHT

DISAPPOINTMENT OBVIOUSLY CLUNG to him, Sam decided, as he carried Samantha's crate to the car. He wondered if he was contagious that way. Maybe the blind dog he tucked carefully into the back of the vehicle felt the same way, now that her two buddies had found homes and she was still hiding in her crate. The two of them seemed doomed for failure.

"Well, well, are we ready?" His father rubbed his hands together in great anticipation of a drive with his one and only son. The fact that his son might like to have a private hour or two in Rhode Island with the luscious Jess Hall had never entered his father's mind, or if it had, the man hadn't given it much thought.

"We're ready," he said. "As soon as Jess says goodbye to Mom again." Sam hid a grin. His father might be spoiling his romantic daydreams, but he was also inheriting Ozzie, the barking Pekingese. Jess had found another home for one of her West Virginia orphans, much to his father's dismay.

"I should have known what your mother was up

to the minute I heard you say you had dogs with you." His father tucked a cooler packed with meatball sandwiches on the floor behind the front seat and hoisted himself into the back. "She's always wanted a little dog—no offense, Darcy."

The mastiff whined and edged closer to his traveling companion.

"Don't lick me," Sam Senior warned the dog. "I'd like to stay clean for a few more minutes."

"You can change your mind." Sam dangled the car keys and opened the driver's door. "It's going to be a long day in the back seat with Darcy."

"But we'll get to talk on the way home. Been a long time since we had a chance to do that," his father reminded him.

The back door opened and Jess stepped out, Martha behind her ready to wave at the departing car. It was foolish to wait for Jess to smile at him, but he did. Hard to imagine he could have been on his honeymoon and never met her… Which was a surprisingly chilling thought considering that last week he had thought himself in love with someone else.

"That is one very nice young lady," his father declared. "Think you'll see her again?"

"It's possible."

Jess hurried over to the other side of the car and climbed into the passenger seat.

"You're welcome to come back and visit here anytime," his father said, leaning forward to pat her shoulder. "But if you bring any more homeless dogs with you, I'm not sure I'll let you stay for dinner."

"He's kidding," Sam said. "That dog will be sleeping in his recliner with him by next weekend."

"Your mother's not going to let that hairy little thing out of her sight," he grumbled. "I think she'd have kept the other one, too, if it hadn't needed surgery. What did you say was wrong with it, Jess?"

"Hernias, we think." She turned in her seat to face the older man. "I hope it's not anything worse, but she has two tumors on her belly."

"Good Lord," his father said. "That's why you drove all the way to Virginia, to save this dog?"

"One of the reasons, yes."

"Tell him about the fabric and the Christmas stockings," Sam suggested.

"Now you're teasing," she said. But she shot him that knockout smile and fastened her seat belt as they drove down the street and north, toward the interstate.

The hours passed too quickly, despite the Monday morning traffic and the stop for coffee at a roadside truck stop. They bought coffee-to-go and a box of powdered sugar doughnuts, most of which were shared with Darcy. Jess lived in Newport, an island town in Narragansett Bay, accessible after two bridges and one small traffic jam on a waterfront street. She directed him up a hill to Bellevue Avenue, past opulent mansions half-hidden behind hedges and iron fences, to a winding road lined with less imposing homes. The house she pointed to was yellow, a neat two-story Cape with a paved driveway and an elegant black door.

"Nice place," Sam's father said, as Sam pulled into the driveway. "Did you grow up here?"

"This was my grandparents' house," Jess explained. "We lived on another part of the island, but that place was sold after my mother died."

"And your father?" Sam couldn't help asking. He hated the idea that Jess was alone in the world, though he told himself that it was none of his business.

"He remarried three years ago—she's a very nice woman—and they moved to Florida, where her sons live." She unbuckled her seat belt and invited them inside. "Come on in. I'll put on some coffee or water for tea," she said.

"It's started to snow," his father pointed out. "We probably should head back before it gets worse."

A vision of making love to Jess while the snow swirled outside flashed into Sam's head. "I'll unload the car," he said.

"The backyard is fenced," Jess said, hopping out of the car. "Darcy is welcome to run around back there for a few minutes."

Great. Hauling boxes of old fabric and watching a mastiff pee was not the fantasy he'd dreamed of last night in his cold and lonely bed.

"COME VISIT US ANYTIME when you're on one of your rescue missions," Mr. Grogan said, enveloping Jess in a hug as they stood in the middle of her tiny foyer. "We'll take good care of that little dog, don't worry."

"I'm not worried." Ozzie had it made, as did Harriet. Only blind, elderly Samantha was left to keep her company tonight.

"Darcy and I will wait for you in the car," Mr. Grogan said, tugging on the dog's leash. He whined, sniffed Samantha as if to say goodbye and trotted reluctantly out the door with Sam's father.

Jess turned to Sam and plastered a bright smile on her face. *It was fun while it lasted,* she wanted to say. Would he say those dreaded words, *I'll call you,* and would she carry her cell phone everywhere she went in hopes that it would ring?

"Well," she said. "Thanks again for everything."

He stood there looking down at her as if he had forgotten where he was.

"Sam?"

Those green eyes met hers. "I wish we had another day."

"Yes," she admitted. "Me, too."

"This is crazy." Of course he kissed her, a soft meeting of lips that meant *goodbye, it's been fun, see you around, sweetheart.* And of course she looped her arms around his neck and kissed him back. *I like you, I'll miss you, I don't know what to think about these past two days.*

"Absolutely insane," she agreed.

"I'll—"

"Oh, please don't say it." Jess winced. "Not unless you really mean it."

"I was going to say I'll call you." He frowned. "You don't want me to?"

"Surprise me," she said. "My phone number is on the adoption form your mother is filling out."

"I can do better than that." His hands cupped her waist, slid to her back and held her body against his in a most arousing way.

"You can?"

"Meet me next weekend. I'm doing a game in Miami. You could join me and we'll spend a long weekend on the beach."

"I can't. I'm working the next twelve days straight with only Sundays off. The holidays are coming and everyone wants more hours." And she needed the money, especially now that she'd be making car payments on whatever she bought.

"The week after that, then. Let's go somewhere special."

"More special than Baltimore?"

"What about Boston?" he said. "I think that's the weekend the Raiders play New England."

She hesitated. "Maybe we should quit while we're ahead."

"Coward," he whispered against her mouth. "I thought you had guts."

"Now you're talking like a jock."

"Meet me somewhere, Jess. Just the two of us, without dogs and parents and broken cars."

"I don't know." She could have invited him back to Newport, but that was somehow too personal. She didn't want to remember him in her house, in her bed, after this ended. It would hurt too much to have had him here, in her life, and then be lonely in her own home.

"Will you have a car—a reliable car—in two weeks?"

"I'll have a car in two days."

"Meet me in Boston in two weeks. On a Sunday night."

"Where?"

"Name it and I'll be there right after the game. I'll do the wrap-up in record time."

"The weather—"

"I'm not going to worry about the weather. We'll figure it out. Just say yes."

"Where are you staying?" Jess stalled for more time to think. Oh, it was tempting to see him again, to spend a few days alone together because they wanted to and not because of a string of accidents.

"At some hotel next to Logan. Meet me downtown, at the Westin. Everything will be decorated for Christmas and I'll even go shopping with you and carry your bags and we can pretend we've known each other forever."

"Sam, I don't know."

His expression changed, the light leaving his eyes. "I'm sorry, Jess. I thought you were feeling the same way I am."

Her breath caught in her throat. "Which is?"

"That we've found something too special to walk away from." His hands tightened on her back. "You don't have to decide now. If you don't think we're somehow meant for each other—and I know how corny that sounds, but what the hell—then don't come to Boston. I'll hate the fact that you're not there, but I'll understand."

"You can change your mind, too," Jess managed to say. "That's only fair. If you're not there, that's okay."

"I'll be there. Six o'clock. We'll have dinner, drink champagne, tell each other the story of our lives."

"Six o'clock," she repeated. "But either one of us can change our mind if we come to our senses."

Sam rolled his eyes. "Sweetheart, don't you believe in love at first sight?"

"Love?" She gulped. "Not this soon, not this fast. Do you?"

"Ah," he said, smiling into her eyes before giving her one final long, promising kiss. "I'll tell you the next time I see you."

And with that he was gone, walking out of her little house without looking back.

CHAPTER NINE

DARCY REFUSED TO EAT. The mastiff turned his nose up at every kind of food offered and slunk back to his enormous pillow bed in the corner of the living room. Sam took him to the vet, but the woman couldn't find anything wrong.

"It must be emotional," she suggested. "Has he had any disruptions in his lifestyle lately?"

"No." Sam could hardly explain that Darcy had participated in a Pekingese Underground Railroad rescue mission or caused an old van to crash into a Dumpster. "He ate a lot of doughnuts last weekend."

"Chocolate?"

"No. Glazed sugar."

"That wouldn't be the problem," the vet said, giving Darcy a pat on the head. "Is he grieving for someone? A death in the family, perhaps?"

"No."

"Maybe he senses your own stress," she continued.

Sam self-consciously relaxed his clenched jaw muscles and tried to take a deep breath. He didn't feel like telling this no-nonsense animal doctor that he'd fallen in love with a woman he hardly knew the day he'd been dumped by his longtime fiancée.

"He's not running a fever and he's certainly not dehydrated. I think something's bothering him, though. Emotionally." She studied Sam as if it was entirely his fault. "Maybe he's spending too much time alone."

"I'm on vacation this week. He sleeps with me every night." Except for last Saturday, when the dog had insisted on sleeping in Jess's room, in front of the crate that held the female Peke.

"Give him a few more days," she advised. "If he seems as if he's in pain, bring him back and we'll run some tests. Boil some chicken breasts and white rice, keep him on a plain diet, see what happens. He's sure to perk up once he gets over whatever it is that's upsetting him."

If only it was that easy, Sam mused. A little boiled chicken and bland rice wasn't going to make either Darcy or his owner forget what had happened last weekend.

They were doomed to suffer for a while longer.

Until Boston.

SHE CHANGED HER MIND a thousand times.

"Go," her best friend Mary ordered. "How many romantic weekend offers do you get?"

"Don't do it," her favorite client said. "He sounds as if he'll break your heart, and I should know *something* about men by now. I'm on my third divorce."

If you don't think we're somehow meant for each other...don't come... The words echoed in her head at the oddest moments, such as when she was at home clipping the snarls behind Samantha's ears or scrubbing tile in a Bellevue mansion kitchen or stuck in traffic behind the wheel of her newly purchased, very reliable, two-year-old Toyota RAV4.

"How can you not go?" Mary asked. "You're in love with him."

"No," Jess lied. "I'm not. Not really."

"I'll keep the Peke for you," her friend replied. "Don't forget to buy new underwear."

Sam's mother sent her a note attached to the adoption form and fee: "We loved meeting you, dear. Make sure Sam brings you back again. Ozzie and I are doing just fine together and hope to see you soon."

There was no word from Sam, so Jess fell in love...with Samantha, though Jess had sworn she wouldn't grow attached to another little dog quite so soon. The auburn Pekingese, having survived surgery, shots and an ear infection, quickly learned that the best place to be was with her new human. Preferably on the bed.

And that was exactly where Jess spent her evenings, watching television and wondering how her life could have changed so much during one brief weekend trip to West Virginia. And what would happen if she really did have the courage to go to Boston.

If he was there—well, it could mean the beginning of something extraordinary.

And if he wasn't there? She couldn't think about that. She'd be like those women on the television show with the bachelor, the ones who didn't get a rose and went home sobbing in the limo.

Maybe it would be better to stay home and never know.

"Ignorance is bliss, Sammy-girl," she told the little dog.

IF EVER THERE WAS A GAME that shouldn't go into overtime, this was it. Sam looked at his watch again and hoped the Redskins would complete a pass into the end zone so they could all call it a day and leave Foxboro.

Two minutes, thirty-eight seconds later, that's exactly what they did, leaving Sam scribbling game notes and getting ready for a final wrap-up.

"Who's the woman?" Rick, the cameraman, grinned at him. "You keep looking at your watch and that was the fastest report you've ever given. You got a hot date back in D.C. tonight?"

"I'm staying here in Boston for a few days," Sam said, deliberately not answering the second question.

"You and your bride made up, huh? Cool."

"Uh, no." But there was no time to explain.

Sam hurried toward the waiting car he'd hired to take him to downtown Boston and the hotel where he hoped Jess would be waiting. He'd stopped himself from calling her every night and most mornings. He'd taken Darcy for long walks, until the dog refused to move another paw. Neither one of them had recovered their appetites. He'd imagined what it would be like to make love to Jess, but he'd booked a two-bedroom suite, just in case she needed more time. He'd give her all the time she wanted, as long as he could see her again.

It was insane, feeling this way. But he'd stopped thinking about what others would say and he'd started concentrating on what he wanted out of life. There was something about Jess that made him wonder how he ever would have been happy married to Susan, a woman who didn't care for dogs and had waved aside any discussions about having children. She'd left a couple of messages on his voice mail, but he hadn't returned the calls. He didn't want to hear her apologies or her explanations and he didn't want to try to convince her that he was fine and yes, this was for the best, because she wouldn't believe that was exactly the way he felt.

"We've got us one hell of a traffic jam," the driver muttered. "Could be here on 95 for a while."

"How long is 'a while'?" He still had time to get to his hotel, pick up his things and head to the Westin. He'd kept the room by the airport—just in case Jess didn't show up. He wasn't going to spend the night in the suite by himself.

"Don't know, not yet. Might be traffic from the game, might be an accident, could be both. Hard to say on game days."

Sam grabbed his cell phone, called the Westin's front desk and introduced himself. "There will be a woman, Jess Hall, arriving at six to check into my suite. Tell her I'll be there as soon as I can, please?"

He had told her six o'clock, knowing damn well the game would be over by three-thirty or four. Leave it to the Patriots to have a replacement quarterback who could complete passes.

The miles crawled by, at a pace so slow he could have jogged beside the car and not fallen behind. He cursed himself for picking Boston, worried that Jess wouldn't come at all, called the hotel and left two more messages in case he didn't arrive in downtown Boston until midnight.

When he finally made it to the airport hotel, he told the driver to wait while he raced inside to collect his things. There was no time for a shower, no time to change his clothes and shave again. On his way out he stopped near the gift shop and bought a bouquet of some kind of colorful flowers wrapped in green tissue and tied with a gold bow.

"Are those for me?" someone asked, and Sam, recognizing trouble when he heard it, looked up to see his former would-be bride.

"Susan."

"You remembered my name."

She smiled and several men covertly watched her. Elegant in a black suit, sexy with a low V-neck blouse and exquisite in thick gold jewelry she'd most likely designed herself, Susan commanded attention.

"What are you doing here?" Sam kissed her cheek and gripped the flowers tighter.

"Looking for you. I found out where you were staying and, voilà! Here I am." She hooked her arm through his. "You should have returned my calls, Sam. Take your coat off and let's get a drink while I apologize for the shabby way I behaved at our wedding."

"Apologize," he repeated, totally aware that time was ticking away. It was after six now, closer to six-thirty. "You don't have to apologize, Susan. Your father already did that for you."

She frowned and tossed her sleek black hair off her shoulders. "Don't be cranky, Sam. I've come to mend fences."

"I have a date," he said, holding up the flowers to prove it.

"Oh, please. Don't tell me you're finally flirting with the cheerleaders. Or is she someone from the local network?" She waved her manicured hand as if to make the other woman disappear. "Let's fly to Hawaii and *not* get married. A few days of sun will be good for you. You're looking pale."

"I'm late." Sam removed her arm from his sleeve. "And we're not going anywhere."

"You're angry with me." She looked as if she was

going to cry, but Sam couldn't stop to comfort her the way he used to.

"No." He gave her a quick hug and then stepped away. "I'm just not the right man for you."

"You've met someone else." Her perfect eyebrows lifted. "Lucky you."

"You don't know the half of it," Sam said, moving past her toward the door. If he'd had any doubts at all about which woman he wanted to spend the rest of his life with, they were gone now. The day he hadn't gotten married had been the luckiest day of his life.

"NO, MR. GROGAN HASN'T checked in yet," the desk clerk said. "And you are?"

"Jess Hall. I believe he made reservations?" She'd arrived exactly at six o'clock, dragging her wheeled suitcase behind her from the train station as she worried that she would be too early or too late, or would be sitting alone in a lobby filled with poinsettias until the security officers escorted her onto the sidewalk.

"Yes. Would you like to check in? I'll have someone show you to the room."

"Oh, no," she said quickly. The thought of waiting for Sam in a hotel room felt strange. What would she do—unpack her one outfit and new black nightgown, watch the news, pace rings in the carpet? "I'll wait for him here," she said.

"But Miss Hall—just a moment, please." The

woman answered the ringing phone by her elbow and proceeded to try to solve some kind of emergency regarding Andrea Bocelli's accomodations. Jess decided to drag her suitcase over to a chair by the Christmas tree decorated with silver angels and blue tinsel.

So Sam had made a reservation. So far so good.

At six-thirty she moved to the bar and watched the front door admit rain-soaked guests, none of them Sam Grogan. She drank hot buttered rum and nibbled crackers. At seven she decided that it was time to take the last train back to Newport. Mary had promised to come get her and bring a box of tissues should her heart be broken, but Jess would call her from the train and request they stop for dinner and some wine instead. She absolutely refused to cry, at least until she was home with Samantha.

So much for love at first sight.

SO MUCH FOR HIS ROMANTIC evening. He arrived at seven-fifteen only to find that Jess wasn't there after all. He hadn't asked at the desk if she'd checked in. If his dreams were going to be trampled, he'd prefer to endure the trauma in the privacy of his own room. So Sam stood in the middle of a suite of rooms worthy of visiting royalty and realized it was depressingly and undeniably empty. He held his wilting flowers, his leather suitcase and his damp overcoat, and lost any hope that the woman he'd fallen in love with had come to Boston because she'd missed him as much as he'd missed her.

He tossed the flowers in the wastebasket and poured a scotch from the nicely stocked bar in the living room. He waited several moments before calling the desk downstairs. Maybe she'd been here. Maybe she'd left a message.

And maybe he'd stay here after all and get drunk.

SAM NEEDED COFFEE. He could have made it himself with the coffeemaker in the kitchen or he could have called room service and had a carafe sent up, along with pastries and a fruit plate.

But if he stayed in the suite of rooms much longer he knew he would go mad. Last night had been hell and this Monday morning was so unlike what he'd pictured it would be that Sam knew the best thing he could do was keep moving. The hotel had a coffee bar. And where there was coffee there were doughnuts and bagels and Danishes, all waiting for a freshly showered man with a hangover, a packed suitcase and the knowledge that he'd missed something very special.

He stood in line at the overpriced coffee stand with a crowd of people wearing conference badges. He bought a large coffee and two croissants and, when he turned to leave the register, he bumped into a woman in a red sweater, a black suitcase beside her.

"Hey," she said, and Sam looked up and focused

on the face of a woman he had never expected to see at eight o'clock in the morning. She smiled and the air disappeared from his lungs. "I wondered when you'd notice me."

"How long—"

Jess ordered coffee and a Danish pastry before explaining. "I was here at six last night. Where were *you?*"

"Stuck in traffic. Buying flowers. Leaving messages for you. Having a nervous breakdown."

"You bought *flowers?*" She looked at him as if he'd presented her with three dozen roses.

"You didn't get my messages?"

She shook her head. "I waited in the bar until seven and then I went back to the train station, but there was a delay out of New York and the train was going to be horribly late, so I came back here and got my own room."

"Here, take these." He handed her his coffee and the bag of croissants so he could pay for her order, then he touched her back and guided her toward the nearby bank of elevators.

"We're going to my—our room now," Sam said, when the elevator emptied and they stepped inside. "Unless you're planning to leave right away."

"I was just getting coffee to take with me," she whispered, though they were alone in the elevator. "And I saw you—though I didn't think it was you at first, not until I heard your voice. I couldn't believe you were here after all and I didn't know it."

"I thought you'd changed your mind." He pushed the numbered button for his floor and contemplated putting their food and drinks on the floor so he could take her in his arms, but instead his mouth found hers again until the elevator stopped at his floor.

"I did," she said, following him down the hall. "Many times."

"I still have to work in D.C., though. Any chance you could start a dog shelter in Virginia?"

"Sam, slow down."

He winced. "Sorry. I've spent two weeks trying to figure out how we could make this work—or at least give it a chance."

"I meant slow down because I can't walk that fast." She laughed, and Sam didn't realize until then how much he'd missed that sound. He stopped in front of the door to his room and turned to her.

"Come on, Jess. Give me some hope."

"I'm not sure how we'll do it," she admitted. "But I do know that I want you in my life."

He let out his breath. "So I was right about love at first sight?"

"Not exactly. I think it started when you tried to get Darcy off the bed and kissed me."

"I was pretty amazed myself." He unlocked the door and ushered her inside. "You know, we have to stop meeting in public places for coffee."

"Do you have a better suggestion?" She set the

coffee cup and the bag on the glass-topped table just inside the door.

Sam led her into the bedroom where he intended to show her how much he loved her. "I think I do, yes. And believe it or not, there are no dogs here. I can kiss you without being barked at."

"Speaking of dogs," she said, looping her arms around his neck, "I'm keeping Samantha."

"Wait till I tell Darcy," Sam added, pulling her closer against him. Where she belonged.

FAMILIAR PURSUIT
Caroline Burnes

For Poe,
a true inspiration.

Dear Reader,

I've always been an animal lover—I love the normal ones, and have even loved a few unusual animals such as an opossum, an eagle (briefly) and a snake. But most of my pets have been cats and dogs, with a few horses thrown in for good measure.

Domestic animals, if they aren't loved, often have tragic lives. When Kristine Rolofson called and asked if I would contribute a story to this anthology, with the idea that the proceeds would go to an animal rescue organization, I was delighted to do so.

My own black cat, E. A. Poe, is a constant source of story inspiration, and it is a lot of fun to try to think like a cat. I have to confess that Poe helps me out a good bit.

For my animal charity I chose Best Friends Animal Sanctuary. This is a compound in Kanab, Utah, that takes in all living creatures. Homes are found for those that can be adopted, but other animals, the sick or old ones, have a place to live out their lives. You can reach them at Best Friends Animal Sanctuary, 5001 Angel Canyon Road, Kanab, UT 84741 (www.bestfriends.org).

I urge you all to spay and neuter your pets to help cut down on unwanted animals, and to offer a home to the homeless. For the record, I practice what I preach—six cats, six dogs and six horses, most all of them rescued.

Best,

Caroline

CHAPTER ONE

Ribbon cuttings aren't normally my thing, but at least I've got a good view. Thank goodness this spur-of-the-moment event is occurring in the spring. Mobile, Alabama, can be sweltering during the summer. I remember my last visit here, when I helped solve a kidnapping. I'm not on a case now, though, just a bit of family business. My humanoid, Peter Curry, DVM, has strung some old Christmas ribbon across the door and he's given his niece a pair of surgical scissors to cut it. This is her first vet clinic, and she is blushing with pleasure. Dr. Penny Jameson has healing hands and I don't think I've ever seen hair that shade of golden brown. So long and shiny. Lordy, lordy, I'm tempted to buy some kennel time in this new clinic.

There goes the ribbon, snipped in two, and the clinic is officially open. Whoever thought that I'd end up in Mobile, Alabama, again. Beautiful trees, nice friendly people, and the most magnificent spring I've seen since my last visit to the Port City. The county has really developed. Peter's niece found this old strip mall to use for her clinic. Renovation is the ticket, not further development. When I run for office, that's going to be my motto—no new asphalt. I could run on the Tree Hugger ticket.

Dr. Jameson has done a great job of taking care of the trees, and the ferns, flowers and grass—not to mention the four-legged critters under her care. Like her uncle Peter, she has a way with all living things. Tender Loving Care is the right name for this place. Another good name might be Easy on the Eyes. Penny Jameson is the best-looking veterinarian I've ever seen. All that hair, those dark brown eyes, and a figure to die for, even if she is only five feet tall.

I think I feel a serious illness building, one that will require loads of calories and lots of stroking and maybe even a little cream. Ah. But what's this? Here comes a short, female humanoid carrying a cardboard box. And she's crying. Uh-oh, looks like Penny has her first client and it doesn't look like a happy case.

From the cries coming from that box, I think she has a litter of young felines. I'll just stroll over and take a look. Oh, they are so cute. Why is the little girl crying? I suppose I'll soon find out.

PENNY JAMESON REMOVED the cardboard box from the young girl's arms. "What's wrong?" she asked, gazing at the five squirming kittens. She saw that the little girl with braids had been crying.

"My dad won't let me keep them," the girl said.

"He says they're feral. He thinks I'm going to get bitten and get rabies. The mother cat only scratched me because she was frightened. Now she's run away and left her babies." She brushed a tear away and worked to hold back her emotions. For a moment her face gained some composure, and then she started sobbing. "They shouldn't have to die just because I scared their mother away."

Penny looked over the box at her uncle, Peter Curry. He shook his head.

"How old are the kittens?" he asked the little girl, kneeling so that he was on her level.

"I found them this morning. In the laundry room. I waited until now, hoping the mother cat would come back. But she didn't." Her breath shuddered as she fought for control. "Dad says the cats are dangerous. He spent a long time explaining to me how they have diseases. But these don't. They're just babies. Can you help them?"

Peter lifted the young girl's chin so he could look into her eyes. "What's your name?" he asked.

"Miranda."

"And you live around here?" he continued.

"Yeah. Not too far away." She looked at Penny. "You're a veterinarian. Will you help them?"

Penny felt her own eyes tearing over. The kittens didn't look much over a day old. Even if they could survive, they'd require feeding every two hours, stimulation—care she simply didn't have the staff to give. In fact, she had no staff at all except a part-time receptionist who wasn't due to start until Monday, and her uncle, who'd offered to help out for a few days until she got on her feet. She'd just opened the door to the clinic not fifteen minutes before.

Sighing, she watched the big black cat, Familiar, walk over to the box and peer in. The tip of his tail twitched. Peter had brought the cat with him from Washington, D.C., with a ton of stories about Familiar and his escapades solving mysteries all over the world. Penny didn't believe everything her uncle said. Sometimes he enjoyed pulling her leg.

"Peter?" She looked at her uncle. "What do you think?"

"Where're your parents?" Peter asked Miranda.

Penny saw the distress in the young girl's face.

New tears welled up. "My mother's gone. It's only me and my dad." Her expression dared anyone to comment on her life.

Feeling a constriction in her chest, Penny put her hand on the girl's shoulder. That explained her uneven braids and un-ironed clothes. "Where's your father?" she asked gently.

"He's probably looking for me," she said, suddenly timid. She cast a worried look out the door. "He doesn't know about the kittens."

Peter stepped forward and picked up the box. He gave his niece a knowing look. "Penny, why don't you have a chat with Miranda's dad? I'll give the kittens their first feeding. Miranda, you can help if you'd like."

"You'll save them?" the little girl asked, her face suddenly filled with hope. "Thank you. I knew you'd help them. I want to be a veterinarian when I grow up so I can help animals. Look!" She pulled a piece of paper from her pocket. "I've named every one of them. And I looked up on the computer how to take care of kittens. I can help."

Penny bit her bottom lip. Peter was no tougher than she was. He'd caved at the sight of the helpless kittens, so that meant he'd stay long enough to get them to the point where they could eat on their own. She let out a sigh of relief as she hurried out the door to talk with Miranda's father. Perhaps he'd be willing to bring his daughter by for several of the feedings so she could help out. And maybe if the cats were tamed...

Just as Penny started out to the parking lot, the little girl tore by her. Miranda's small feet flew over the asphalt and she disappeared between two huge azalea bushes in the yard next door to the clinic. Penny surveyed the parking lot. She'd assumed Miranda's father was waiting outside for her, but no one was parked. Miranda had lied, and then she'd vanished.

Suckered once again, Penny thought as she headed back into the clinic to help Peter with the kittens.

MACK SANDERS took the steps two at a time. He burst through the door of the TLC veterinarian clinic and into the empty waiting room. Just perfect. The clinic was totally empty. He'd felt certain Miranda had come over here. She'd been talking about the new vet clinic on the corner and how much she wanted to work there. She was only nine, but she thought she was old enough for a job. He'd tried to explain to her that even though she was advanced in school, there were laws about child labor. Now, though, he was worried. He'd found a note she'd left, saying she'd gone "to take care of something important."

"Hey! Is anybody here?" he called out in the empty clinic.

A young woman in a white clinic coat stepped out of a back room. His gaze swept over her lovely face, her gentle brown eyes and her slender figure. He took it all in, but what he focused on was the concerned expression on her face. And the name tag on her white coat—Penny Jameson, DVM.

"Can I help you?" she asked.

"I'm looking for a little girl. About four feet tall. Her name is Miranda Sanders. I thought she might have stopped by here—to ask for a job." He felt the scrutiny of the young woman rake over him. He was making a bad impression, but he didn't care. "I'm her father, and she's disappeared. I'm a little worried."

"There was a young girl named Miranda here. She didn't leave her last name, but she did leave a box of kittens. They're too young to be without their mother." Penny's tone held disapproval. "She was very upset."

"So the cat had kittens." He shook his head. "And now she's disappeared. I was afraid this would happen. Now Miranda will have her heart broken again."

"She said the kittens were feral. That's an impressive word for a little girl to know."

"She's been trying to trap the mother cat, even though I told her it was useless. A wild animal can't be tamed. I figured that cat would dump her kittens and take off, but Miranda was determined to save them. She thinks she's a combination of that crocodile hunter guy and Harriet the girl spy. Do you know where Miranda went?"

"She took off through the yard next door," Penny said. "Do you think she could come by and help with the feedings?"

"Sure. Miranda would love that. She wants to be a vet. Did she say where she was going?" He leaned on the counter. Penny Jameson was an easy sight to look at. He could see the intelligence shining in her eyes. For the first time in a long time he felt interested in a woman.

Penny shook her head. "No. She was upset about the kittens."

"How upset?" He could feel his face tightening. "Miranda doesn't need to be upset."

"She'd been crying," Penny said. Her face showed surprise.

"I have to find her." Panic made Mack speak sharply. He realized Penny thought he was acting like a lunatic. "She didn't say anything?"

"I'm sorry. I can't help you."

Mack turned abruptly and headed out the door. At any other time, he would have liked to stay and chat with his pretty new neighbor, but he had to find Miranda. Emotional situations were the worst thing for his daughter, and he could easily imagine how torn apart she was. She'd been watching for days for the kittens, and now she had them and no mother cat. He'd tried, unsuccessfully, to make his daughter see that trying to tame a feral cat would only bring heartache, if not painful medical treatment. Feral cats, when cornered, were ferocious fighters. As he'd expected, the cat had dumped her kittens and moved on to greener pastures. His daughter was left with a broken heart.

He jogged across the parking lot and into his own backyard with the terrible feeling that he'd made a big mistake. He should have helped Miranda catch the cat. Now he had to find her, before it was too late.

"HE'S A VERY STRANGE MAN," Penny said as she picked up a tiny bottle and began the process of teaching the yellow kitten to suck.

"That was the father?" Peter asked.

"Yes. He seemed very concerned about his daughter. He has the idea that a feral cat can't be tamed. He thinks the mother cat has left her babies—but cats normally don't abandon a litter if the kittens are healthy, and these are good-looking babies."

"Did he have any idea what might have happened to the mother cat?"

"No. But only injury or fear would have made her leave her babies. How awful for her." Penny smiled as she felt the kitten latch on to the rubber nipple. It began to suck with great force.

"Any chance he'll take the kittens when they're old enough?" Peter asked.

"I doubt it. People have strange ideas about strays. Even if she is a stray, people should step up to the plate and help a little. He could have caught her and had her spayed. Then there wouldn't have been kittens. But no, that's just too much trouble and responsibility for most people."

She could see that her uncle was smiling at her. Not unkindly, but with tolerance. "It isn't something to smile about," she said. "If every single family would spay one stray animal, there wouldn't be the overpopulation problem we have today."

"You can come down off the soapbox anytime now," Peter said. He put his hand on her shoulder before he reached for another kitten to feed. "I know where you're coming from, Penny, but getting yourself worked into a lather won't do any good."

"I'm stuck with these kittens, aren't I."

His smile widened. "I'm afraid so. They're awfully cute. Look at this little black-and-white one's tail. It's all crimped up."

"Kinky," Penny said.

"Don't name them," Peter warned. "You'll never be able to give them away. Besides, Miranda has named them all." He got the note out of the box. "I believe that one's Sylvester."

Penny picked up the little black-and-white female.

The kitten yowled so loudly that Penny put a bottle in her mouth. It latched on instantly. "This one's going to have a strong personality, and I override Miranda. Her name is Kinky," she said.

"Heaven help us," Peter said, grinning. "This clinic can't stand another female with a strong personality. I see only trouble in the future. By the way, where is Familiar?"

CHAPTER TWO

HUMANOIDS LACK THE ACUTE SENSE of smell that we felines are blessed with, so I've taken it upon myself to track down little Miranda. This isn't exactly a mystery that requires my indubitable skills as a private investigator, unless someone would want to explain how a grown man could traumatize his daughter by failing to notice a passel of helpless kittens. What lessons is that man teaching his daughter? Jeez, just when I begin to think that evolution is taking hold in the humanoid species, I discover something like this.

There are a few evolved members of the human species, like Peter and Eleanor, the two who saved me from extermination in an experiment lab. I had that blasted microchip implanted in my hide and those villains were determined to kill me and anyone who tried to help me. Thank goodness Eleanor had a tender heart and picked me up and took me to Peter. And that began my career as a feline detective who specializes in matchmaking, but only for sensitive and kind humans.

Penny is a fine example of a sensitive humanoid.

But sometir. :s, I think the human genes aren't capable of true development. Humanoids like to believe that they're the only species with feelings and needs.

Hmm, a little less philosophizing and a little more detecting are in order. I've picked up Miranda's trail, and it doesn't look good. The clinic is in a very upscale neighborhood, but a mile away, things get a little dicey. Miranda is headed into what appears to be a really rough area. I saw the signs along the road that say this is going to be another exclusive subdivision, Stone Hedge. Some big developer has bought up all these old places, but for right now, it's a haven of decline. I spy an old sofa on the side of the road, abandoned cars, houses with rotted porches and idle men sitting around in the front yard. Uh-oh, if Miranda has followed the mother cat into this neighborhood, they're both in trouble.

PENNY WATCHED HER UNCLE walk around the parking lot calling for Familiar. Peter didn't seem exactly worried, but he acted as if the cat was up to something. But what? Surely all those crazy stories she'd heard about Familiar couldn't be true. She'd been surprised when Peter had arrived with the black cat in tow, and then Peter had made a strange comment, something to the effect that the cat couldn't be left alone. She knew Eleanor was in California researching some obscure Native American language, but that didn't explain why the cat couldn't have been left at a responsible kennel. Peter had just smiled and said something about Familiar being smarter than the average cat. Right.

She was about to walk outside and ask her uncle about the cat when a black Volvo careened into the parking lot, tires squealing. A young mother with her two children ran into the clinic.

"Please, can you help us? Our dog was hit by a car!" The two children were wailing and crying, and the mother was fighting back tears. "Please."

"Where is your dog?" Penny asked.

"He's in the back seat."

"Let's get him." Penny ran out the door and Peter met her at the car. Penny opened the back door and felt her pulse accelerate at the sight of the dog. He was breathing shallowly, blood leaking from his mouth onto the leather seat.

"I'll get him," Peter said, picking up the little Jack Russell terrier and gently carrying him inside the clinic.

"We'll have a look at him," Penny said as she followed Peter into an exam room and closed the door. She'd been trained for all types of animal emergencies, but she was certainly glad Peter was here. He had years of experience. It made her feel more secure as she stepped up to the table and began to assess the terrier's condition.

Thirty minutes later, Penny walked out to the waiting room where the mother and her children tensely waited.

"He's going to be okay," Penny said, smiling. "He's one lucky dog."

"His name is Roscoe," the little boy said, wiping a tear from his cheek with the sleeve of his shirt. "I left the gate to the backyard open and he got out. I don't remember leaving it open, but I must have. It's my fault he got hit."

Penny knelt down beside the boy. "It isn't your fault, sweetie," she said. "Roscoe made a bad choice when he ran into the street."

"I left the gate open," the boy said again.

"We can't be perfect all the time," Penny said softly, ruffling his brown hair. "You made a mistake and Roscoe made a mistake. We all make mistakes. And the important thing is that Roscoe is going to be just fine."

"Thank you," the mother said. "I've been trying to make Jeffrey understand that accidents happen. He's just a child that takes on way too much responsibility."

"I know that pattern," Penny said, rising to her feet. "It's too big a burden for a little boy."

The mother nodded.

"Roscoe has a broken back leg and some internal bruising," Penny said. "I'd like to keep him overnight, if that's okay."

"We'll be by tomorrow to check on him," the mother said, gathering both children by the hand. "Thank you. It's just a blessing you were open today."

Penny felt her uncle step up beside her and together they watched the family get in their car and pull away.

"That hits home, doesn't it?" Peter said, putting his hand on Penny's shoulder. "I know you always felt responsible for your mother when she was so sick. You were just a kid."

Penny sighed. "Life isn't fair."

"I had no idea what you were going through until Margaret passed away," Peter said. His arms went around her and he held her tightly. "I'm so sorry."

"It wasn't your fault. It just happened. After Dad died, Mom and I were so close. I wouldn't have had it any other way."

"Still, it's a hard life for a little girl who should have been going to parties and tormenting the opposite sex."

Penny patted her uncle's arm and stepped away from him. She welcomed his help and experience, but not his pity. "I have the rest of my life to torment men," she said, forcing a bright smile.

"Not today," Peter said, nodding toward the parking lot. "Here comes another patient. Looks like you picked a great location."

MACK WALKED DOWN Wellington Street, his sharp gaze sweeping both sides of the road. He'd managed to get his panic under control and decided on a block-by-block search of the neighborhood. So far, he hadn't seen hide nor hair of his daughter or the calico cat that had dumped a litter of kittens in his laundry room.

Miranda had named the cat Gumbo, an appropriate name. Too bad the cat wouldn't ever be tamed. She was feral, and it had been his concern for Miranda that had made him resist her pleas to tame the cat. He'd been afraid that if she got her hands on Gumbo, the feline would panic and claw and bite her. He'd offered to go to the pet store and buy her a cat, but Miranda had only wanted Gumbo. She'd wanted to save the cat. Now Mack realized how serious his daughter had been. This was just another in a long line of recent mistakes he'd made with her.

The series of memories that flashed through his mind were painful. Miranda had gotten up every morning and taken a saucer of milk out to the cat. She'd waited and waited for the cat to come out, until it was time for school. When she'd come home in the afternoons and the milk was gone, Miranda had believed she was making progress. She'd set her heart on making the cat a pet, and now, too late, he realized he should have helped her.

Now Gumbo was probably gone for good. After dropping her kittens, she'd fled. And the one thing his daughter didn't need was another loss—especially after her mother had just abandoned her and disappeared.

He'd tried to tell his daughter not to set her heart on the impossible. Belinda had taught him that bitter lesson, and he'd tried to protect Miranda from learning it, because he couldn't stand to see Miranda disappointed. She'd been so brave after her mother had left. Now, she had to live the loss again with a dang cat. At least the cat hadn't bitten Miranda. Mack had a vivid memory of his sister being bitten by a wild cat. She'd had to undergo the horribly painful shots to prevent rabies. He could still hear her screams.

He'd finished scouring his neighborhood and had crossed into unfamiliar territory. He'd heard that a new neighborhood was coming in, but what was left of the old one was sad. This must be where Gumbo had come from. Someone had abandoned her, or she'd been part of a litter that went feral. Mack didn't like the idea of Miranda in this neighborhood.

A black cat flashed by the corner of a house, and Mack slowed. The cat was a mighty sleek-looking cat for this area, where even the children looked as if they didn't get enough to eat.

"Miranda!" he called. "Miranda!"

The black cat peeked around a corner, then disappeared. Funny, it was almost as if the cat were assessing him. He shook off the feeling and continued walking, calling his daughter's name.

An hour later, Mack couldn't tamp down the panic he felt. He touched the inhaler in his pocket. Miranda would need her asthma medicine soon. He had a terrible image of her, unconscious behind some old house. He shook it off and started jogging, his voice reflecting the urgency he felt.

PENNY SIGHED and plopped down into the empty receptionist's chair. "Lock the door," she said to Peter, who took a seat on the visitor's sofa. "I had no idea we'd be swamped."

"You're going to need some staff, at least some technicians to assist you. You won't be able to manage this alone. Good grief, you've had twenty cases already," he said. "I can hang around until you interview some folks."

"Thanks." He was a great uncle, even if he was a little overprotective. "Look," she said, sitting up taller in the chair. "Here comes Miranda's father again. And he doesn't look happy." The tall, broad-shouldered man was striding across the parking lot. If he weren't so grim, with his brow furrowed and his generous mouth in a taut line, he'd be handsome, she thought.

The door swung open with a thrust and Mack stepped into the office. "I hate to ask you again, but it seems you were the last people to see Miranda. I've been searching for her everywhere, and I can't find her. Did she say anything about where she planned to go?"

"I'm sorry," Peter said. "She didn't. She asked if we could take care of the kittens. She was going to help with a feeding, and then she suddenly ran away."

"The last we saw her, she was headed south," Penny said, "as I told you. That was over four hours ago." She saw the tension on Mack's face increase.

Mack nodded. "She cut through our yard, but I have no idea where she went from there. I've been all over this neighborhood, and even down into the area they call Birdville. I'm worried. She doesn't have her asthma medicine with her."

"She's asthmatic?" Penny asked, felling a tug of worry herself. Miranda's father hadn't made the best first impression, but he was very worried about his child. She could see that.

"She has serious trouble with her breathing when she gets overexcited. And I have no doubt she's terribly upset."

That explained a lot about his behavior. "Can we help you look?" Penny asked, surprising herself. She was dog tired and ready for a bath and the sofa, but Mack Sanders looked as if he were coming apart at the seams.

"I'd appreciate any help." Mack brushed his thick sandy hair off his forehead. "Miranda's such a sweet child. She trusts everyone." It was obvious to Penny that he fought to control his voice. "I never wanted her to be afraid of life. Maybe I should have put a little more caution into her."

Penny's concern rippled into fear. An innocent child with open trust could get herself in serious trouble, especially in Birdville. "Had you two argued?" she asked gently. "Is it possible she ran away from home?"

Mack's eyebrows drew together. Instead of bristling at Penny's question, he looked stricken. "I think I made a terrible mistake."

The note of bitterness in his voice warned Penny to tread carefully. She exchanged a glance with Peter.

"While you were hunting for your daughter, did you happen to see a black cat?" Peter asked.

Mack's left eyebrow rose. "I sure did. Why?"

"Let's go to where you saw the cat," Peter said. "My best guess is that where we find Familiar, we'll also find your daughter."

CHAPTER THREE

MACK FELT A STRANGE WAVE of gratitude as he watched Penny slip back out the half-shut door of an old shed. It had been a long time since anyone had volunteered to come to his aid. The new veterinarian and her uncle were helping him conduct a thorough search of his neighborhood. Two strangers had taken on the burden of his missing daughter. The thought of it humbled him.

He'd walked a large area calling Miranda's name, but now that he had help, he was looking under houses and checking in garages and sheds, doing the thorough search he hadn't had time to do alone. At first, he'd thought Miranda was hiding because she was angry with him. Now though, he'd begun to let darker thoughts float through his mind—and those dismal images put fire under his feet.

"Does Miranda have any friends in the neighborhood? She might have gone to a playmate's house," Penny said, wiping a smudge of dirt from her cheek.

He almost lifted his hand to brush her face, but thought better of it. Many years had passed since he'd felt the impulse to make such an intimate gesture with a woman. Penny Jameson, with her caring eyes, invited such thoughts. Instead, he followed through on her question.

"I've called all of her friends from where we used to live, but there is one new friend. Good thinking." He whipped out his cell phone. "Amy Bradshaw. Miranda's had a tough time making new friends in this neighborhood, but she likes to go play with Amy." He dialed the number to the Bradshaw house, feeling his hopes lift.

Penny was a genius. There were times when he so needed a woman's thinking or feeling. He worked hard at being a good father to Miranda, but he wasn't a very good mother. This episode with the cat was showing him that.

He heard a woman answer the phone. "Mrs. Bradshaw, this is Mack Sanders. Is Miranda there, by any chance?"

He felt as if his heart had turned to stone as he listened. "Thanks, anyway. If you see her, would you call me?" He put the phone back in his pocket, trying hard to hide his sudden fear from Penny's gentle scrutiny.

"It was a good idea." He forced a smile as he looked at Penny. Her soft brown eyes reflected his disappointment. He really wanted to know her better. There was something in her expression that tore down the defenses he'd built, the desire to remain solitary, his distrust of women. Once Miranda was found safe and sound, he was going to ask Penny on a date. He stored that thought away as he scanned the backyard of an abandoned house for some sign of his daughter.

"The farther we get from the clinic, the worse the neighborhood looks," Penny said. Mack followed her gaze to where her uncle was forcing open the door of an old abandoned house. "Would Miranda really have come here?" she asked.

"If she thought the mother cat was here. Miranda's really a good kid. She's never done anything like this before. She just wanted to help that cat." He bit his bottom lip. "She was obsessed with it. She didn't want to move here, and as I said, she hasn't made a lot of new friends. I thought I was doing the right thing, but I see now that Miranda invested all of her time and energy into saving that cat."

"She has a tender heart," Penny said. "And I'm sure she's fine. She probably just got caught up in her imagination. Kids are like that, as best I remember."

Mack smiled at Penny's efforts to comfort him. In all likelihood, she probably viewed him as a terrible father, yet she was working to keep his fears at bay. "Miranda could be unconscious somewhere." Mack fought back thoughts of serious possibilities. "Someone could have taken her."

"Let's assume that she's simply gone farther away from home than she intended," Penny said. "Did you check at your house? Maybe she called home."

Mack rubbed his forehead and then retrieved

his cell phone. "About half an hour ago. Maybe she's called since then." He punched in his home number and checked his answering service. "Nothing," he said as he put the phone away for the second time.

Penny Jameson didn't know Miranda, but as Mack watched her expression, he saw her eyebrows draw together in a frown. He could see the concentration on her face.

"Does Miranda have a secret place? When I was a child, I had this one tree that I'd climb whenever I was mad at my parents or upset." Penny pointed to a grove of woods. "Maybe there. That looks like a good spot for a secret fort."

Mack shook his head. "We moved to this neighborhood about four months ago, after Belinda…" He stopped talking, biting back the angry words that threatened. What was going on with him? He seldom felt anger at his ex-wife anymore, and he never talked about his private business with anyone.

"Belinda is your wife?" Penny asked.

He sighed. "My wife left us. One day she was cooking breakfast and the next day she was gone. It's been hard on Miranda. We had a place on the north side of town, a less affluent neighborhood. This house came up for sale, and I thought it would be good for Miranda to move. She kept asking and wondering each day when she came home from school if her mother would be back. And the new house is closer to Glenda, her sitter. I thought she'd love the swimming pool and the big backyard." He looked down. "I was pretty much wrong about everything."

"I'm sorry," Penny said.

Her touch on his arm was featherlight, but it carried a powerful sensation.

"I'm not sorry Belinda's gone. I'm just sorry that it hurt Miranda so much. Moving may not have been such a bright idea." He felt the burden of all the things he hadn't done in the past year. "I work too much. I've left Miranda with the sitter too much."

"Over here!"

They both started as they heard Peter's call.

"He's found something," Penny said as she began to run toward her uncle.

PETER WALKED TOWARD THEM holding what looked like a book bag with the initials MLS. It was filled with cans of cat food. "Do you recognize this?" Peter asked.

Penny knew the answer even before Mack spoke. She could tell by the pain that passed over his face.

"It's Miranda's," he said. "She told me yesterday she had lost it. Where did she get money to buy cat food? I give her an allowance, but not enough for that much food." He looked stricken. "She must have saved her school lunch money. She's been going without food."

"She was determined to catch that cat," Penny said. "I would have loaned her a kindness trap. It's a cage with a trap door. When the cat goes in for food, the door closes."

Mack took the book bag from Peter, his hands

grasping it as if he could force it to tell him where his daughter had gone. "I just didn't realize how much she wanted it."

"I don't think she wanted the cat as much as she wanted to help her," Penny said. She put a comforting hand on Mack's arm, feeling the strength of his muscles beneath the sleeve of his shirt. He might have made mistakes with his daughter, but not out of a lack of caring. There was no doubt in her mind that he loved Miranda more than anything. "Mack, you did what you thought was right."

Mack ran his hand over the canvas bag as if he could summon his daughter like a genie. "She talked about Gumbo incessantly. I told her not to name the cat. I warned her that she'd probably disappear once she had her kittens."

"Cats don't normally leave their babies," Penny said gently. "Not even feral cats. And if we find Gumbo with Miranda, sometimes a feral cat can be tamed and become a lovely pet."

"That's true," Peter said. "But I'm worried about Gumbo, as well as Miranda. The cat must have been frightened, or hurt, to leave her babies."

"If I'd had any idea…" Mack said, shaking his head.

"Is there anything in the book bag that might give us a lead?" Penny asked.

"Let's find out." Mack dumped the contents on the ground. It was mostly cans of cat food, but there was also a small notebook.

"I hope Miranda will forgive me for reading this,"

Mack said as he opened the notebook. "She writes down everything. She's a big reader, and she reads a lot of books and watches a lot of shows about this girl spy, Harriet. And Nancy Drew. Along with being a veterinarian, she wants to be a private detective."

The first page was dated a week earlier. "The two men in the green truck are back again. They put out another cage at the old blue house," Miranda had written. "They caught a yellow cat, but I let it go."

Penny watched as Mack's face turned ashen. He flipped the page. "The green truck is driving all around here. Mrs. Wilson said her gray cat went missing. She hasn't found him."

Mack's eyes were blank with fear. "Good Lord, Miranda's been spying on these men."

MACK FELT AS IF he were trapped in a nightmare.

"Call Mrs. Wilson," Penny urged. "Call Information and get the number."

"I don't really know her. She lives a couple of doors down." Mack talked as he got out his phone. He called Information, and in a few moments the operator had connected him. He counted the rings. On the ninth ring he heard an elderly voice say hello.

"Mrs. Wilson, I'm Miranda's father—"

"Such a lovely girl. She was so concerned when I told her that Buster was missing. She helped me look for him. She is such a dear girl, Mr. Sanders. You've done a fine job of raising her, even without a wife."

Mack fought to control his impatience. When he

spoke again, his voice was calm. "Have you seen Miranda this afternoon?" He tilted the phone so that all of them could hear the response.

"No, not since this morning. She was looking for that calico cat she calls Gumbo. She said the cat had kittens. She was worried to death that the kittens would die if the mother cat didn't come back."

"Mrs. Wilson, did Buster ever come home?" Mack asked.

"No, he didn't. I've hunted high and low. I even offered a reward. No one has seen him."

"Did Miranda mention anything about two men in a green car?" Mack asked.

"Yes, she did. She seemed to think that maybe they'd trapped Buster and kidnapped him. She said she was going to find him and set him free. She said that was what Nancy Drew and Harriet would do." She laughed softly. "Miranda has such a lively imagination. Why would anyone go to the trouble of stealing someone else's cat? There are plenty of cats to be had at the animal shelter."

"I don't know," Mack said, but when he saw Penny's face, he realized that she had an answer to that question, and it wasn't going to be one that he liked.

"When you talked with Miranda this morning, did she say where she thought the mother cat might be?"

"No, she didn't. But she was bent on saving the kittens. She said once she tamed the kittens, the mother cat would calm down, too. She's determined, that one is."

"Thank you," Mack said. "I have to go now."

"Stop by for some coffee and pie sometime, Mr. Sanders. And if you ever need someone to look out for Miranda, just give me a call. She's a darling child."

"Thank you. If you see her, would you call me?"

"Absolutely."

He turned off the phone. "Why would someone steal a pet cat?"

Penny grasped his forearm as her uncle answered.

"They steal the pets and sell them for animal experimentation," Peter said. "A lot of pounds won't allow the cats and dogs in their care to be used in that way. These brokers go through neighborhoods trapping pets and selling them."

"I had no idea," Mack said. He could hear the anger in Peter's voice, and he saw the censure in Penny's eyes. She gave his arm another squeeze and then let go.

"If that's what's going on, we need to catch these people," Penny said. "And we need to get Miranda back. If she's following men like that, she could be in more danger than we thought."

"If my daughter is in danger, it's my fault. I should have listened to her. I should have tried to help her instead of coming up with reasons not to."

"You're a parent, not a god," Peter said. "We do the best we can, and you obviously love your daughter. Blame doesn't help anyone."

"Miranda tried to tell me something about this

last week, but I didn't have time to listen." Mack's voice was choked with fear and grief. "If I'd taken ten minutes, I could have helped her. If this is really going on, I want those guys as bad as you do. But first, I want my daughter home safe and sound."

Penny nodded, then turned to her uncle. "What should we do?"

"Find Familiar. He was an animal research cat when Eleanor found him. He'd escaped from a lab, and he has a real aversion to folks who trap animals. Eleanor and I both were nearly killed in our efforts to protect him."

Penny gave her uncle a long look. "I thought that was just a story you made up."

Peter shook his head. "It's true, and if anyone can help us, it's Familiar. Let's just hope that my hunch is correct, and he's with Miranda."

"Should we call the police?" Mack asked.

Peter shook his head. "First we should make certain that she's not simply hiding from us. The police won't do much of anything for twenty-four hours. If we find evidence that she's in danger, I think you should contact the police. Men who sell animals to be used in such experiments are capable of almost anything."

"Okay," Mack said. He could feel the nervous energy shifting through his body. "Let's get busy looking. We have to find Miranda. And Familiar. And Gumbo." He nodded at Penny. "We have to find all the animals those men have, and save them."

CHAPTER FOUR

I WASN'T UPSET until Miranda dropped that bag of cat food and crawled under an old house. I'm not the squeamish type, but there are spiders here. And rats. Yeah, I know cats are supposed to catch rats, but you haven't seen the size of these babies. When they sit up, they're as big as poodles. They have really sharp teeth and a bad attitude. And red eyes that glare like they're possessed.

Uh-oh, Miranda's down on all fours. She's got that determined look on her face. And there she goes! I'd just as soon skip the haunted crawl space tour, but it's my catly duty to follow this young humanoid and keep her safe. But why this house? Why this crawl space?

Ah, I see—and hear—the attraction for Miranda now. It's a cage. And inside the cage is a charming black-and-white cat of juvenile years. He says his name is Bossy and he's been in the cage for two days. Without any water. The men who set these traps are worse than I thought. But let's hear what Bossy has to say. Maybe he can give us some clues.

Bossy is a free agent in this world, so no one has

missed him or been looking for him. And he's scared. He says that lots of cats have disappeared from the neighborhood recently. He says that about two weeks ago, these cages filled with food started showing up in out-of-the-way places. The cat goes in, the trap closes, and he's there until someone comes to get the cage. And once a cat is caught, he isn't ever heard from again. This sounds really bad. This is evil at work.

Miranda is working the catch on the cage. And yes, she sprang him! Bossy stayed around long enough to give her a rub and a purr, and now he's on his way. And Miranda is destroying the spring on the cage so that it won't work anymore. She is one smart little girl.

Now she's crawling out the other side of the house and moving on. The problem is that she's still going away from home. I've tried snagging her pant leg and pulling her back toward home, but she isn't going to listen to me. It's not that she doesn't understand; she's very perceptive for a humanoid. It's that she simply ignores me. She has a mission, and she's not going to back off.

I'm liking this situation less and less, though. I just saw two men sitting on a porch and watching her. She doesn't realize that there are mean people around—people who will hurt her as quickly as they will a stray cat. Those men are looking at her and laughing. I don't like that a bit. If I had my way, we'd go home and get Peter and Penny.

Sure, it's a good thing we're doing, freeing cats

in cages, but I think we need some reinforcements. Besides, it's time to eat. Miranda doesn't show any sign of fatigue or hunger, but by my schedule, I'm two hours overdue for some grub.

Okay, here's another cage. This one has a...Chihuahua! And she's one pissed-off little canine. I normally don't condescend to talk to dogs, but this one is chattering away, and oh, the language! I'm just glad Miranda can't understand what's being said.

Her name is Bitsy, and she's telling me that cats and dogs are disappearing. She was looking for her friend, Prissy, who disappeared yesterday. Prissy went out to relieve herself and she never came home. Bitsy is terribly upset that she can't find a trace of her friend.

This doesn't sound good at all. It sounds like someone is kidnapping dogs and cats, and the only reason for that would be to sell them to people who want to cut them up or torture them. I know firsthand how horrible the life of a lab animal is. I spent nearly a year as a lab cat. I never got outside my cage except when they caught me to inject some horrible drug into me. No one even bothered to give me a name. The pain was bad, but the loneliness was even worse. If that's what's going on here—and Bitsy believes so—then I'm going to put a stop to it.

There Bitsy goes, her little tail straight out behind her. At least she knows her way home, and I'll bet she never walks into a cage again.

Another good deed, and another cage destroyed.

What's that I hear? Some sort of commotion. Let me take a peek around the corner of this house. Hmm. It's two men in a green pickup, and they're highly agitated. They look lean, mean and upset. They've got the cat cage Miranda just destroyed. One man is shaking it and yelling. The other is looking around. Miranda and I need to kick up some heel dust.

The men have put the cage in the back of the pickup. Now they've crossed the street to talk to those two older men on the porch. And now they're looking at us.

Oh, no. I think it's time to go—and no fooling around. Those men are pissed off big-time and they're headed our way.

"Run, little humanoid!"

PENNY PAUSED at the porch where two older men sat in plastic chairs that moaned under their weight. One had white hair and the other had an earring in his right ear. "Have you seen a young girl, about nine years old, brown hair in braids?"

The men looked at each other and then down the street. Neither of them answered.

"Her father is looking for her." Penny pointed across the street toward where Mack was looking under a house.

When the men still didn't answer, Penny stepped closer. Something about their silence made her feel uncomfortable. "Have you seen a little girl?" she asked again, and this time with an edge to her voice.

One man looked away, but the other simply stared into her face.

"It's a simple question, yes or no," she said, feeling her anger begin to mount.

"What if we did?" the one with white hair asked.

"Then you'd better tell me," she said.

"Or what?" the other man asked, sneering.

"Mr. Sanders!" she called. "Could you come here a moment?" If the men wouldn't talk to her, maybe they'd talk to Mack. He was at least a hundred pounds bigger and, when it came to his daughter, very convincing.

Mack trotted across the street and came to stand beside her.

"These men may have seen Miranda," said Penny. "Unfortunately they don't want to tell me anything."

Mack put one foot on the step. "My little girl is missing," he said softly. "If you've seen her, please tell me."

"What's it worth to you?" the man with the earring asked.

Penny saw the flush of anger touch Mack's face. Instead of snatching the man out of his chair, though, he reached into his back pocket and pulled out a twenty-dollar bill.

"It's worth this." He handed it to the man.

"I saw a little girl. She and a black cat were under that house over there." He pointed across the street. "They left."

"How long ago?" Mack asked.

"Maybe half an hour."

"Which way did she go?" Penny asked.

"She ran toward that old junkyard," the man said, a cruel smile playing across his lips. "She was runnin' fast, too."

Mack turned, ready to go. Penny put a hand on his arm and detained him. "Why was she running?" she asked.

"'Cause those two men who were after her were mad," the man said, laughing out loud. "She was giving it all she had, but I don't think she got away from them."

Penny's hold tightened on Mack's arm and held him in the yard. He was about to climb up on the porch and do some damage. "Why were the men after her?"

"I reckon because she was tearing up their traps."

"What kind of traps?"

"Animal traps. They've been catching cats and little dogs for a couple of weeks. Catching 'em and hauling 'em off. There're enough stray cats and dogs around here, we won't miss a few."

"Did the men hurt her?" Penny asked.

Both men shrugged. "She tore up their stuff. They were mighty upset about what she'd done. They said they were going to get her."

Mack stared at the men. "I'm going to find my daughter, and after I do, I'm coming back here," he said. "If you're sitting out here on the porch watching the events of the day unfold, I may feel the need to include you in a few of them."

He turned abruptly and started jogging toward the old junkyard the men had pointed out.

Penny glanced again at the men and was glad to see the smirks had fled their faces. She hurried after Mack.

RESTRAINT HAD ALWAYS BEEN a byword of his life, but Mack felt his ability to control his anger slipping. He focused on the rusted metal fence that enclosed the junkyard.

"Miranda!" he called.

Only silence answered him. He saw Peter about a hundred yards down the block, looking in an old freezer. Behind him, Penny was catching up.

"Mack, she's okay," Penny said. "They saw her not half an hour ago. Surely she couldn't have gotten too far away in that time. Those men were probably mad, but they wouldn't hurt a child over a trap that can be replaced."

"We don't have a clue what really happened," he said bitterly. He knew she was trying to comfort him by putting on the best face possible. She was the kind of woman who wouldn't add to a father's torment. No, she was kind. But Miranda was still in danger. "Those two men just sat there and watched my daughter run while two men chased her. How could they do that?"

"I don't know." Penny followed him through a rusted-out hole in the fence.

"I think it's time to call the police," Mack said. Dusk was falling, and in front of Mack was an ocean of wrecked and abandoned cars. "She could be anywhere in here." Dread slipped over him. "They could have hurt her. She may be lying here...unconscious."

Mack turned at the sound of a cat meowing, his gaze going over an old BMW that sat on rusted axles.

"Familiar!" Penny darted in front of him and scooped up the black cat out of an old tire. She held him a moment, then held her hand out in front of her, disbelief showing on her face. Her hand was covered in blood. "Familiar's bleeding!" she said. "Will you find Peter while I check him out?"

"Sure," Mack said, heading back to the hole in the fence and taking out his cell phone. "And I'm going to call the police. Maybe Miranda is nearby, but we're not going to have enough daylight to hunt on our own. After what those two men said, I think we have enough evidence to prove she may be in danger."

PENNY FOUND THE WOUND on Familiar's side and quickly began to stanch the flow of blood. It looked like the cat had been shot. While her hands were busy with Familiar, her mind was going back over the conversation with the two men on the porch. Neither of the men had said anything about a gunshot. Then again, they hadn't been very forthcoming with any information.

She saw her uncle duck through the hole in the fence. "I think he's okay," she called to her uncle. "He's been shot. Small-caliber."

Peter hurried over and knelt beside her. As his hands moved over Familiar's sleek black hide, Penny filled him in on what she'd learned.

"Let me take Familiar to the clinic," Peter said. "It looks superficial. I think the bullet grazed his side, but I want to make certain. You stay and help Mack look for Miranda. Mack called the police and they're on the way. This is looking serious—but I don't have to tell you that."

Peter scooped the cat into his arms. As he stood, sirens sounded in the distance. "I'm really afraid something terrible has happened to his daughter."

"I can't believe this is happening. Surely Miranda is okay. I keep thinking we should have detained her at the clinic."

"How could we have known?" Peter said. "Look, do what you can. I'll be back as soon as I check Familiar out."

"Do you need my help?" Penny asked.

Peter shook his head. "Familiar's going to be fine. You stay with Mack. I think he's going to need someone he can lean on."

"Are you sure?" Penny asked.

"Positive." He kissed her forehead. "I'll be back as soon as—" Before he could finish, Familiar jumped to the ground.

Meowing, he started weaving through the junked cars.

"Familiar!" Peter called. "Come back here."

Penny saw the tip of his black tail disappear. "I

think he wants to stay here," Penny said, amazement in her voice.

"He's the most stubborn animal I've ever known," Peter said with disgust. "He's been in trouble from Ireland to Egypt and back. He has a nose for getting into the middle of things."

Penny turned to her uncle. "He's after something. He keeps looking over his shoulder to see if we're following." Penny started after the cat. "Come on, Uncle Peter." Familiar had already disappeared from view into an old rusted chasis.

She began wading through the wrecked cars as the sound of the sirens grew louder. When she turned back, she saw that Peter had stopped to examine the ground. "What is it?"

"A footprint. It might be evidence."

Penny let out the breath she'd been holding for what felt like centuries. "Do you think someone took Miranda?"

Peter nodded. "I can't think of anything else. I'm frightened to imagine what they may have done to her. You go get Mack and see if the police will send some officers to help with the search."

"The cat disappeared," Penny said. She pointed to the area. "He just vanished."

Peter nodded. "I'll look for him. You go help Mack. Familiar's out here somewhere, and our job is to have the backup he needs, when he needs it."

CHAPTER FIVE

SHOCK PASSED OVER Mack's face as he watched Penny walk up to the patrol car. It took Penny a few seconds to realize that blood colored her blouse and hands. The police officer, wearing a sergeant's chevrons and a tag with the name Stanley Greene, got out of the car with a questioning look at the blood.

"My uncle's cat was shot," Penny said, and saw the color drain from Mack's face. She gave him a tight smile of reassurance, then continued, "He's going to be okay. At least, we hope so. He took off among the cars. We lost him." Familiar was everything her uncle had said, and then some. Even though he was injured, he wouldn't give up the hunt.

"Did you find any sign of Miranda?" Mack's face showed naked fear.

Penny slowly shook her head. "Familiar is searching the area. If she's there, he'll find her. Uncle Peter says he's one heck of a detective."

"A cat?" the policeman said incredulously. "You have a tracking cat?"

Penny nodded, casting a glance at the junkyard where her uncle still searched. "You could say that."

"I hope you're right." Mack's voice was hoarse with worry and stress.

Penny couldn't help herself. Mack looked so distraught. She put her arm around his waist and gave him a comforting squeeze. "Miranda's going to be okay," she said. "We'll find her."

"I told the officer everything," he said. "He's going back to question those two men on the porch."

"They might be more willing to talk to a law officer," Penny agreed.

"If not willing, at least afraid not to tell the truth. And the officer radioed to bring in some tracking dogs," Mack continued. He spoke as if he were in a daze. "They don't really know for certain that Miranda is in danger, but they're going to help. It's going to be dark in another few minutes. Miranda has never been away from home in the dark." His voice grew rougher. "I know she's going to be terrified."

Penny's hand automatically began to rub Mack's back. Touch carried an amazing ability to comfort. She knew that from her work with animals. Whenever a cat or dog was frightened and upset, she spent time petting and rubbing it, soothing it so that it would relax and begin to heal.

"Uncle Peter found a footprint," Penny told the officer. "It could belong to anyone, but it could also belong to one of the two men who chased Miranda into the junkyard."

"We'll take care of it." Sergeant Greene got on the radio and put out a call for other units. "We'll get this search started," he said, looking up at the sky and shaking his head. "It's only going to get harder when it's dark."

"Let's go call for Familiar," Penny said, taking Mack's hand and pulling him away from the patrol car. She thought of Miranda, the girl's desire to help a stray cat. She felt a wave of anger and then grief. Surely nothing had happened to the child. But she couldn't escape the fact that Familiar had been shot. She could only assume that it had been the men who'd gone hunting for Miranda.

"She has to be okay," Mack said, more to himself than to Penny.

She tightened her grip on his hand. "Just visualize her alive and safe."

"Why are you doing this?" Mack stopped suddenly, an expression of amazement on his face. "You just moved into the neighborhood and all you know is that my little girl brought you kittens that were going to die. You don't know me or Miranda. Why do you care?"

"I care about cats and dogs and even a little girl I don't know." Penny's smile was slow. "I care about all things, and I don't like to see animals or humans suffer." Her smile widened. "I have a sneaking suspicion that Miranda is a very lovable little girl—when she isn't driving you crazy with worry."

"She's a great kid," Mack said, exhaling a long breath. "Better than I deserve. I just don't want her hurt again."

Penny suspected he was talking about the past as much as the present. "Children are a lot tougher than you might think," she said.

"You sound like you're talking from experience."

Penny nodded. "My dad died when I was twelve. He was in an accident. And then my mother got breast cancer. She died when I was nineteen. It was a long, hard illness."

"And you took care of her?"

"I tried." Penny felt the unexpected surge of tears. She'd thought she'd grieved enough. "There wasn't anything to be done. The doctors tried everything."

"At least your mother didn't abandon you," Mack said, with such bitterness that Penny stopped and turned to face him. In the failing light, she could see the anger and hurt in his eyes.

"Death is a form of permanent abandonment."

"Your mother didn't choose to die and leave you."

Penny shook her head. "Toward the end, she did. And I was glad when it was over. It isn't about abandonment."

His arm went around her shoulders and she felt a sense of comfort she hadn't expected. "Thank you," she said, stepping back from him. "You're a very gentle man—though I didn't think so at first."

"I can only imagine what you must have thought, with Miranda bringing in those kittens, probably acting like she didn't want me to know."

Penny shook her head. "It wasn't the best first

impression. But I understand now. You were only trying to protect Miranda from an animal you thought was dangerous. I understand how it is not to want to lose someone." For some reason she found it easy to talk to Mack, a man who was virtually a stranger. "I'm guilty of avoiding relationships because I don't want to chance risking another loss." She laughed self-consciously. "I think that's why Uncle Peter is here, to urge me to date a little before I'm a dried-up old maid."

Mack's large hands slid to her shoulders, and he started a slow, gentle massage of the tense muscles. "You don't have any worries in that regard. You're too pretty to stay alone for long."

Penny began to relax as he kneaded her tired shoulders. "I don't know about that, but I appreciate the sentiment."

"I guess I'm so mad at Miranda's mom because it upsets me to think about how she must hurt. But that's my problem, not Miranda's. I shouldn't let how I feel affect how I deal with this. I should be focusing on her feelings, not my own." His hand slipped around Penny's shoulder and he pulled her close to him. "Thank you," he whispered into her hair.

Penny closed her eyes. Mack smelled of laundry detergent and the heat of his own body. She felt as if she was trembling all over, but she knew it was emotional, not physical.

"She's going to be okay, Mack. We'll find her." She stepped away and turned, giving him a long look.

MACK THOUGHT HIS HEART would break. His fear for his daughter was overwhelming. And yet he found room in his thoughts for the remarkable young woman who stood staring into his eyes. She was a good person, a woman with tender feelings for a child she hadn't met for more than a few minutes. And she was beautiful. Her brown eyes held depths that urged him to gaze into them forever. There was something in her that made her want to help—even him.

"When we find her, I want you to help me with that cat. Gumbo." He said the word as if it might hold the magic to bring his daughter home. "If we can really tame her, I want Miranda to have her."

"We'll find the cat, and if we have to, we can trap her. Then we'll tame her a little, and when the kittens are weaned, we can spay her. Once she is loved and wanted, she'll probably come around."

Penny continued to talk about the cat, and Mack was grateful. Her voice was the thread that held him together. It didn't matter what she said, and she seemed to sense that. She was one of the most giving and tender people he'd ever met. How would he handle this without her—a woman he'd just met a few hours before?

"Gumbo is a great name for a calico," Penny said, leading him away from the crackle of the policeman's radio and the words that cut through his heart. He heard "stretcher" and "hostage situation" and "kidnapping" and "medical examiner." And it was the last that nearly broke him.

He let her lead him toward the junkyard where all of his hopes and fears waited.

"We should probably do something in a pattern," Penny said as she tugged at his hand. "Why don't we begin here? Maybe we can find some clue before night falls completely. It'll take the police a little while to get organized. Of course, they'll have lights and all the right equipment, but we can get started."

Penny Jameson was an angel. Mack found himself staring at her, wondering where she'd left her wings. She was getting him going, keeping him moving, starting off on her own search while he followed behind her like a big, dumb animal. No, not like an animal. Like some hunk of rock or a tree trunk. He shook himself, forcing himself out of his stupor.

A minute later he saw the footprint. He bent to examine it.

"That's where we found Familiar, in that tire," Penny pointed out.

"It would probably be safe to assume that Miranda was somewhere near here, then," Mack said. "It looks as though the cat was trying to guard her."

He moved past a crunched BMW and found what looked like a rough path among the cars. In the fading light, he stooped and picked up an empty can of cat food. The label was still pristine.

"It's new," Penny said when he held it out to her. "I think Miranda was here."

How long had his daughter been coming to this junkyard? Mack felt as if he'd left his world behind and stepped into a nightmare. "Do you think she brought it today?"

Penny nodded. "Could be. Maybe she isn't hurt, Mack. Maybe she's feeding the stray cats."

He prayed that was true. Once he found Miranda, he was going to buy food for *all* the cats in the neighborhood—and help her put it out, too. Once he found her, things were going to be different. He was going to come home at three o'clock, when she got out of school. He was going to be the best father in the world.

"Look!"

Penny's excited tone pulled him free of his thoughts. "What is it?"

"It's a sheet of paper." Penny held him back from picking it up. Instead, she used a stick to unfold it.

Mack leaned closer. "That looks like the type of writing tablet Miranda had. She was always making notes and drawing pictures." He got another stick and helped hold down one end of the note.

In the center of the sheet was a drawing of what looked like a dragon. Beside it were two words: "bad teeth."

"Is that Miranda's handwriting?" Penny asked, her voice rising with concern.

"Yes, and it's the purple pen I gave her last week. There's no doubt she left this." He knelt down, careful not to touch the note. "Bad teeth," he said out loud. He looked up at Penny's worried face.

"I think she's trying to identify the men," Penny said slowly. "One could have had a tattoo of a dragon and the other bad teeth."

"At least it's a start," Mack said.

"We have to assume Miranda is okay," Penny said. "She was able to draw that image and write those words, and she left the paper for us to find. Mack, she's not only okay, I think she's smarter than her abductors."

Mack acknowledged Penny's words, but he wasn't certain it was a good thing. He knew his daughter. "She's a very smart little girl. They wanted to put her up two grades, but I wouldn't let them. She's smart," he said, "and she's very determined. Sometimes that's a dangerous combination."

WAIT UNTIL I get my hands on those two creeps. They shot me and grabbed Miranda. Dang it, they snatched her up and took off with her. But I have a plan. I know the humanoids are going to use the typical police procedure to find Miranda. That won't be quick enough.

From the conversation I overheard between Dumb and Dumber, they've got almost a full shipment of stray cats and dogs, even though some of the animals they captured aren't strays. Like Buster. I'm certain they have him. Their plan is to load up the cages and take the animals tonight. They didn't say where, but I have no doubt that it's someplace no cat or dog wants to be.

Even worse, they have Miranda. I don't know

what they plan to do with her, but it can't be good. One of the men mentioned selling her, like she's a tub of green beans or basket of potatoes. Or an animal. It just made my skin crawl. The good news is that I'd recognize both of the men if I saw them again. One has had a real dental apocalypse. The three teeth I saw looked like candidates for removal. And the other has this unique dragon tattooed on his right forearm. Really, he might as well wear a name tag. And that's what bothers me. If he were worried about being identified, he'd have tried to cover up the tattoo. So that must mean that he doesn't plan for Miranda to be able to give a description to anyone. And that means nothing good for Miranda.

My side stings a little where the bullet nicked me, but I've been hurt worse. I'll be okay, at least until I find the humanoid. After that, I think I'll swoon and let the good Dr. Jameson tend my wound. First things first, though—I'm off to the rescue. I only hope Peter can see well enough in this poor light to understand what I'm doing.

CHAPTER SIX

MACK WATCHED Sergeant Greene collect the piece of paper that bore the drawing of the tattoo and the words "bad teeth."

"Those two old gents on the porch reluctantly confirmed that one of the men chasing your daughter had a dragon tattoo and the other had bad teeth. Looks like your daughter is pretty smart," the officer told Mack. "That's in her favor. Now that we know she's been abducted, we can focus our search."

The police officer and Penny, heads bent together in a whispered conversation, walked back to the patrol car.

Mack felt his dread deepen. *Abducted.* There was no doubt now. Miranda had been taken by unprincipled and possibly violent men. His nine-year-old daughter was beyond his protection.

Mack's fears were compounded by the total fall of darkness. Officers had almost finished searching the junkyard, and so far there was no sign of Miranda or the cat. With the moonlight touching the last bits of shiny metal and glass on the sea of cars that stretched out for acres, Mack felt hopelessness settle over him. Miranda could be anywhere.

"She's going to be okay." Peter walked up behind Mack. His voice held determination. "Let's head back to your house. If she can get home, that's where she'll go. If the officers find anything, they'll contact you at home. Penny is giving them all the pertinent information."

Mack turned and followed Peter down the block. "I hope so."

"I don't blame you for being skeptical, but keep in mind, Familiar is on the case."

"He's a cat." Mack couldn't help himself. He didn't intend to hurt Peter's feelings. After all, Peter was a total stranger, yet he had just spent the past four hours searching for Miranda. They were moving slowly away from the junkyard, and he looked back over his shoulder. "There's not much a cat can do at this point." Penny was rapidly catching up with them, and he felt a sense of relief.

Peter's laugh was easy. "So you might think. Just remember, even though Familiar was wounded, he still went after your daughter."

"How would he know where they took her?" Mack wanted to believe. More than anything he wanted to hold on to the idea that someone—even a cat—was on the trail of Miranda.

"Cats are uncanny creatures," Penny said. "They have a sixth sense about things, and Familiar is the most observant living creature I've ever known."

"We both know that those men didn't take Miranda because they wanted to buy her an ice-cream cone." Mack pushed aside the thoughts of what they might be doing to his daughter.

"What about ransom?" Penny asked.

Mack felt as if he were under water. Ransom! He'd never even thought about it. "I need to check my phone," he said. He dialed his home number, got the answering machine, coded in his key and began to retrieve the one message. At the rough sound of the strange man's voice, he felt as if everything around him had stopped.

"Your little girl says you'll pay for her," the voice said. "If that's true, and you want her back alive, you'll need some money. Lots of money. A hundred-thousand dollars, cash. And if you involve the police or anyone else in this, you can kiss your kid good-bye. I have a source in the police department, so don't do anything stupid. I'll call back and tell you the arrangements."

The message ended, and Mack felt as if his heart had frozen.

"You got a call, didn't you," Penny said.

"You've been a big help," he said to her and Peter, "but I can handle it from here." Mack's gaze sought the police officer walking toward them.

"The tracking dogs will be here in about five minutes," the officer said.

"We don't need them." Mack was abrupt. "My daughter called home. She was at a friend's. I'm going to get her now." He brushed past Peter, Penny and the officer and started toward home. The worst thing that could happen now would be for the kidnappers to think he'd called the police. The ransom call had been left almost ten minutes earlier, on his home phone. Miranda must have given the kidnappers information on how to reach him. Now he had to get home and wait for the next call. And he couldn't involve Peter and Penny.

"Is she okay?" Penny had jogged to catch up with him, and she was stretching her legs to maintain the brisk pace he'd set. "What happened?"

"She's fine." Mack glanced down at Penny's worried face. "I can't stay here. Please tell Sergeant Greene how much I thank him." He sprinted into the darkness without even a backward glance.

PENNY KNEW SOMETHING was terribly wrong. One minute she was working with Mack Sanders to find his little girl, and the next she was standing in a junkyard, dismissed as if she were of no significance. And to top it off, Mack had left her to thank the police officers, while he disappeared. Beneath the initial hurt, she felt the warning of trouble.

She walked back to her uncle and Sergeant Greene, trying hard not to show she was troubled. "Mr. Sanders said to thank you, Sergeant. I guess he was so excited at finding Miranda that he rushed away."

"He sure has a great way of showing his appreciation. Let me radio the dogs and send them back. He said the kid showed up at someone's house, right?"

"That's what he said," Peter answered.

Penny swung around at her uncle's tone of voice. When she started to say something, Peter put a hand on her arm, cautioning her to silence.

"Well, the important thing is the kid's safe. You two need a lift?" Greene asked.

"No, thanks. My cat is still missing," Peter said. "I think we'll hunt a little longer."

"Be careful. This isn't a great neighborhood. Would you like me to stay with you?"

Peter shook the sergeant's hand. "I'm sure you have better things to do than hunt for a lost cat."

"I'll contact Mr. Sanders. He'll have to come by the police department tomorrow and fill out some paperwork. I'm just glad we had a good result in this one. I was getting worried when he found that note."

As soon as the sergeant was gone, Penny turned to her uncle. "What on earth is going on?"

"Miranda isn't safe. I think Mack must have gotten a ransom call. He checked his messages, and then suddenly, his whole personality changed."

"I'll say," Penny said, realizing how bad her feelings were hurt. "If someone has taken Miranda for ransom, Mack needs to tell the police."

Peter shook his head. "I'm sure he was warned not to, and I have to say, I'd do the same thing in his situation."

"What are we going to do?"

"Our ace in the hole is Familiar."

"Uncle Peter, I know you love him, but he is just a cat."

Peter put his arm around Miranda's shoulders. "So you may think. Let me tell you about the anthropologist he saved in Egypt, or the horse in Ireland, or the sheriff in Colorado, or the stuntwoman in Hollywood, or—"

"Okay, I get the point. So, what do you think Familiar is up to?"

"I only wish I knew," Peter said. "I do know that he won't fail to risk his life for that little girl, and if she is being held for ransom, Familiar is her best hope."

"I can't just go home and wait this out. We're going by the clinic to feed the kittens, and then I'm going to Mack's house and demand that he let us help out."

Peter hugged Penny's shoulders. "That's my girl."

HUMANOIDS FIND NIGHT, more often than not, to be a disadvantage. Not me. Night is my ally. I'm sleek and black and equipped with eyes that see better in darkness than those of Homo sapiens. No big surprise there, though. Felines are generally superior in all regards.

Let's see. I've made it at least four miles from the junkyard. The neighborhood has gotten worse and worse, and I've passed two cages with felines already trapped. They looked bad. I did my best to reassure them that this was all going to work out, but

I don't think they believed me. They were hungry and thirsty, and I needed Miranda to help me work the release mechanism. I just couldn't do it on my own. Which tends to make me want to rethink my plan. I just don't have time to cook up something better.

So, here's an empty cage. Baited with...sniff, sniff...peanut better? These guys are great. They not only trap animals for some nefarious purpose, but they're too cheap to even spring for some decent food. If these stray cats weren't starving, they wouldn't fall for peanut butter. Just wait until I get my hands on these cretins. I'm going to make them pay in ways they never imagined. That is, of course, if Miranda has been taken by them and if she's conscious and able to help me.

My whole plan centers on that little girl. I spent enough time with her this afternoon to know what a big and courageous heart she has. She's been saving her lunch money from school to buy food for the strays. She goes hungry all day.

And when she grows up, she's going to be a vet, just like Penny and Peter. Except she says she's going to have a mobile vet clinic and drive through neighborhoods like this to help the stray animals that no one else helps.

She did talk to me a bit about her mother leaving. Her little heart is bruised but not broken. She says she has to be brave for her dad. She says that he is so sad, he can't even talk about it.

I doubt that's true, but this is one of the major

problems with humanoids. They get an idea in their head and then they don't talk to anyone, especially the person who should hear it. Sigh. I could teach seminars in this. Felines, and to some extent even canines, are superb at making their feelings known. We want food—we demand it. We want sleep—we curl up and dare anyone to annoy us. We want danger— well, here it comes. I'm stepping into the cage. Speaking of wants, I don't really want to do this. I've been trapped and caged before, and it wasn't a positive experience. But I have to find Miranda.

I can't help but believe this is exactly what's happened to the mother cat, the one she calls Gumbo. I took a look at those kittens. They'd been cleaned and loved. Gumbo didn't leave them voluntarily. I can only hope that when these creeps come to fetch me, they'll take me straight to Gumbo—and Miranda.

CHAPTER SEVEN

MACK SAT in the leather chair beside the telephone at his house and replayed the message. The words were even more chilling the second time around. The male voice was cold, cruel. The idea that such a man held his daughter's fate was almost more than Mack could bear.

From the little he knew about ransoms, mostly from television and movies, Mack thought that a hundred-thousand dollars wasn't an excessively large amount of money to ask for. Still, it would be difficult to raise on short notice. Time was the problem. Things in the financial world didn't move fast enough. He didn't have a choice, though. He would get the money, no matter what he had to do.

He had a heart-stopping mental image of Miranda, frightened, cowering in a corner of a dark room. Each minute Miranda spent in the company of those men was a minute too long.

The phone rang and he grabbed it. "Yes."

"Can you get the money?" Threat laced the man's voice.

"Yes. I have to wait for the bank to open. I need some time."

"Okay, you have until ten o'clock. I'll call you and tell you where to bring the money. Remember, if you notify the police, I'll know, and your kid will die."

"Wait." Mack gave his cell phone number. "And I want to talk to my daughter."

There was the fumbling of the phone before he heard Miranda's voice. "Daddy, they have all these cats and—" His daughter's voice was cut off.

The same man came back on the line. "You heard her. She's alive. Just do what we tell you and she'll stay that way."

"If you harm her in any way—"

"What will you do?" the man jeered. "Instead of wasting time thinking about that, you'd better worry about getting the money." The line went dead.

Mack sat back and let his heart rate calm. He had some money in savings, but he'd have to cash out his stocks. And he could borrow from the bank. There was no doubt he could get the money, but could he get it by ten? The bank opened at nine. He'd have only an hour.

Sweat rolled down his back. He got up and began to pace. He had to have everything figured out by morning so that all went like clockwork.

He heard a knock on his door and stopped. Moving stealthily, he stepped to the window and looked out. The petite woman who stood on his porch could not be anyone but Penny. The very sight of her made his heart lift.

He opened the door and, without a word, quickly pulled her into the house. "Is anyone out there?" he asked. "Did you see anyone?"

"No," she answered.

He held her for a moment and then released her. "You can't be here. You have to leave."

"What?"

"You have to get away from here. There's danger. For you, and for Miranda if anyone sees you."

"I know those men have Miranda." She looked into his eyes. "I'm not leaving, Mack. Not by a long shot. Peter and I are involved in this and we aren't leaving until Miranda's home safe and sound. Right now, Peter's at the clinic. And don't forget, his cat is out there, too. We're all going to help."

The rush of emotion caught Mack by surprise. How long had it been since he'd felt someone was really on his side? Years. Even when his ex-wife had been at home, he hadn't felt he could rely on her. Belinda had been totally self-centered. Her needs had always come first. Penny was a stranger, a woman he'd just met. Yet she was standing right in front of him, refusing to leave until Miranda was safe.

"I can't involve you in this," he said, his hand touching her cheek. "Your offer means more to me than you'll ever know. But these men are dangerous. They could hurt you." He paused. "They could kill you. Or they could hurt Miranda if they know I've got anyone else involved. I can't let that happen."

Penny's smile was crooked. "You don't have a

choice, Mack Sanders. I'm here and I'm not going anywhere. Peter's at the office waiting for my call. If you don't let us help, then he's going to call the police."

"That's blackmail," Mack said.

"Yep, it is." Penny took his hand. "So learn to enjoy it. Remember, I'm not leaving. This is one time you aren't going to be left all alone."

"Okay, then," he said. "Listen to this." He played the original message for Penny, and then the conversation he'd just recorded.

"It's the same man both times," Penny said.

He saw his own fear reflected in Penny's eyes, and somehow, that made him stronger.

"I can get the money. In the morning. But I don't know if I can get it in an hour."

Penny nodded. He could see that she was thinking hard. When she spoke, though, he was surprised at her clarity and daring.

"I think we should use paper. Cut it, bundle it just like money, wrap it and put it in the bottom of a case. Cover the bundles of paper with some real money, so the kidnappers would have to dig down to find out that we'd tricked them."

Mack recognized the wisdom of her words intellectually, but emotionally he felt only fear at the idea. "I can't play with my daughter's life," he said.

"I know," Penny said. "But consider this. If you go to the bank and attempt a large withdrawal, the banking authorities are going to notify the police.

You'll have a risk either way. Which risk is worse—trying to trick them or getting the police involved?"

Mack realized she was right. "Damn!" he whispered harshly.

"I have some cash at the clinic. It's not a lot, but with what you can get and what Peter may have, we can pull this off." Penny's warm hand, so small and fragile but so strong, grasped his. "Remember, Miranda's a lot smarter than her captors. She left us a clue. We have to be as smart as she is."

Mack knew the plan she offered was the only one that had a chance of working. He'd never get the money without alerting the police, even if he could get it at all by the deadline. Once the police were involved, he believed the captors would kill his daughter. The kidnapper had said he had a contact in the police department.

"Okay," he said.

There was a knock at the door that made both of them jump. Mack checked through the window and saw Peter standing on the porch.

"Come in," Mack said as he opened the door.

"No time." Peter's voice was clipped. "I have an idea. I'm going to say I was attacked. I'll go down to the police station and see if I can look at some mug books. We don't have a lot to go on, except the tattoo. I believe these men have been in trouble before."

"That's a good idea," Mack said. He bit his lip as he took Peter's hand and gripped it tightly. "Be careful. The kidnapper says he has someone on the inside at the police department."

"No problem," Peter said. "I'll call if I find anything. And you call me if you find Familiar."

Mack watched Peter stride down the sidewalk to his car. When he closed the door, he turned to find Penny watching him closely. "What do we do until morning?" he asked.

"Wait," she said simply. "That's all we can do. I'll make something to eat, and then we're going to try to rest for a few hours. I'll set an alarm so I can get up and feed those kittens."

Mack put his hands on her shoulders. With her soft, curly hair framing her face, she was lovely. "Through all of this, you have the energy to nurse a litter of abandoned kittens?"

Penny shook her head. Her smile was wry. "The good news is that when we find Miranda, I think we'll also find that mother cat—and then she can take over her responsibilities. Now, show me the kitchen. We have to eat while we can."

He didn't argue with her. Didn't have the desire. She was right, and she was beautiful. As she opened his cupboards and began to look for something to cook, he couldn't help but think how natural it felt to have her in his life.

PENNY PUT the angel-hair pasta on the table. For a man who lived without a wife, Mack kept a well-supplied kitchen. Penny noticed several bottles of good wine but didn't open one. They were both too tired, too stressed. Wine might dull their ability to react—should it become necessary.

As she set the table she felt his gaze lingering on her. Instead of making her uncomfortable, it made her realize how at ease she was with him. She'd missed so much, living a solitary life. Independence and being comfortable alone were both good things—things she'd struggled to attain. But in the rush to be independent and avoid the risk of caring for another person, she'd lost a lot, too. Like this feeling of partnership, and the underlying tingle of sexual attraction. Now wasn't the time for kisses, but…she wanted to kiss Mack. She thought about it, and when she did, she felt alive in a way that she'd never felt before. Deliciously alive.

Once Miranda was safely home, she was going to explore her feelings for Mack Sanders. Yesterday, she might have been too shy, but Miranda's disappearance had taught her a valuable lesson—no one knew what the future held. There wasn't always plenty of time to waste. And while trying to keep from again losing someone she loved, she'd lost the joy of loving.

Things were going to change.

"Dinner's ready," she said.

Mack held her chair as she sat. He had good manners. She liked that in a man. In fact, she liked a great many things about Mack Sanders. When he was seated across from her, she smiled.

"I know you don't feel like eating, but try."

He took a bite. "It's delicious. It's just that—"

"I know," she said. "Eat a little anyway."

Instead of eating, he looked at her. "Tell me something about yourself. Something good." He glanced at the clock on the kitchen wall. "Time is passing so slowly. Talk to me."

She put down her fork. She wasn't hungry, either. "I've always loved animals. When I was a child, my best friend was my dog, Clover. She went everywhere with me. And when my dad died, Clover was the only one who could comfort me."

"You've had a lot of loss in your life, haven't you?"

She nodded. "Mom died when I was in my teens. Uncle Peter paid my way through college and veterinary school."

"You two seem close."

She nodded. "We are. Now you tell me something about yourself." She sipped the iced tea she'd made and decided to ask the question that had lingered in her mind all day. "What happened with your wife?" She held his gaze. She'd just stepped right into the middle of Mack's personal business. Her new motto, though, was not to waste time. All of it was precious, and if he was still in love with his ex, she needed to know.

"Miranda is the best thing that came from that relationship. I realize now that I never loved Belinda, or if I did, that love died in the first months of our marriage."

"How did you meet?" Penny knew that the best thing was to keep him talking. She could see that his memories were painful, but sometimes the best way to heal was to talk.

Mack looked at his plate, but before he spoke, he shifted his gaze to her so that he was staring deeply into her eyes. "I knew Belinda in college. She was beautiful, and always laughing. I never dreamed she'd go out with me, but she did." He paused. "She got pregnant. She wanted to have an abortion, but I wanted the baby. I begged her to marry me, and she finally did. Miranda was born, and from the first day Belinda got home with the baby from the hospital, she was leaving."

Penny frowned. "What do you mean?"

"She'd stand at the kitchen sink, looking out the window at the backyard. I think she was imagining herself anywhere but where she was. She was terribly unhappy. I did try, but I didn't know what to do to make her happy."

"She didn't love Miranda?"

He looked down at his plate. "I don't think she did. I don't think she loved anyone, even herself. In the long run, that may have been a blessing. Miranda didn't take her departure all that hard. I think on some level she realized Belinda had always been gone. I see now that I'm the only one who took her leaving so much to heart, and I've been attributing all of that to Miranda. I just hope it isn't too late to straighten it all out for my daughter."

Penny felt a sense of sorrow for the long-gone Belinda. How was it possible to have a child like Miranda and not love her?

"Do you know where your wife is?"

"*Ex*-wife. I divorced her in absentia. And no. I never heard a word. I tell Miranda that she calls and asks about her, but it's a lie, and I think Miranda knows it." He frowned. "I've made so many mistakes."

Penny didn't approve of lying to a child, but she certainly understood Mack's reasons for doing so. Heck, in his shoes, she might have done a lot more. But there was a question niggling at her. "Do you think it's possible your ex-wife might be behind this abduction?"

Mack gave it a moment's thought before he spoke. "No. Because I don't think Belinda would ever have thought Miranda was valuable enough to ransom. Her mind just didn't work that way. I suspect she's in Vegas or some party town living it up. She's a beautiful woman, and as long as her looks last, she won't even think about what she left behind in Mobile, Alabama."

"So, tell me about your little girl," Penny said, hoping to lighten the conversation. They had hours to get through before it would be time for another phone call from the kidnappers.

"Miranda is the best. She has the liveliest imagination. I can sit for hours and listen to her talk about what she does and thinks. She writes every day. I've never seen anything like it. Of course, I'd never read her diary before, but she's told me about it."

The frown had left his features, and Penny drank in the sight of Mack smiling. He was a handsome man, a strong man with a big heart filled with love for his daughter.

"When Miranda gets up in the morning, she makes toast for both of us," Mack said. "She puts milk out for the cat. She has such a routine." A pang crossed his face. "When she comes home, I'm going to buy a truckload of cat food for her and help her set traps to catch all those feral cats. I should have helped her."

"Maybe she needed to do it herself," Penny said. "Sometimes, people have to do something alone, Mack. Maybe this was what she needed. Now you can help her in the future."

"Maybe so." He took a deep breath and forced a smile. "Anyway, she's good to all the older people in the neighborhood. On Saturday she gets up and takes the newspapers in from the walk for them." He smiled. "She's a marvelous child with a huge heart."

"She's a lot like her father," Penny said, feeling a stirring in her heart that was both wonderful and frightening. She *liked* Mack Sanders. "I see similarities—"

Penny didn't get to finish. The harsh jangle of the phone made both of them jump to their feet and dash to answer it.

CHAPTER EIGHT

I'M NOT SURE that climbing into that cage was my brightest idea. We've been booking it for the past forty minutes—over the hills and through the woods. I could only wish to grandmother's house we'd go. Instead we're headed for the wilderness. For the last fifteen minutes, I haven't seen a light or any sign of civilization. This guy is taking me out to the boonies.

We're slowing, and at last we're coming to a stop. I enjoy a little breeze, but riding in the back of this pickup truck in a cage isn't my idea of suitable transportation. I feel like my whiskers have been whipped off. Stupid bipeds. Two other felines are shivering with fear. When I get my claws on this moron, I'll give him a double dose of pain.

The humanoid, the one with the tattoos, is taking the cages off the truck and hauling them away. My goodness! This place we've arrived at stinks. I can smell my fellow felines, not to mention canines. They must have a hundred animals here. And I can only imagine the condition some of them are in. These guys obviously aren't concerned with water, food or sanitary conditions.

Here comes the other one, and he's yelling orders and cursing. It seems Toothless Wonder is the brains of the business, and that would add up to about a teaspoon of gray matter. But he's mean. He kicked a little dog that tried to get away, and the poor little guy is still shivering and whining. I need Peter. He could help him.

Here we go. Tattoo man is picking up my cage and taking it around back. Yes, indeed, there are at least a hundred cages filled with all kinds of animals. This is a big business.

I wonder where Miranda is. She has to be here. I don't think they had time to take her to another place. I'll practice my two-yawl warble. I taught her that sound this afternoon, and she's a smart kid. I'm sure she'll recognize it. If she can get to me, I'm sure she will.

"Me-ow-ow-ow. Me-ow-ow-ow."

I see her face at the window of that old shack! She's waving to me, just a slight curl of her fingers. She looks scared, but she doesn't seem to be hurt. Thank goodness. I know she'll try to sneak out here and release me. She can always use the ploy of having to go to the bathroom. Dumb and Dumber won't catch on. We're so far out in the boondocks that they realize she can't get away from them. If my opinion of these two creeps is correct, they won't believe a nine-year-old girl will give them any trouble. Bingo! Here she comes. Dumb, aka Toothless Wonder, is watching from the door to make sure she goes to the bathroom. Good work, Miranda. She's slipping behind a stack of cages and coming at me from the back side. There's her little hand, releasing the spring on the cage.

And I'm free! I'm just going to sit here for a moment and wait for my chance.

Whew! I was getting cage fever. Too many bad memories, I suppose. At least my bullet wound is no longer too painful. But Miranda is going back in, and the door is closing. Yes! I'm outta this cage and headed to initiate stage two of my action plan.

"I'LL GET THE MONEY as soon as we feed the kittens," Penny said. She was glad that Mack had decided to come with her—and a little surprised. The telephone call had been one last threat by Miranda's abductors, warning Mack not to call the police. The exchange was still set for ten in the morning. Now they had to wait for Peter to call and report his findings. Mack wanted to call the police, but if the kidnappers did have a mole in the police department, that phone call would seal Miranda's fate.

Penny knew the best thing to do was to keep Mack busy so that the time would pass faster. She prepared two tiny bottles and gave Mack one along with the little black-and-white kitten with the kinky tail. The kitten was half the size of Mack's hand, but she watched with amusement as Mack gently held the squirming bundle. As soon as he put the rubber nipple to the tiny pink mouth, the kitten latched on and began to suck ferociously.

"She's so strong," he said, a smile splitting his face.

Penny couldn't help but think how handsome he was when he smiled.

"These kittens will be fine," she said. "If we find Gumbo soon enough, she'll still nurse them. But we'll keep them where we can handle them and teach them to be domesticated. That will help us tame Gumbo." She gave him an encouraging look. "For Miranda."

Penny nursed the yellow kitten, and then they both took black ones. The last one, a gray tabby, went to Mack.

"You did a good job," she said, putting the kittens back in a small incubator.

"I want Miranda to help feed them. She'll get a kick out of it." He looked up with naked pain in his eyes. "I just didn't want her to be hurt."

"I know," Penny said. "When she gets back, though, she can help." Penny put her hand on his cheek. He was such a gentle man at heart. "She's fine, Mack."

He bent toward her, slowly. She knew what was coming, and she kept her face turned up to accept his kiss. She'd known that it would be powerful and affecting, and she was right. She felt as if she were melting into his arms, and he held her with strength and tenderness.

When she put a hand on his chest, he broke the kiss. "I'm sorry," he said. "My timing is all wrong."

"No, it's not," she said. "I've never been more ready for a kiss in my life." She smiled. "I just don't want you to regret anything."

He nodded in understanding. "I'd never forgive myself if something happened to Miranda while I was falling in love with you."

Penny heard the words and felt an unexpected rush of joy. She wanted to kiss him, to feel his arms surround her with all of the emotions she'd denied herself for so long. But now wasn't the time, and they both knew it. They had to keep focused on Miranda.

"I have lots of copy paper here," Penny said, stepping around him and pointing to a case of paper on the floor by the desk. "And here's the money. I didn't have time to stop by the bank and make a deposit, so that's good." She pulled the money drawer open and gathered up the twenties. "We should put twenties on top. That looks more realistic."

"I know this is a risk," Mack said. "But this is less risky than going to the bank. Do you think I could rig some type of explosive device in the money? Something that would disable one of them so I could go after the other?"

"That's an idea," Penny said thoughtfully. "Do you know how to do that?"

"In the military I had some training."

His eyes had grown flinty, and Penny knew that as sweet and caring as Mack could be, he was also a force to be reckoned with.

"I'll take this home and rig it up." He lifted the box and was almost out the door with it when the cell phone in his pocket shrilled. He pulled the phone out and answered. In a moment his face lit with joy.

He turned to Penny. "It's Miranda. She's okay. She's being held in some shack out in the woods." He spoke swiftly into the phone, telling Miranda that he loved her and that he was going to find her and save her.

"Tell me where you are," he urged. He listened for a moment. "Familiar is there with you? How?" He listened again. "Okay, honey, put the phone back where you got it. Try to stay calm and don't get excited. I have your asthma medicine and I'm bringing it to you. I love you." He slowly lowered the receiver.

"Familiar is with her?" Penny asked, relief in her tone.

"He is. He got himself caught in a trap. Miranda let him out, and he's with her. In fact, the cat got the cell phone out of one man's jacket pocket and gave it to Miranda so she could call. The good news is that the men aren't watching her closely. She's been pretending to be dumb, and so they've begun to believe she's too slow to try anything. The problem is that she doesn't know where she is."

"Not to worry," Penny said. "Did she describe anything?"

"A few things." Light touched Mack's eyes. "We can figure it out."

"Yes, I think we can. I grew up around here. I know a lot of the landmarks. What did she say?"

"She said on the drive she remembered hearing airplanes really loud. And they went over a long bridge with water on one side."

"That's old Shell Road!" Penny couldn't contain her excitement. "That's not that far from here. What else?"

"She said there were some round tin buildings—"

"Silos! I know where that is."

"And then they turned left on a bumpy dirt road."

"We can find them, Mack. I know we can."

He lowered the heavy case of paper to the floor. "Can you really find her?"

Penny nodded. "I have a pretty good idea where they are. It's isolated there. Back in the fifties, it was a haven for moonshiners."

"Let's go." Mack's hand was on the doorknob, and the eagerness on his face was a little unnerving. "Don't bother with the ransom money. There's a change of plan. We're going to take them by surprise, if you can find the location."

"I'll find it," Penny promised.

"I'm going to slip in there, get my daughter, and then make those bastards pay."

"I do need to call Peter," Penny said. "He swears that Familiar can handle these things. And he's done a pretty good job so far. He seems to have got himself trapped and taken to Miranda. He got her to free him, and he managed to get a phone into her hands. I'd say that if we have Familiar on our team, we're going to be able to get Miranda without anything happening to her."

"Call him," he said.

MACK LET THE MOTOR IDLE as he waited for Peter at the crossroads. He was glad to have Penny and Peter along, but now he was focused on action. In his stint in the military, he'd learned to move covertly, to slip in behind enemy lines and do what had to be done to protect his men. It was a part of his life that he wanted to leave behind. He'd done what was necessary, and now it was past. Never had he imagined that his training would be necessary in his civilian life. But the two thugs who'd taken his daughter had brought this fate down on their own heads.

"Mack, there's Peter."

Penny's voice was filled with excitement and trepidation. He grasped her hand as he watched Peter's car turn in and park. In a moment Peter was sliding into the truck seat. Penny moved to the middle, her hip and thigh pressed against Mack's as he put the truck in Drive and floored it.

"The man with the dragon tattoo is a convicted felon," Peter said, not wasting any time. "His name is Emmon Fells. He's a tough character."

"How tough?" Mack asked, his heart pounding even harder.

"He did ten years for murder." Peter hesitated.

"Tell me the rest of it," Mack said. He felt Penny's hand creep onto his thigh, a touch of comfort and strength.

"He murdered a child. A young boy. They got into an argument over some trash on the road."

The silence in the truck was thick and oppressive.

"How did he get out of prison?" Penny asked. "That doesn't make any sense."

"He did his time. Before the murder charge he was up for animal cruelty, a six-month sentence, and several counts of aggravated assault."

"Well, it's good we've ID'd him," Penny said grimly. She grabbed Mack and Peter as the truck careened around a curve. Up ahead were the silver guardrails of Big Creek Lake. "Easy, Mack. We can't help her if we're wrecked and at the bottom of a lake."

He nodded and slowed the truck a fraction, but he kept the speedometer at eighty.

"Anything else on the toothless guy?" Penny asked.

"No. If you go through the mug books you'd be surprised how many felons have poor teeth. But one of the cops said that Fells had been arrested a couple of times with a guy named Junior Bennett. I'm guessing that's the other man."

Mack didn't know why he felt better, knowing the kidnappers' names, but he did. It made them real, and if they were real, they could be defeated.

"You did an amazing job, Peter," Mack said. "We'll get Miranda and we'll save those animals."

"I want those men behind bars. An animal-theft charge doesn't carry much time, but when they kidnapped your daughter, they bought themselves a long, long visit in a state correctional center," Peter said, his voice raw with anger.

"I wouldn't be surprised if these guys didn't steal dogs out of backyards," Penny said. "I've seen it done." She thought, too, about the little Jack Russell terrier that had gotten hit that morning. Maybe the young boy hadn't left the backyard gate open. It could have been the two animal thieves.

"We'll get them," Mack vowed.

"Go right here," Penny said. "And I think we should turn off the truck lights."

Mack did as she suggested, slowing to a crawl. A three-quarter moon illuminated the road enough for them to see clearly, at least where huge oaks didn't block the light.

"Under other circumstances, this would be a lovely place," Peter said softly. They'd all dropped to whispers.

"I'm going to block the road," Mack said as he did a turn so that they were pointed in the proper direction for a fast getaway. "This stand of trees is perfect." If the men tried to make a dash for it with Miranda, they would be effectively blocked.

He parked, and the three of them got out. Mack felt his body and mind shift. His training had taught him that stealth and surprise were lethal weapons. When it came to saving his daughter, he'd be as lethal as he had to be. He waved Peter and Penny back and slowly crept forward to scout out the situation.

CHAPTER NINE

THE TWO MEN *are sitting around an old card table eating cold stew out of cans and drinking what smells like lighter fluid. Good. It won't be long before I make my move. My plan is to jump in through this open window, leap onto Dumb's face and blind him with my claws. After that, Dumber should be a piece of cake. He's too stupid to come in out of the rain.*

Some of my fellow felines have been in those cages for over a week. They haven't had food or water. I don't know if two of them are going to survive. I have to say that it's going to give me great pleasure to put a hurting on these guys.

Miranda is sitting on a sleeping bag on the floor. She knows I'm here, and I've warned her to duck under the table when all hell breaks loose. She understands me perfectly, because she listens with her heart, not her ears. This is one child I'd like to keep.

Oh, what is that I spy sneaking through the woods? I do believe the cavalry has arrived. And not a moment too soon. I'm going to make my presence known to the good guys.

"PENNY. PETER." Mack's whisper was a guideline through the darkness for Penny. She moved through the trees, careful not to step on dry limbs. Her uncle was beside her, moving as silently as she. Mack was up ahead, a dark shadow among the gray trees, a man determined to save his child. He was some man.

She stopped when she saw his signal. In front of them was a ramshackle house, illuminated only by candles.

A cat's soft meow sounded.

"It's Familiar," Penny said, amazed even though Miranda had told them the cat was there. "He really did it."

"I think we should charge the house," Peter said.

As Peter stood, the cat grabbed the cuff of his pants with a paw.

"No," Mack said. "We have to make certain Miranda is safely out of the way before we rush the house."

He felt the cat tugging on his jeans. So far, Familiar had been nothing less than astounding. He knelt down. Familiar darted forward, then turned and waited for him. When Peter tried to move forward, Familiar hissed at him.

"I think he's trying to tell us something," Mack said amazed. "I think he wants to go in the window to make sure Miranda is safely out of the way. I'm going with him. The two of us will go together, and then you follow."

"We should all go together," Penny objected. "Those men could have guns."

"Trust the cat," Peter said. "Mack is right. Familiar will go in first."

Mack nodded. "Good. We'll give Familiar two minutes to get Miranda somewhere safe, and then I'll kick the door in. Penny will go through the window, and Peter, you cover the back door."

"Sounds like a good plan. Familiar knows how to handle himself," Peter said, slapping Mack lightly on the back. "He'll take care of your little girl."

They waited at the edge of the woods as the black cat scuttled across the yard. In a moment he jumped to the front window, and then disappeared. Mack checked his watch.

There was a scream and the sound of scuffling.

"Kitty! Kitty!" Miranda's young voice broke through the night.

Mack started to rush the house, but Penny restrained him with a touch. "Give the cat time."

There were screams of pain from one of the men. Penny felt Mack's muscles bunch beneath her hand. The cabin went dark.

"Fire!" one of the men yelled. "Fire!"

Mack bolted across the yard. He kicked the front door open and fell to the ground just as a gun roared. Junior Bennett rushed out, pointing the gun where Mack was rolling out of the way. In a moment Mack was on his feet, moving sideways, staring down the barrel of Junior's gun.

"Get Miranda!" he yelled. Then he turned his attention on the man with the gun. "Put it down," he said. "You don't want to add murder to kidnapping."

Penny and Peter were already moving. Out of the corner of his eye, Mack saw Penny aim for the window and leap through it just before a small black animal hurtled out. Penny was now in the cabin with Miranda. Mack focused on Familiar. The cat hit the ground, sprinted around the front yard and, in seconds, was clinging to Junior Bennett's head with his claws.

Bennett waved the gun wildly in the air as the cat rode his head. Familiar's claws opened a gash at least four inches long across the felon's forehead and blood ran into his eyes.

"Get off me," he screamed, swatting at the cat. "I'm going to kill you!"

"I don't think so." Mack stepped close to Junior and snatched the gun from his hands. He nodded at Familiar, who jumped clear, and then Mack's right fist connected with Junior's jaw with such force that Penny heard the bone snap. Junior went down in an unconscious heap.

Mack ran toward the cabin. "Miranda!"

"I'm okay, Daddy." She came to the door of the cabin and hesitated, Penny right behind her.

Mack dropped the gun and opened his arms for his daughter to run into them.

"I knew you'd come. I knew you would." Miranda snuggled against her father's chest. "You're the best daddy in the world."

"Are you okay?" Mack asked. He held his daughter back from him and ran his hands down her arms and over her back and legs. "Did they hurt you?"

"No," Miranda said, but she was trembling.

Mack stood up, his daughter in his arms. He went to Penny. "Are you okay?"

"Yes, and Peter's fine, too. He just called the police."

"Thank you," Mack said. He leaned forward and kissed Penny. "Thank you for so much."

"Daddy, Dr. Jameson, you have to help all the cats and dogs. Some of them are dying. It's terrible. They have Gumbo in a cage." Miranda choked back tears. "Did the kittens die?"

Mack signaled Penny to his side. "Could you tell Miranda about the kittens?" he asked. "I want to take a look around. The other kidnapper is in the house."

"Don't worry about him," Miranda said. "Familiar clawed his face. I don't think he can see. Familiar's the one who knocked the candles off the table. Peter's putting the fire out now."

Penny drew Miranda into the crook of her arm and held her as Mack went into the cabin. "The kittens are fine," she said. "Your father helped me feed them tonight. He's pretty good at it."

"He is?" Miranda, seeming a little calmer already, brushed her bangs out of her eyes. "He fed them?"

"He did. I think he's fond of them."

"He won't let me keep them."

"Oh, I think he might," Penny said, hugging the girl. "I think your father may have had a change of heart about feral cats."

"If he did, then all of this has been worth it. Can we go see the animals in the cages?"

Penny hesitated. Some of the animals were probably in bad shape. It might not be good for Miranda. "We should wait," Penny said.

"I know some are very sick. They need water and food. I want to help," Miranda said. "I'm not a baby."

Penny made a decision. Mack Sanders had tried to protect his daughter from every hurt in the world. It was a noble goal, but impractical. The important thing was knowing that beneath pain and suffering there could also be happiness—a lesson she would remind herself of every day as she allowed herself to fall in love with Mack.

"Okay," she said. "Let's get a water hose and get some of those animals something to drink."

EMMON FELLS AND JUNIOR BENNETT were trussed like turkeys and lying on their sides in the yard. Penny put the last pan of water in a cage with a cute little Yorkshire terrier. The dog looked in bad shape. It was dehydrated and starved. But it made an attempt to lap the water.

"He wants to live," Miranda said, reaching a finger into the cage to stroke the dog. "And he has a collar."

Of the twenty dogs they'd watered, seventeen had collars and tags. Penny put a hand on Miranda's head.

"We'll make sure the healthy animals get home, and we'll take the sick ones to my clinic. Peter and I will try to help them."

"And me, too," Miranda said. "I can help."

"She sure can," Mack said, lifting his daughter into his arms.

"I'm going to be a veterinarian," Miranda said. "Just like you, Penny."

"Hey!" Peter called from the back of the cages. "Come on over here, Miranda. There's a calico cat here that wants to know where her kittens are."

"Gumbo!" Miranda's legs churned the air until Mack put her down. She dashed behind the cages to Peter. In a moment there was a squeal of pure delight. "Peter says she's okay. That she can still nurse her babies. And here's Buster, too! We can take him home with us."

"It's just amazing. She didn't have a single asthma attack. In fact, she doesn't seem to be traumatized in any way," Mack said as he lifted Penny's face for a gentle kiss. "I can't thank you enough. And Peter. And of course, Familiar."

"I might make some appointments with a psychologist. Just to be on the safe side," Penny suggested.

He nodded. "And I'm going to spend a lot more time with her. I don't want her with a sitter after school. I've been using work to avoid my own loneliness, but that's over and done with." He smiled. "There're going to be a lot of changes in my life. Good changes."

Penny hesitated. "Would you consider letting Miranda come to the clinic in the afternoons? She could help with some of the feedings and she could go along with one of the assistants I hire to help walk the dogs. Things like that."

Mack's face split into a grin. "You are an angel."

"No, I'm just a veterinarian."

He kissed her, a long, passionate kiss. "No," he said, giving her a considering look. "You're an angel. Veterinarians don't taste as good as you do."

She laughed, and mingled in with the sound of her happiness was the blare of police sirens. Emmon Fell and Junior Bennett were going to jail for years.

"Let's start loading these cages," Mack said. "I want to get these pets home as soon as possible."

"We'll need to make several trips," Peter said. "We'll load the sickest ones first, Mack, while you take care of your business with the police."

"And then I'll be at the clinic to help," Mack said, taking his daughter's hand.

CHAPTER TEN

MACK WATCHED PENNY as she leaned into a cage and doctored Chauncey, a golden retriever mix that had been one of the largest dogs they'd saved from Fells and Bennett. The dog had not had a tag or collar, but she was a sweet female who loved affection.

After administering the eye drops, Penny snapped the leash on the brand-new purple collar, vaccination tag jangling. Chauncey jumped out of the cage, shook herself, and then danced on the leash as Penny led her to the waiting room.

"She's beautiful," the little boy said as he knelt beside the dog and buried his face in her long, silky fur.

"She is lovely," the boy's mother said. "Are you sure she doesn't belong to anyone?"

"I don't think so," Penny said. "We've advertised in the paper for the past two weeks. No one claimed her. But she's been wormed and had her shots. Use up all the eye drops and be sure to bring her back to have her spayed."

"We will," the woman promised. "Come on, Jeremy. Let's take Chauncey home and show her where she's going to live."

"Yeah! I can't wait." The young boy took the leash and he and the dog were out the door, running. Chauncey leaped high into the air, twirled and landed beside the boy, running again.

"Thank you for everything," the woman said. "Jeremy has wanted a dog for so long, and this one is perfect." She followed her son and the dog at a slower pace.

When she closed the door behind her, Mack turned to Penny. "Another good deed," he said. "So how much are you going in the hole on this business?"

Penny laughed. "It'll all work out. Peter and Familiar promised me that it would."

Mack pulled her into his arms. For the past two weeks he'd spent every day at the clinic. He'd told Penny it was because he wanted to help, but actually, he just wanted to be near her. And he'd learned a lot—about taking care of animals, and about caring and loving again.

Penny had doctored all the sick strays they'd rescued. Luckily, she's begun to find homes for most of them. But no one was footing the bills. Just Penny. His angel. "Sounds to me like you could use a benefactor."

"I'm just doing my part to make the world a tiny bit better," she said with a little grin. "I'll get some paying clients."

Mack tilted her face up to his. He loved kissing her. He loved the way she felt and smelled and kissed him back. He loved the idea of her, and he found himself thinking about her at the strangest times. At home, in the shower, in bed.

"Miranda loves being here with you." He kissed her again. "And so do I."

"I could become addicted to having the two of you around," Penny said, kissing him back.

"Penny, I've fallen in love with you." He hadn't meant to say it so bluntly. He should have brought flowers. Heck, he'd never even taken her to dinner. Not a real dinner. They'd been so busy with all the animals that they'd ordered pizzas and picked up burgers.

She looked up at him. "I've been afraid to love anyone," she said. "I guess I thought if I cared about anyone else, I'd lose them, too. But you and Miranda got past my defenses. I love you. Both of you."

Mack had never heard sweeter words. He kissed her again, and this time the kiss held more than passion. It held the promise of a future together.

They were still kissing when two clients came in the door. And they didn't stop.

SO, ALL'S WELL that ends well. Miranda has a soon-to-be stepmother who will cherish her and her animals. Mack will get a wife who adores him. And Penny will have a man who loves her beyond all reason. And don't forget Gumbo and her five kittens. They've found a wonderful home where they'll have the finest care.

Peter has given me the sign that it's time to head for home. I'm ready, too. This episode with animal abductors has brought back a lot of ghosts for me. But letting the past go is the road to happiness. That's what I have to do, because there's always adventure around the corner for Familiar, the black cat detective.

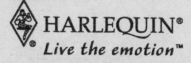

California's most talked about family, the Coltons, is back!

"Just how close to me do you intend to get?"

CLOSE
PROXIMITY

by bestselling author
Donna Clayton

When attorney Libby Corbett started receiving death threats, Private Investigator Rafe James whisked her away for round-the-clock protection…and soon realized that the only place she would truly be safe was in his arms.

Coming in August 2004.

"Donna Clayton pens a cozy romance with a lot of humor, heart and passion."
—*Romantic Times*

THE COLTONS
FAMILY. PRIVILEGE. POWER.

Where love comes alive™

**Someone wanted him dead.
She just *wanted* him.**

THE TARGET

Bestselling Silhouette Intimate Moments® authors

Justine Davis
Linda Turner

The combination of passion and peril can be explosive
in these two full-length novels.

Available everywhere books are sold in August 2004.

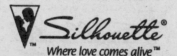

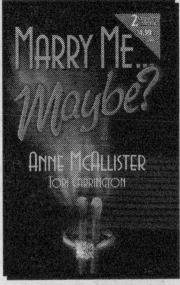
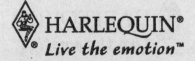

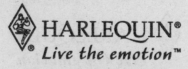